LURKING
IN THE
MIND

1

Published by CHBB Publishing
Text Copyright 2017 held by CHBB Publishing and
the Individual Authors
Edited by Jaidis Shaw
Cover by Jaidis Shaw
Formatted by Jaidis Shaw

Table of Contents

<u>Dedication</u>

If you have ever felt alone while standing in a crowded room, been overwhelmed with insecurities, or heard whispers calling your name, this collection is dedicated to you.

Disclaimer

While the stories within this anthology are works of fiction, some very real mental disorders, fears and/or characteristics are discussed. Stories may contain sensitive topics such as depression, suicide, self-harm, split personalities, schizophrenia, and more.

Please be advised.

Twisted

Jaclyn Osborn

"Please," the thin blonde woman with the pale blue eyes begged, as a tear made its way down her cheek, reaching the tip of her pierced nose, and then falling soundlessly to the ground. She stood on trembling feet and shook profusely, the faint smell of urine rising into the air. Her wrists were rubbed raw from the numerous failed attempts of slipping out of the chains that held her prisoner against the cold, concrete wall.

Standing in front of my weapon shelf beside her, my eyes scanned over the vast amount of instruments of torture. Oh…the possibilities. Choosing an old—but still very sharp—knife, I held it up to the dim light, admiring it. Dried blood from the last unfortunate soul to venture to my basement was still on the blade.

The woman's breath caught in her throat.

I took the knife and slowly made a deep cut down her forearm. Blood escaped the wound, trickled down her raised arm, and formed in a small puddle on the dirty floor beneath her. A blood-curdling scream escaped her quivering lips, and I closed my eyes, savoring the moment.

She thrashed around and tried to kick me away, but the heavy chains binding her feet halted her action. Leisurely, I began to peel away the skin on her arm, exposing muscle and smiling as her screams echoed throughout the room.

"No, no, no, *please*!" Her voice cracked on the last word, and she let out an agonizing howl.

My body stirred as the sound of her pitiful pleas reached my ears. Her fear was palpable and I could taste it. My eyes rolled into the back of my head, and I bit down gently on my bottom lip, letting the sensation run all throughout my body and causing me to whimper aloud.

I laid the blood-drenched knife on the shelf beside her, as her body went through severe spasms and I scanned the shelf once more. Choosing a crowbar, I tested the point of it with my middle finger to make sure it was nice and sharp for my lovely guest.

When the steel bit into my finger, I groaned. Damn, it felt good.

"Oh, come on, sweet cheeks. Give me one reason why I shouldn't," I said in a mocking tone, sliding the tip of the weapon over her good arm and teasing her with it.

She didn't answer me. Instead, she turned her head to the side and vomited all over the floor.

I growled. "What do we have here? You made a mess on my floor; I don't like that." Blood was one thing. Vomit was something else entirely. Without waiting for a reply, I drew back the crowbar and aimed it at her slightly open, trembling mouth.

"No—"

She was cut off as the weapon was thrust with excessive force into her mouth. The point of it appeared out of the back of her head and stopped abruptly as it collided with the wall behind her. A gurgling noise came out of her mouth, along with a mouthful of crimson delight.

Admiring my work, I watched humorously as the dark blood oozed from her parted lips, adding to the already formed puddle on the ground. I followed the trail of blood with my eyes, having an uncontrollable urge to taste it. Soon, the life in the blonde's eyes faded away, leaving behind the cold sensation of death.

She was dead.

Daniel, my best friend and murder accomplice, came strolling down the cellar stairs with an apple in his left hand. He was shirtless and barefoot, wearing only a pair of tattered jeans. His perfectly sculpted chest clouded my vision with the green devil envy. Daniel was stunning, and it annoyed the fuck out of me for some reason.

I nodded to him and then turned back to the dead girl. Tilting my head, I looked at her for a moment before pulling the crowbar out of her mouth, causing it to make a popping sound. Blood still dripped from its tip.

"Well done, buddy." Daniel smiled and walked back upstairs.

I watched him walk away until he disappeared from my sight. Setting the tool aside, I looked down at the combination of puke and blood on the floor and groaned. This was the part that I hated the most. Clean up. With a sigh, I started cleaning the mess, getting myself all nice and filthy in the process.

After a while, everything was spotless, and the girl's body was disposed of. And by disposed of, that meant she was chopped up and looked like raw hamburger meat. That was more Daniel's doing than my own. He had a taste for human flesh, but I had never grown accustomed to it. What couldn't be eaten was burned in the furnace in the basement.

It was just one of the many bonuses of living out in the country, secluded from everyone and away from prying eyes.

Reaching the top of the stairs, I started making my way to the bathroom. "I'm gonna clean up first, and then I'll be in for lunch."

"Dude, it's closer to dinner now than lunch," Daniel called from the other room. I heard movement and then saw him poke his head out of the living room to look at me. "Don't take too long in there." His voice was amused, and he stared at me with a slight smirk on his handsome face.

He knew me all too well. I was slightly obsessive-compulsive when it came to cleanliness. Drench my victims in their own blood, sure that's fine. But don't get it all over me. It made me anxious. Already, my skin crawled with the thought of the blood and grime covering me.

I flipped him the bird and then walked into the bathroom, shutting the door behind me.

***

Daniel sat at the table, reading the day's newspaper when I walked into the kitchen. His tousled, dark hair fell into his eyes. *He needs to get another haircut*, I thought to myself.

His dark eyes flickered up to meet mine and I quickly looked away.

Making my way over to the refrigerator, I pulled out a bottle of water and twisted off the cap before taking a huge gulp. Observing the room, I made a mental note to do some cleaning later. The place wasn't exactly messy, but it sure as hell wasn't clean enough for my liking. As I leaned against the counter, I noticed that there were a few dirty dishes in the sink. My insides cringed.

Tap. Tap. I tapped my fingers against the bottle I held in my hands. Dishes. Mess. I replaced the cap on the bottle and placed it back in the refrigerator. Clutter. Disorder.

Damnit.

Rushing over to the sink, I began washing the dishes. *Everything must be perfect.* Once they were clean, I dried them and placed them in their proper spots in the cabinet. Relieved, I braced myself on the edge of the counter and hung my head as I took a deep breath. I opened my eyes and was about to grab a plate for a sandwich when I froze. Noticing a crumb on the counter, I wet a rag and started wiping down all the surfaces.

"Going off on another freaky cleaning spree, Xavier?" Daniel asked in an amused, husky tone.

"You know that I can't help it, so I would appreciate it if you would wash your dishes every damn once in a while," I snapped.

He ignored me and went back to reading the paper. Hearing him chuckle I looked up, curious as to what he found funny about this situation. But, his chuckle was dark and held a sardonic quality to it as he looked at the paper in his hands.

"What a bunch of fucking idiots," he said with a sneer. "These people care more about trivial matters such as what new sales the stores are having, or about who some bullshit politician had an affair with than the deaths of their citizens."

"What do you mean? I'm sure they care." I tried to convince him.

"Don't be a fucking moron, Xavier. I'm talking about our killings here. Not one of those fucking pathetic fools we butchered made the front page of this goddamn paper!"

He was angry. It was never a good thing when he was angry. Mentally, I chuckled at my thoughts, reminding myself of the *Hulk*.

"I don't want to kill anymore." It slipped out uncontrollably. I'm not exactly sure what possessed me to say it to him.

Killing people made me feel powerful, it made me feel alive. But, deep down, there was a small part of me that wanted it all to end. It was like there were two sides to me: the side that awoke and thrived from other people's torment and then the side that felt guilty about it.

Seeing Daniel's ravenous features, I took a step back and bumped into the wall.

Within seconds, he was across the room with his hands tightly around my throat. I imagined my windpipe busting into a million pieces, as his hands became tighter. Grabbing onto his arms, I attempted to pry open his grip, to no avail. He pulled my head forward and then smashed it back against the wall, causing my vision to blur.

"How dare you fucking say that, you asshole," he hissed between clenched teeth. "Why care about those brainless imbeciles? Huh? They have never done *anything* for you. They wouldn't care one bit if I just choked you out right here."

I stared pitifully into his black eyes and saw nothing. They were unfeeling and cold.

He released his hold on me, and I fell hard to my knees and gasped for air.

"You are weak," he spat and then stormed out of the kitchen.

Sitting on my knees, I stared down at the floor as tears of frustration formed in the corners of my eyes. My chest ached. I hated when he was mad at me. Everything I did, I did it for him. Daniel was everything to me. More than my best friend.

It was like he was a part of me and I'd be completely lost without him.

Pulling myself to my feet, I no longer had an appetite. I felt empty inside. But it was the kind of emptiness that couldn't be filled. I needed to find a way to make things right with Daniel...to make him love me again.

***

Daniel must have been very upset with me. He was nowhere to be found in our home, so I assumed that he had gone somewhere to cool off for a while. Hopefully, when I saw him again, we could talk things out, and I could explain that I wasn't going to stop killing people. I'd say it was just a moment of insecurity and it meant nothing.

He needed to understand that I would never abandon him.

After moping around for a while, I jumped into the car and headed to town. Our house was in dire need of some groceries. Town was about thirty minutes away, so the drive to the store was quiet. Finally arriving, I pulled into a parking spot and walked in, beginning my usual routine around the store. Meat aisle first and then the spices, followed by a trip down the drink aisle for more bottled water.

I passed by countless people, wondering if I had killed any of their loved ones. The blonde woman, was she a mother? A wife? I felt a sudden pang of guilt, and then I saw Daniel in my mind, calling me pathetic and weak.

Clank.

"Damn!" A girl exclaimed.

I had been so wrapped up in my thoughts that I had run right into her with my cart, knocking her down.

"Watch where you're goin', dumbass," the girl snapped. She had neatly styled, shoulder length brown hair and looked as if she had just come back from a visit to the salon. Her hazel eyes watched me scornfully.

12

I offered to help her up, but she slapped my hand away in a fit of rage.

"I…I'm sorry," I stuttered, shocked at her reaction.

"Well, you should be." She stood up and winced. "I think I sprang my ankle when I fell."

I didn't hit her *that* hard. She was over exaggerating. "I'll help walk you to your car if you need me to," I responded in a polite tone.

"I didn't bring my friggin' car. I walked here, you filthy bastard." I saw her role her eyes and then flip her hair back with her right hand.

A filthy bastard. Bastard…

"Bastard!" My mother yelled and threw me to the ground.

"Mama! Please don't, Mama." I flinched as her foot collided with the back of my head.

"Don't you beg for mercy, you little fuck." She kicked me harder.

I tried standing up, but she grabbed onto my shaggy hair and threw me back onto the tile floor in the kitchen, grabbing my face and angling it toward the carpet in the living room.

"How dare you spill grape juice on my new carpet." Her voice was venomous. "Look at what you did! Brand new carpet that is now ruined."

"I sorry, Mama. Please, I not mean to!"

With one last slap to the back of my head, my mother stormed off.

Looking up, I saw Daniel standing in the hallway and he was staring at me with pity in his eyes.

"Are you stupid?"

I blinked and looked around, confused. The brunette girl stared at me with disgust penetrating through her brown-green eyes.

"How about I give you a ride home, it's the least I can do." I smiled at her, playing nice. "I really should be more careful, and I just feel awful for hurting you."

She hesitated, the anger slowly draining from her features as confusion took its place. "Sure. That would be great, thanks."

Smiling as kindly as I could, I said, "Perfect. Let me go pay for my items, and you can meet me outside."

I walked away from her, my eyes scanning the people around us and making sure that no one saw us speaking. The grocery store only had one security camera, and it was located at the front of the store. So, as long as no one had seen the altercation between the woman and me, the suspicion should be off me if something were to happen to her.

I grinned at the thought.

Once I paid for my groceries, I walked out and loaded the bags into my truck. As a habit, I always parked as far away from other cars as possible, so my vehicle was somewhat out of sight. The woman walked out a few minutes after I did, and turned her head as she searched for me.

I whistled to get her attention, and she made her way over to me.

I scoffed. She wasn't limping whatsoever. *Bitch.* We got into my truck, and I drove a little ways down the road. Once we were clear of the busy part of town and the scenery changed to farm fields and dirt roads, I made sure there were no other cars around and reached under my seat to grab onto the dull hammer I kept hidden.

Damn, I loved the way it felt within my hand. I always carried it in my truck, especially for these types of occurrences.

"What are you—?

I hit her over the head with the butt end of the hammer, careful not to use too much force. I wanted this one alive...for now at least. She fell back against the seat as a small trickle of blood dripped from where I hit her. Smiling, I pushed her down into the seat so no passing cars would be able to see her.

This was how I would make amends with Daniel.

***

Walking through the door of my house, I threw the girl down on the floor of the living room. Daniel was sitting on the couch and turned his head to look at me. His eyes scanned the body of the girl, and then his gaze returned to mine, a smile playing at the edges of his mouth.

"I'll show you weak," I told him as I grabbed the girl by her ankle and began dragging her unconscious body down the stairs into my chamber of death.

About ten minutes later, the girl woke up. Confusion marked her face as she squinted and took in her surroundings.

"Hello there, princess. Have a nice nap?"

Her eyes clouded with terror. "What do you want? Oh God, please don't hurt me." She began to thrash around, causing the chains to clank against the wall.

Music to my ears. Smirking, I grabbed a pair of pliers and caught her tongue. "There is no God here, sweet cheeks."

She moved her head from side to side, attempting to make me lose my grip. *Stupid girl.* I pushed down harder on the pliers, causing her to scream.

Daniel walked down the steps at that time and went over to our weapon shelf, grabbed a small pair of gardening shears and walked over to where the girl was thrashing wildly. He looked at her, but she didn't look back at him.

Her panicked eyes were still focused on me.

Shrugging his shoulders, he roughly grabbed her face and sliced off her tongue. It fell to the floor, making itself a home. The room was then filled with a chorus of shrieks and wails. Blood gushed out of her mouth continuously, staining and drenching the front of her shirt.

"I want to make her squeal like a little pig," Daniel said, his voice filled with humor.

I watched as he walked over to the shelves that held our numerous tools and saw his eyes scan the shelf as if he were unsure of what he wanted to use.

Then his wandering gaze landed on a chainsaw.

"Time to have some fun," he murmured to himself.

Daniel walked over to the panicked girl and pulled the switch on the chainsaw; the sound of it sent shivers down my spine. The next half hour was a complete blood bath. The body of the once beautiful, but arrogant girl was now unrecognizable.

Body parts were strewn all over the room. The only intact parts were the girl's arms, which were still dangling from the chains on the wall. For once, I was thankful that I didn't participate in this killing. The mess was of epic proportions, and I wasn't in the mindset to be *that* wet and sticky with blood.

A wave of gratitude washed over me as I looked at Daniel.

He had always been there for me. All of the times that my mother used to go through her episodes of rage—blaming me for my father walking out on us, and using me as her personal punching bag—Daniel had been there.

One night my mother had her new boyfriend, Mike, over at our house and I heard her yelling. Jumping up from my bed, I ran into her bedroom to check on her. She was on top of Mike and bouncing up and down on his lap.

Confused, I stared at them, not knowing what was happening. They were both naked and panted very heavily.

"Mama?"

She sharply turned to me. "Get out of here, you little fuck."

I spun around and ran out of the room, fear swirling inside of me. Before I made it to my bedroom, my mom called to me. Turning, I saw her barging toward me down the hallway. She beat me so bad that afterward, I had trouble standing up and walking. As I crawled down the hall toward my room, I heard her pleading for Mike to stay. His voice boomed as he threw insults at her. I heard the door slam, and that was the last of him.

Daniel was waiting for me inside my room, ready to comfort me as always.

A little while later, once my strength had returned to me, Daniel had a marvelous idea. "A way to end it all," he had whispered to me as we sat on the edge of my bed.

Quietly, I walked into the kitchen and headed straight for the knife rack. Grabbing the biggest one, adrenaline jolted throughout my small ten-year-old body. I crept into my mother's room with Daniel at my side.

The faint sounds of her breathing could be heard. Inhaling and exhaling.

Once beside her bed, I watched her sleep. Her long dark hair was tangled on the pillow and her dainty body was curled into the fetal position. Raising the knife above my head, I hesitated.

I couldn't do it. No matter how much she hurt me, I couldn't bring myself to harm her.

Daniel grabbed onto my arm and took the knife into his hand. When I looked at him, he nodded his head as if he understood my dilemma. Moving his gaze to my mom, he lifted the knife and put an end to her. I remember that I cried afterward, afraid of what was going to happen next.

But, Daniel calmed me down. He told me that she could never harm me again and that whatever happened next, at least we would be together.

That had been the beginning of our new life.

Mike was convicted of butchering my mother; his DNA was all over the crime scene. Daniel had been smart about everything and made sure we were taken care of. We moved from foster home to foster home until we were old enough to set out on our own.

And here we were now.

I must have blacked out for a minute because I noticed that Daniel was no longer down there with me. Shuffling upstairs and out of the basement, I locked the door behind me and went to look for him.

"Daniel?"

No answer.

Trying not to worry, I headed for the bathroom, thinking that maybe he was cleaning himself up from the massive mess he had made. I stopped suddenly when I saw my reflection in the hallway mirror.

I was covered in blood from head to toe.

Confused, I wiped the blood away from my face with my right hand, which was also drenched in red, so it didn't help much. How did I get bloody? *This makes no sense.* I hadn't killed that girl, Daniel had. Gazing at my reflection, I gasped.

My eyes were not my eyes; they were darker. More sinister. They were Daniel's.

Daniel was standing there staring back at me through the mirror. I raised my hand and he mirrored my movement. I touched my hair and noticed it was Daniel's raven black hair that was now growing out of my head. Only now, it was clumped with dried blood.

My head began to spin.

"What the fuck is wrong with you?" I told my reflection.

I could see him smile. He was mocking me, taunting me.

"You are weak," he hissed. "Always weak. Always making me do your dirty work for you." He smiled a menacing grin.

I flinched and staggered backward, hitting my head with my fists and trying to get the voices to cease.

"Stop, stop, stop!" I shouted pitifully.

A plethora of voices stirred around me. *Weak. You're weak. Pathetic.*

"Xavier," my reflection spoke, causing me to look up and see him watching me.

His dark eyes were always watching me...

"Please, just leave me alone. I want to be...alone," I whimpered. "Please."

More voices stirred until only one voice was audible. His. "You are alone."

Alone.

Everything became quiet.

I was alone. I always have been.

Lonely Hearts

Amber Hassler

Gusts of air ruffled the dying leaves from an aging oak tree that sat on top of a hill, alone, until it became a scraggly piece of thick wood.

Mila Webber watched the brown leaflets float to the ground, helpless to their fate. She pulled her black pea coat tighter against the crisp wind. Despite the fall chill, she welcomed it.

Another year and another season had passed. It was her last year in high school, and she had no plans for after graduation. *Depressing.*

The crunch of light footsteps on the brittle ground broke through Mila's solitude, warning of someone approaching from behind. An aroma of coconut swirled in the air giving away the presence of her best friend, Cindy.

"What are you doing out here?" Cindy stepped into view. Her strawberry blonde hair whipped around her face, blocking her features.

"I needed some air," Mila replied while pulling her jacket closer around her thin frame.

"Well, come on, Mrs. Bleevie has started roll call. You don't want her calling home and telling your mom you ditched this field trip." Cindy didn't wait for an answer; she rotated on her heels, leaving an indent in the soft ground and headed back inside.

Mila glanced at the fragile tree one last time. Its branches seemed to reach for her as they shifted from the air's intensity. Her long, vibrant auburn locks, in turn, searched for a connection with its limbs, wanting to accept the invitation to sit among its protruding roots.

With a sigh, she reluctantly spun around and followed her friend's trail. In her mind, the leaves appeared to scream in protest under her feet as she stepped on the ones she couldn't avoid while fighting against the wind.

Nearing the base of the hill an elongated, two-story, brick building loomed ahead of her. Within the walls, it provided a false hope of change. A change that was to come from what she would learn today. *It was just a waste of time. She was certain it was a setup; it had the parental stench of poor planning. So, why did she agree to come on this field trip? And how in the heck were they able to convince Mrs. Bleevie to make a class trip out of it; that was the real question.* A scoff followed Mila's thoughts.

Mila entered the lobby right as Mrs. Bleevie called her name.

"Here." She spoke without missing a beat and then crossed her arms over her chest while leaning against the wall.

Mrs. Bleevie didn't seem to notice she was absent beforehand as she continued rifling off the last few names from her clipboard.

Mila shifted both feet and glanced at her enthusiastic classmates, moving from one to another, and listening to them gush about the haunting decor. She didn't stop until she caught Cindy eyeing her with one of her criticizing looks. She brushed it off and paid attention to the once thriving entryway.

Even though it had been classified a museum, there wasn't an entry fee. As long as no one took advantage by vandalizing the grounds, then it was free for the public to enjoy. It also meant, no tour guides or floor employees to give direction when needed; except for a lone security guard that moseyed along the property's perimeter. For there being no crew to upkeep the place it looked intact. Apart from a few spots where the plaster had flaked off the wall, and chunks of rocks littering the floor that had fallen from the ceiling, everything else appeared as it did when people once walked the halls.

With the current state of the building, a special bond formed between her and it, because it revealed what she felt inside.

"All right class, quiet down," Mrs. Bleevie's voice filled the room. "No wandering off. Stay close. We were only given an hour to explore. No shenanigans. Listen to your assigned chaperone."

The decibels in the hollow space immediately increased followed by the scuffling of feet as students and parents tried to figure out where to go.

An ear piercing whistle caused everyone to go silent and look at Mrs. Bleevie who removed her thumb and forefinger from her mouth.

"Welcome to Stayville Asylum. Some historians believe the majority of unconventional testing were done here. All their efforts were to understand the brain and how it functioned under certain circumstances. Each room is equipped with a glass case that holds the tools used and a plaque that gives you the reasons behind the experiments performed. Take notes, because I will expect a three-page paper on your findings, due first thing in the morning. Now, explore."

When Mrs. Bleevie spoke the last word, the hair on Mila's skin rose, sending chills down her spine. It could have been the way Mrs. Bleevie said 'explore' that made it sound dark and daring, but it gave her an uneasy twinge in her stomach as if she was doomed.

The small groups of students and parents dispersed in different directions to begin their tour into the depths of history.

Cindy dodged through the masses and emerged on the other side, showing her irritation that they didn't make it easy for her to cut across. "Do these boys ever take a shower? *Ugh.* And what the heck is up with this lack of organization? You'd think Mrs. Bleevie would have already made a list of who goes where before we got here. It's complete chaos," she sneered.

Mila ignored her comments and didn't hold back her own irritation. "An asylum. Really? What made my parents think this would be a great idea?"

Cindy furrowed her brows together, confused. "Umm, what do you mean by parents?"

"This is why I had to come to school today?" Mila spoke over her friend, continuing her rant.

All she wanted to do was take the day off, lay in bed and catch up on rest. So, it still made little sense as to why her parents were persistent on her attending class today. She may have found out the where, but it was the why that plagued her.

Cindy dropped her line of sight to the ground and used a rock to divert her attention by pushing it back and forth with a leather boot. "Maybe, it's because you have been distant with her lately."

"I'm a teenager, what do they expect? A cheery cheerleader?"

"It's more than being a teenager, Mila. You have gone through how many therapists in the last year? And all it's done is turn you into a recluse."

"I can't help that they did absolutely nothing for me. But forcing me on this field trip? What did they think it would accomplish? To show me where I might end up?" Mila dramatically rolled her eyes with a head shake.

Cindy continued to rotate the rock under her foot, avoiding eye contact. "Maybe."

Mila growled in a low voice, "Unbelievable."

***

Mila pushed herself off the wall with her shoulder and left Cindy behind to figure out why she was mad. She headed after her group, steering clear of the fallen debris that scattered over the tile.

It was disappointing that this place wasn't sacred enough for anyone to keep up the grounds. It had potential; she thought. *And what in the heck made her parents think forcing her on a field trip to the asylum would help express her darkest feelings!*

Anger rose in her chest; the betrayal a little too surreal. She marched around the corner, following the faint voices of her group. While trying to catch up, Mila peeked into each room as she passed. The first three rooms had been used for sleeping quarters, its scenery holding no importance, so she continued in a fuming silence.

The fourth room held the same appeal as the others except for an old metal bed frame laid on its side, and a cracked mirror occupied one corner. Mila resumed her stroll down the hall. She had just passed the doorframe when a faint sound stopped her. It had come from the last room.

With eyebrows raised, she rigidly backed up and peered into the room. Mila surveyed the area, searching for the source. Apart from the things she noted before, it was empty.

She waited a few moments, her breathing coming out in thin, short bursts.

It was quiet.

Rotating on her heels, she focused on her classmates, their faint voices echoed from the end of the hall.

"Mila..."

She froze.

Her name whispered with every letter drawn out caused chills to ricochet up and down her spine before using her limbs as an outlet. The blood pumped loud in her ears.

In seconds, a battle raged within her mind. *Should she turn around, or keep walking and then get the heck out of that place?* Not knowing who or what was behind her, added to the fear, making every muscle burn and her joints ache.

Could it be a straggler, someone playing a trick on her, or taking their time as she was? Unless, it was Cindy, but, *why would she whisper?*

A burst of laughter from down the hall made her realize the group had proceeded further into the depths of insanity.

"Mila..."

This time, the hair around her ear moved in the breeze of her name. Her breathing hitched in her throat, heart pounding harder against her chest.

Drawing in a breath, Mila slowly, and cautiously, pivoted to face the unknown.

Her eyes grew wide while she released her breath.

No one was there.

***

Mila stepped into the dingy room and eyed every corner. She noticed a closet with the door half hanging off of its hinges. Inhaling a large breath, she squared her shoulders, then stormed to the vacant space.

Peeking in, she saw it was empty.

Stumped, Mila scanned her surroundings again until she was face-to-face with the broken mirror. Her uncombed, multi-layer appearance stared back at her.

She frowned.

It frowned back.

Mirrors never did her justice, which is why the only one in the entire house was in her parents' bathroom. It only reminded her of how bleak and unwanted she felt, and how it had ways to destroy one's life. *Did she really need to have that constant reminder?*

Mila ran her fingers through her frizzy strands, attempting to bring order to her tresses. With a sigh, she gave up, and before leaving watched a single tear slip down her pimply cheek.

In that moment, her throat ached, and a layer of unforgivable sadness began to suffocate her.

Quickly averting her eyes from the image, she forced her emotions to calm down before they overreacted and resulted in a barrage of tears.

As she took a step toward the door, an airy voice reached her ears. "Why don't you just give up then?"

"What?" Mila choked out. She eyed the room with more persistence, adamant to find the face that went with the voice. But again, she was the only one in the room.

"It's simple, really."

Mila faced the mirror, realizing it was the source, and hesitantly walked toward it. Once again, she was one-on-one with her image.

"I could give you some tips."

Mila gasped. Her reflection was speaking to her.

This could not be happening. She must have knocked her head at some point. There was no way it was a ghost; she didn't believe in the supernatural. Mila freaked.

The reflection put a hand on her hip. "No, you did not knock your head. Yes, it's happening. And you're right; I am not a ghost."

Mila's eyes grew wide at the reflection answering her thoughts. "Then, who are you?"

"Isn't it obvious? I'm you." The reflection smirked.

"I don't understand."

She sighed. "You are talking to yourself, Mila."

Mila raised her eyebrows.

"Think of me as your evil conscience. I'm the one who makes you hate yourself. Oh, and don't bother looking for Jiminy the Cricket, he was quite tasty."

Mila swallowed hard. A thousand questions ran through her mind, but she didn't know which one to ask first.

"I've been biding my time, waiting for the right moment to explain a sensitive situation to you. Deep down you know your parents and Cindy are only pretending like they give a damn."

"Why would they do that?"

"To make you think you're going crazy, so they can lock you up and never deal with you, ever, again."

Mila's throat tightened while a trickle of tears flowed down her pale flesh.

"It would be smarter to end it before they do. Because you know if they caged you, you will find a way, it's inevitable."

"What if I talk to them?"

The reflection belted out a throaty laugh. "Don't kid yourself, Mila. A damaged soul is a damaged soul. There is no fixing that."

A steady stream of liquid, now released from Mila's bottom lids.

Disgusted, the broken image rolled its eyes. "Stop crying. You clinging to your worthlessness is your fault, so there is no need for the pity party."

"But... but..."

"Mila!" Cindy's voice rang from down the hall.

Mila quickly wiped at her eyes and watched her reflection performing the same action.

"There you are." Cindy's face filled the doorway. "Everyone is already at the meeting location. It's time to head back."

"An hour has passed already?"

"Yeah. Were you in here the whole time?"

"I suppose I was." Mila breathed, surprised.

"Well, come on," Cindy motioned with her hand. "It's time to go."

Cindy was out the door before Mila could protest.

Mila turned back to the mirror, shocked to see her disconnected form wink while the corner of her mouth twitched.

Turning to follow Cindy, a voice echoed in her head, *You know I'm right.*

***

The noise in the lobby overpowered the small space. Mila hugged the wall until she found a section that wasn't being occupied and then crossed her arms over her midsection. She listened to the different animated conversations on what they found.

Look at them, so, happy. Maybe, someone should tell them, life is one big disappointment.

Mila scoffed. She thought of what she experienced. Besides, trying to comprehend what had happened, there was nothing her alternate self-said that wasn't true.

Of course, I'm right. We are of like minds. And, it would be so simple, Mila. Who would even miss you?

"You know I'm here for you if you ever need to talk."

Mila jumped and then snapped her head to the right to see Cindy supporting the wall with her.

"What makes you think I need to talk?" Mila hissed, ready to strangle her prey if it continued to interrupt her thoughts.

Sensing the hostile atmosphere, Cindy pushed off the wall and faced her friend. "I'm not blind, Mila. You've been acting standoffish ever since we arrived." She sighed. "An asylum probably wasn't the best choice–"

"You think?"

"But we thought it would help."

Mila straightened, her eyebrows furrowing together. "We? So, you had a hand in this too? What was this, an intervention?"

Heads close by turned, startled by Mila's tone. They watched the exchange between the two friends, probably wondering if they would see a fight.

"Mila, please calm down." Cindy let out a breath. "Why do you act as if we are committing a crime by showing how much we care for you?"

She's lying Mila.

"If this is caring, then I want no part of it."

"You're being ridiculous, Mila."

"Am I?"

Cindy sighed and then lowered her voice. "Why won't you talk to me?"

"Because there is nothing to talk about Cindy. I'm fine. I'm standoffish because this place is depressing, just like this conversation."

Nice save, the voice within her praised.

"You don't have to be so mean about it, Mila." Cindy pouted.

"All right class. Let's get back on the buses," Mrs. Bleevie announced, saving Mila from having to apologize for her behavior. *She shouldn't have to relent when it was them who needed to grovel.*

Automatically, the students migrated to the door. Cindy followed, but Mila lingered behind, waiting for an opportunity to leave without bumping shoulders with people. Her friend glanced back, but Mila gave no indication that she had forgiven her.

***

The bus ride back was overpowered by noise from students teasing over who got scared in one of the rooms with some disturbing tools the doctors used on their patients. Mila rolled her eyes, deciding to not listen to the details, then rested her head against the back of the seat. She thought about the choice words she was going to share with her parents. *Forcing her on this trip and telling her she would not get the car promised if she didn't go. It was beneath them to blackmail her.* Mila seethed.

As the night sky descended upon them, the jokes and excitement slowly died down.

"Are we good?" Cindy's whispered voice broke through her red fog.

The bus pulled in front of the school and came to a stop. Everyone stood up at once, eager to get home.

Mila faced her friend; green eyes stared back. They had been through a lot since freshman year and were close. It was hard to stay mad at her... sometimes.

"Not right now, Cindy. You tricked me. And that is not what friends do." Mila sidestepped around Cindy and joined the crowd.

"But–" Cindy's words faded as Mila shuffled her way off the bus.

The moment Mila's foot hit the pavement the night air stung her cheeks. She brought her coat closer around her while scanning the parking lot. She didn't see her parents' car. *Oh, how nice of them to not even pick her up.* She growled under her breath.

There's your proof that they don't care, Mila.

"I'm sure there is an explanation," Mila uttered out loud.

Why do you keep making excuses for them?

"I don't know."

***

By the time Mila got home, her extremities were numb from the cold. A blazing fire crackled and popped as she entered the foyer. The warmth began to bring her limbs back to life but not without an uncomfortable tingly sensation.

She stripped off her jacket and was greeted by the *clip-clop* of nails on the tile as the family's chocolate Labrador, Rex, hurried toward her wagging his tail in excitement at the sight of her.

Mila kneeled next to Rex and rubbed behind his ears. "Hey, buddy." She placed a kiss on top of his wet nose, and he returned the gesture by giving her a lick across the cheek.

"Mila? Is that you?" Kora, her mother, called from the living room.

"Yeah, Mom."

"Come in here and keep your aging mother company." One glass clinking another echoed from the room.

She's at it again, I see.

Mila strolled to the archway and stopped. Two open bottles of wine sat on the coffee table in front of her mother. Kora had her legs curled under her, and a wine glass gripped between two hands.

There's your explanation.

"Not today, Mother. I haven't quite forgiven you for forcing me on that field trip today."

"Oh, honey. You're being silly. I was only trying to help." Her mother took a sip from her glass.

"Right. I'm sure that's *all* it was. I'm going to bed." Mila turned.

"Mila, hold on!" Her mother raised her voice as she got up from the couch, attempting to go after her. "I have tried to be sympathetic to whatever you are feeling inside. But enough is enough. I want my daughter back. Is that so much to ask?"

Mila whipped around to see her mother standing in the doorway.

Not much of an effort.

"I've always been here, Mother. I never left. If you had just paid attention, you would have seen that." Tears pricked Mila's eyes. She forced down the bubble of sobs in her throat. Her mother's expression left a guilty twinge resting in her stomach.

Reciting what she wanted to say would only cause further pain, and she didn't want that on her conscience, so she spun on her heels and ascended the stairs.

"Mila? Does your behavior have anything to do with Lila?" Kora called after her.

She froze in mid-step.

An overwhelming weight on her lungs began to suffocate her. Hearing that name brought on a slew of forgotten memories. Not ready to relive them, she shoved them back into the darkness and then pivoted to face her mother, rage filling all corners of her being.

"How dare you speak of her! You have no right to." Her insides began to boil.

Kora let out a breath. "Mila, it wasn't your fault."

"You're absolutely right, Mother. It was yours," Mila spewed, then charged up the stairs to her bedroom, slamming the door in her wake.

Lila. She hadn't thought of her name in a year. Then the repressed memories returned, and with force. *Her sister had taken her own life, and their lack of connection at the time had kept her from seeing the signs to stop her.* Thinking of her identical twin brought on emotions she had trapped inside since Lila's death; it was agonizing.

She's not the only one to blame, you know.

"What are you talking about?" Mila challenged.

It was your fault, too.

"How so?" Anger laced Mila's words; she spun back and forth looking for the voice. It didn't respond. "How so?" She growled, demanding an answer.

The silence continued to be the only reply to her question.

"Maybe I *should* commit myself. If I'm talking to myself and expecting an answer, then I must have already lost my mind." Mila disposed of her day clothes with force, tossing them toward the open hamper, but they missed and landed on the floor.

Or, you could just end things and not have to worry about where you belong.

She disregarded the heap, the voice, and then donned her nightwear. Mila skipped her nightly ritual and then crawled in between the sheets.

It didn't take her long to succumb to sleep, and Mila found herself plunged into a red fog, swirling with the mist. Light up ahead forced her hand to cover her eyes from the brightness. When it dimmed, Mila found herself back at the asylum, face-to-face with her reflection in the broken mirror.

A maniacal laugh rumbled in the room. Her image distorted and then morphed into her evil self from earlier.

"Hello again, Mila. You ready to give up yet?" The reflection pushed a hand through her hair, throwing her long tresses away from her shoulder.

"I'm not sure." Mila hesitated.

The image smirked. "You have every reason to. And it won't take much effort on your part."

"What about my parents?"

"What about them?" The reflection let out a breath. "Has it not been blatantly clear that they don't care for you? That they won't miss you when you're gone."

Tears pooled on her bottom lids. She couldn't even have her own thoughts without her evil side having an opinion.

The reflection let out another menacing chuckle. "You were always weaker than me. Never had the guts to live… sister."

Mila froze. *It can't be.* "Lila?" Her mouth dropped open. "How is this even possible? You're… you're dead."

"No thanks to you," Lila spat.

A series of events took over her mind, one after another, knocking her back.

They shifted until it became one continuous reel. It was unclear, but the images twisted and moved in a fluid motion. Even though the picture was hazy, Mila knew what scene was playing out in front of her. It was the day Lila died.

***

Mila threw her tote bag on top of her unmade bed, a smile touching each cheek. Henry Raven, a percussionist in the band, asked her out to a movie. She was on cloud nine. Her heart fluttered in excitement at the thought of showing up to school the next day to see him again.

Water trickling in the bathroom froze her smile. *Was Lila home, already?* She closed the space and tapped on the door with her knuckles. "Lila? You in there?"

There was no answer.

Mila turned the knob and then placed one foot in the room before she realized something was wrong. Her socks soaked in the water puddled on the floor. She glanced down, confused. Eyeing her surroundings, she quickly assessed the situation.

A scream released from her lungs when her eyes lay upon her sister, Lila. Her twin was submerged in the tub; red mixed with the water spilling over the side. The mirror hanging over the sink had been shattered into pieces. Glass shards littered the tile.

Mila pressed her palms hard over her eyes, refusing to watch the scene, again.

"Why are you showing this to me? I already know what happened," she hollered out.

Not everything. You seem to have forgotten the most important part.

The picture replayed, but this time it rewound to before Mila walked in the door. It stopped and played at normal speed. She watched a fuzzy image of herself bash Lila's head into the mirror, the glass splintering, and then picking up a sliver of the mirror, and slitting Lila's wrists before placing her in the tub.

Mila shook her head at the sight. "No! It's not possible! There is no way I would have done that to you! I loved you, Lila."

Well, that's how I remembered it.

"No!" Mila screamed. "No. No. No. No!"

"Mila!"

Another voice called out to her as if on an intercom. Her entire body started convulsing.

"Mila! Stop! Wake up!"

***

Mila's eyes fluttered open. What she thought was her bedroom, at first, melted into white walls around her. With a blurry vision, she tried to focus when she spotted her mother and a man wearing a white coat, standing by the door. Both were whispering intently.

"What is happening with my daughter?" Kora dabbed at her eyes with a tissue.

"It appears she is experiencing a psychotic breakdown."

"How? How did this happen?" Kora choked on the tears flowing from her eyes.

"What were the events leading up to this moment?" The man inquired as he opened a file in his hands.

"I forced her on a field trip. Thought it would be good for her to get out of the house and the funk she has been in for this past year. When she got back, we had a fight. She marched up to her room and went to bed. A little while later I heard her screaming. I rushed in to find her thrashing in bed, and she was holding a piece of mirror to her wrists.

"I couldn't get her to wake up, so I called an ambulance. At the hospital, they found nothing physically wrong with her. The staff decided it was best to place her on suicide watch for a few days. When her condition didn't improve, they committed her."

"That's what I'm seeing in her file." He mentioned, and then flipped through several pages before stopping on a tab that was labeled red. "It also states you were to remove any reflective surfaces that could cause her harm." He snapped the file shut. "So, where did Mila get the mirror?"

Kora's breath hitched in her throat. "I'm afraid I don't know where she got it. I had placed those items in storage. It's possible she retrieved it at some point. She and Lila used to have matching hand mirrors."

"Lila..." He flipped open the file again. "Your other daughter?"

"Yes. Mila had come home to find Lila had taken her own life one year ago, today. I knew she was feeling guilty for not seeing the signs, just based on her behavior. That's why I put her in therapy, but it didn't seem to help." Kora shook her head.

The doctor closed the file again and placed it underneath his armpit, and then the two glanced in Mila's direction.

Mila sat hunched in the corner, the padding providing comfort for the throbbing ache in her head. Her mom knelt beside her, then ran a hand through her untamed locks.

"Mrs. Webber, we will take care of her here at Blayville. I want to ensure you we have a very successful program to help teens with psychological issues."

A heave escaped her mother's throat. "Psychological issues?" She whispered.

"It hasn't escaped my attention as I was glancing through her file of who Mila's father is, Mrs. Webber. Trenton Webber has been a resident here for the last year."

Kora closed her eyes, but the tears still escaped.

"He's been diagnosed with Schizoaffective disorder." The doctor stated.

Mila briefly tuned out their talk and focused on the fact that she couldn't wrap her mind around killing her sister. *Why would she have done such a thing?*

You were jealous.

"Never," Mila growled defensively.

Kora and the doctor returned their line of sight toward her.

Her mother leaned in closer. "Mila?"

In a whisper, Mila uttered, "I killed my sister."

Tears streamed down her face. Lila's laugh vibrated in her ears. She put a hand over each ear and rocked back and forth. "Stop, please. I'm sorry!" Mila clawed at her face, her nails tearing into the flesh.

"Mila, honey." Her mother tried to grab her flailing arms, attempting to hold them down, but she only rocked harder and clawed faster.

"Nurse! Get me a jacket!" The doctor hollered out the open door.

Two burly men in white scrubs rushed in.

Kora maneuvered to the side and watched, helpless.

One man focused on holding her legs down but struggled from Mila kicking them out in all directions. The other man shoved her thrashing arms, with force, into the straitjacket. After a few attempts, they finally succeeded and pulled the straps tight. She continued to fight against the restraints.

"Why?" Mila screamed.

"It appears Mila is hearing voices and hallucinating. Based on your family history so far, I'm led to believe your other daughter might have had a similar form of Schizophrenia, and succumbed to her own inner voices." The doctor concluded.

"Please help her." Kora released her tears. "She is all I have."

"We will do what we can. This disease is a powerful illness and is not curable. But there are treatments out there to keep it stable."

"I loved you!" Mila continued to fight against the restraints.

It wasn't enough.

A sharp pain in her arm caused a yelp to escape. Her world became fuzzy, and her mom and the doctor turned into a ripple from a disrupted puddle.

A single tear slipped down her cheek as darkness took over.

When Emily Was Here

Kathy-Lynn Cross

The bite from the worn mattress jolted me awake. Taking a deep breath as if I had awakened from death caused a dry tickle to form in the back of my throat. A coughing fit soon erupted, dampening my eyes.

Lanterns from the grounds below shone through the caged glass above my bed casting a web-like shadow across the poxed ceiling. After my vision had adjusted to the dim light, I pretended to skip on spider legs from line to line toward the only reminder of my unattainable dream. *Freedom.*

Arms heavy, I pushed myself to stand, and then sluggishly worked my feet to reach the paint-flaked window frame. Running my fingertips across the light, grey wood, I followed the window's frame to the edge. Lightning flashed while I was admiring the tiny notches decorating the entire circumference. Gauging the stretch of silence, I released my misgivings when my fingertips brushed across a smooth spot.

Body quivering, I thought, *Just one more.*

Using the nail on my right phalange, I began to saw a little gash to match the others. Feverishly moving my index finger caused the fingernail to split and break under the pressure I was applying. A wood shard pierced my flesh; instinctively, I locked my jaw to keep from acknowledging the pain. Unmoving, I watched my blood drip into the new indentation. It seemed fitting since it would be my last.

Riding on an exhale was a silent giggle. I spoke only loud enough for confirmation. "Yes, very fitting for today. This makes four thousand seven hundred and forty-nine." I whipped my head to check on the metal door behind me. The view window remained closed.

Relieved to know they weren't watching, I smiled at the silhouette cowering in the corner and motioned for it to move where I could see it better. Holding up its dark hands, I could tell it displayed one finger on the right hand and a three on the left.

"Yes, this does mark thirteen years, doesn't it?"

Another flash of lightning scared Mistie away, so I resumed with the task at hand. There was a smear of blood where I had absentmindedly steadied myself to acknowledge her. My eyes followed the trail on the floor, and then I inspected my shirt.

Damn, if the guard notices, she might alert the doctor.

The room illuminated at the same time an idea struck. I wiped the blood from the wall using my sleeve before pulling the shirt over my head. I turned it inside out and then slipped it back on. Reaching behind my neck, I ripped off the tag. Not sure on what to do with it, I slipped it under the mattress.

Touching the bloody spot, I decided to place the wound into my mouth to stop the bleeding. Liquid salt and iron coated my tongue, replacing the stale, warm Dr. Pepper and dirty penny film. This new flavor was a refreshing change and made me pull harder.

I ran the tip of my tongue over the torn skin to find the splinter. Using my front teeth to extract the foreign object, I deposited it into a pool of saliva that had accumulated in my mouth. The extra liquid helped me spit the nuisance in a crimson diluted spray onto the concrete floor.

A strobe of light brought my attention to the caged glass in front of me. An ashen face of a female stared back. She wore a broad sneer, slightly exposing both canines and enough bloodstained teeth to make me apprehensive about moving forward with my plan. Kaye might try to convince me to bring her along if she knew.

Her eyes narrowed as the darkness from both pupils inked out coloring each orb in a hollow blackness. There was a tightness growing in the middle of my chest causing my breath to hitch. She was vexed.

Instantaneously, a metal latch from the window unlocked, and I took a jarred step back anxious the sound might have woken up my roommate. Several rapid snaps from the last two made me blink as the glass began to splinter and crack from what she had done. My fingers cramped and burned when the cold breeze from the partially open window reached them.

Moisture poured into the room with the promise of rain. This made the little hairs on the back of my neck stand at attention. So many emotions mixed around in my head: anxiety, joy, alarm, jubilation. I didn't know whether to clap with glee or vomit.

Kaye looked down at the one-inch opening. The wood protested and then fractured under the pressure she was applying. I held my breath and waited for the sound of the guard.

Instead, my roommate rolled over and broke the room's silence. "With all the noise you're making, it's going to get us both into trouble."

I crouched so she could hear me. "You know, if you helped me, then we both could escape. Do you want to stay here trapped with only Kaye and Mistie to talk too?"

The human-sized lump, I was talking to, squirmed out to reveal the blank stare of a sixteen-year-old girl. She had a wicked case of bed head, which was common since Arora slept most of the time.

She yawned and used a knuckle to scrub the crusties from her eyes. "You know there is nothing out there for me."

Disgusted, I turned my attention to the door. "You should stop taking those drugs. Eventually, you'll lose yourself to them. Ever watch a zombie movie?"

Arora answered me through another yawn, "Yeah, right before I cut my boyfriend's heart out."

I made a back-throat cough knowing full well she was a compulsive liar. "You are a few sleeping tablets away from being one."

A gust of wind made its way down my shirt. Nature's timing was better than a slap in the face to get my attention. From under the door a thin line glowed, which meant two things, it was five a.m. and Ester was coming.

***

My escape plan would have to wait. Jumping away from Arora's side of the room, I never felt my feet leave the ground, but the landing caused my calves to cramp. Ignoring the pain, I spun around on a heel and then smacked the window shut. Before diving into my bed, I caught sight of Kaye staring at me in disbelief. She opened her mouth to protest, and I quickly gave her the signal to be quiet. Disappointment drained her face of color, but her eyes had changed back to normal.

With a nod, I tossed myself onto the bed, and then grabbed the scratchy cover, pulling it over my head. Across the room, Arora cast judgment with a laugh.

"Stop it," I hissed from under the blanket.

"You'll never get out."

The statement made the band around my heart squeeze. "If you would've helped, we both could have gotten out."

She sighed. "This way is easier. You'll see."

Frustrated, hot tears trickled down and threatened to drip from my chin and nose. I pushed my face into my pillow and screamed. This wasn't easier, and I didn't belong here. Deep down I knew, if I didn't get out, I would die in here.

Click-click-slam. Ester's face peered through the honeycombed screen. "Emily, get up. Wesley will be here in five minutes."

I laid there trying to control my breathing.

"Be a good girl. Don't make me come in there with Wesley."

Oh crap, that meant needles. Sucking in the lint-filled air, I flipped back the blanket. "I'm up. Now go bug somebody else."

I heard the jingle of keys. One slipped into the lock. Biting my lower lip, I shook my head from side to side. Ester extracted the key. I could tell she had moved on when her laugh echoed from down the hall. The guard was on her way to the next victim. As the footfalls grew faint I could breathe again.

Ester's menacing cackle used to invade my nightmares for the first year. Now, it festered under my skin like a crippling disease. One I didn't think a drug could cure or control.

A scene popped into my head as I envisioned Ester choking on her tongue from laughing too hard. This helped me relax, and I wiped my face with a shirt sleeve. If the doctor knew I was thinking ill thoughts then she might up my dosage; but if I kept these sugar-coated wishes to myself, she would be none the wiser. Besides, the daydreams helped me get through times like these.

Arora propped herself up on an elbow. "See, I told you, sleeping is the best escape."

I kicked my legs over the side of the bed. "I'll sleep when they close the lid on my coffin."

***

Religiously, I began my morning routine. Pushing the smelly blanket to the other side of the bed I untangled myself to stand. Once I had stripped the mattress and folded the bedding, Arora moaned from the corner.

"You know, Ester will be back to let Wesley in, better get up. I'm not going to do your chores for you." It was the only free warning she would get from me.

The pile of blankets wriggled next to the wall Arora's bed was up against. Then two hands gripped the pillow she had been using to pull it under the covers. A muffled yawn had filled the silence before she answered me with a flippant casual reply. "They don't care about me."

"Yeah, because you're a compliant captive," I said while placing my pillow and folded pillow case on top of my neat stack of monthly laundry.

"You may not understand my reasons," she sighed. "But being ignored makes me unseen. I like flying under their radar."

"I don't want to be ignored. I want them to listen. My brain works just fine and isn't as twisted as any normal human walking the streets." The springs creaked from my weight when I sat back down.

A bitter chuckle came from her. When Arora calmed down, her head popped out as she turned to face me.

"Sleeping is the best escape. It's like diving into a movie or reading a book and getting lost in it. I'm someone special in my own world."

The morning sun was trying to fight through the rain filled clouds. The overcast light touched her unspent tears. Arora was crabby, uncooperative, a sloth, but when she opened up and spoke about herself in this way it created an imploding star of emptiness.

Not wanting to acknowledge her mental state, my eyes roamed the room, landing on the windowsill I knew was partially unlocked. Then I whispered, "I dream too."

Arora blinked back the moisture before it spilled over and her expression shifted to shock. "You do?"

As the familiar sound of a key slipped into the lock, my coveting gaze went from the window to the door. Waiting, I clasped both hands and placed them in my lap. Posture stiff, I sat on the edge of my bed. The morning's routine was about to begin, I quickly murmured, "Yes, I dream of running. Oh, there are so many ways to run away from here."

***

Arora had scooted to the edge of the frame. She sat across from me in a crossed-legged yoga position, and then regarded me with a warm smile. I started to say something but when the lock clicked she shrugged and swung her attention to the door.

My head mimicked the same action as I stared at the solid metal door swing wider into the room. It mocked me with its rusty creaking, a daily reminder of this reality. I was a caged bird with clipped wings and restrictions on how long I could sing. My existence observed by others through glass and wire.

Squeaky wheels meant my nurse was coming. Wesley rounded the corner looking concerned. His sandy-blond bangs parted briefly with each step, and I could see his eyes. Today the sun's dim light had changed his hazel gaze to a stormy gray.

My hands prickled with the want to caress his face. There was a familiarity about him, a distant relative perhaps or a childhood friend. I could never put my finger on it. He was composed and understanding most of the time. Wesley's gentle demeanor would slip when I pushed Ester too far, and things between us got physical because she would demand for him to intervene.

Ester never made it easy for us to talk in private. In the past, she had mentioned once or twice it wasn't proper protocol for us to be alone. It wasn't like that between us. If I had a friend on the outside, they would be like Wesley.

Solemn, he said, "Good morning, my favorite patient."

Coy, I tilted my head. "I bet you say that to all of your patients."

Taking my morning vitals was the one ritual I complied with and didn't protest about, much. The cart stopped, and then he sidestepped around it while picking up the pressure cuff. Placing the device next to me, Wesley slipped the stethoscope from around his neck. He winced before putting the ear tips in both ears. The nurse had once admitted to me the pressure was annoying.

Ester lingered by the open door looking at her watch while her other hand twirled a key ring with my cell number on it. Mesmerized by the glint coming off of the number seven, I watched it chase a silver key. It was her way of challenging me to make her morning more interesting.

Wesley placed the stethoscope's diaphragm on my chest and told me to take deep breaths. When he moved to my back, I held up my hair but only high enough so he wouldn't see the missing tag. On my last exhale, he dropped the drum with a muffled thunk against his chest. He penciled in my info, and then picked up the pressure cuff to secure it around my arm. Light pumps filled in for small talk as he worked.

Movement from behind the nurse drew my attention. Arora was making silent gagging gestures and air kisses. Baffled by her behavior, I inconspicuously altered my gaze to regard Ester's behavior. *Was she looney?* If the guard noticed Arora's childish actions, she'd get smacked for sure.

There was a pinch down my arm, and then Wesley released the air from the cuff. The *pshhh* died, and he started to turn around. Not wanting him to see Arora making out with her hand, I tugged on his lab coat.

My throat muscle tightened when his smirk began to defrost the emotional ice I encased myself with. I could tell he didn't want Ester to know I had physically gotten his attention. Wesley quickly pivoted as though he forgot to check my pupils. I could detect the lingering effects from a breath mint he had used to mask his vanilla, coffee breath.

Since I missed the opportunity to talk he gave me another chance when his fingers snatched a silver and black Ophthalmoscope. Shining the tool in my eyes, he whispered, "Emily, how are you?"

If anyone here in this godforsaken place should express concern, I was grateful he did. Since Ester could see me, I turned my head so I could direct him to move with me. When Wesley understood my slight movements, his frame shifted to block Ester from my view. I answered with an inaudible, "Fine."

The wrinkles around his dark eyes blended behind short lashes. "Did you want something?"

Nervously, my gaze moved to the door and back to him.

He sighed. "She's on the warpath today. I don't know if we'll be able to talk alone." Moving it to the other eye temporarily blinded me until the one he had checked adapted to the room, and I could see his name tag clearly. Then he said, "I'll see what I can do. If I can come back later, I will."

Arora fanned herself and pretended to faint. Ester turned to stare in her direction, eyes narrowing. She bolted to a compliant sitting position, and I felt myself sigh from relief.

Wesley misunderstood my actions, and hastily added, "Is it important?"

I gave him a slight nod.

He proceeded to pack up the cart when Arora gushed out with, "Me next."

Ester glared.

Wesley smacked his face to cover his reddening cheeks. Then he mumbled, "And things were going so well."

My stomach twisted from his comment, and a wave of nausea crashed against my rib cage. I closed my eyes not wanting to see what the guard was about to do to Arora. Wesley was right; things had been going well.

Guilt clawed within me as I remembered our earlier conversation. Even though my roommate wanted to sleep more than live, Arora didn't deserve this kind of treatment. Heck, we both didn't deserve this kind of life.

Bile burned a trail up my esophagus. With unshed tears growing cold, I forced my eyelids shut. The last thing I heard was the repetitious hand-smacking of Ester's baton. Then Arora grumbled a few obscenities before her screams broke my resolve.

***

I stirred my blob of cold oatmeal. It was beginning to retain to the consistency of ashen Playdough. Pushing the thin plastic spoon into the middle of my creation, I tried to test the laws of physics by flipping the bowl upside down. The cereal and spoon remained stationary.

"Look, magic." I tried to break the depressing stillness in the room.

Arora was back under her blanket. This time, she had tightly pulled the cover around her fetal positioned body. Her sobs had quelled to hiccups and sighs a few minutes ago.

I attempted to get her to eat, but nothing was working this time. Setting my bowl back down, I moved to sit on the edge of my bed. It took some time since I was sore too. Arora's pleas had gotten to me, and I couldn't stop myself as I lunged at Ester's swinging arm. I caught the first of many strikes in the ribs.

Unfortunately, Wesley was forced to assist the nasty woman in restraining us to take a different kind of medicine. Seriously, Ester needed help. I could have sworn the woman got off on beating everyone in her care. I might have imagined it because Dr. Reins says I have a tendency to do that sort of thing.

Mentally, I buried the memory along with all the rest. The place where my soul resided was becoming a bit crowded, standing in the middle of a private cemetery with unmarked moments rioting under layers of negative emotions. At least, they were in a place only I knew about; and no one, not even the doctor could gain access. And as long as my soul kept a safeguard over the primary grave, normalcy was one session away.

A sniffle brought me back to the problem at hand. Arora's impression of a pill bug was getting better. I couldn't tell where her head was, though. Taking in her condition, a thought had occurred to me. *If only I had something to cheer her up.* I turned back to my bed and on the breakfast tray was a clear two-ounce cup of pills. Not even thinking twice about how it appeared there, I shook it like coaxing a pet to come. When she didn't move, I held it out and shook it again, louder.

It baffled me, why guilt had me defending my actions. She knew better than to provoke the passive aggressive hippo. From afar they seem non-threatening, but approach one, and you'll find yourself stuck to the bottom of their foot like ABC gum; already been chewed goo.

My roommate moved gently, and it dumbfounded me how fluently she slithered under the cover. At the foot of her bed, she emerged from the makeshift cocoon. Arora's hair looked like a mound of fresh cotton candy. Swollen eyes, from crying, stared up at me and I snapped mine shut. Turning away, I held the treat cup out to her.

Arora cautiously sat up and sniffed hard enough to stop the dripping. The springs made a twang and popped as she adjusted herself. Wincing, she tried to cross her legs. Arora extended her right arm to expose a scratched hand and waited in a silent demand.

Using my long hair as a black curtain, I peered through the split to look at her. A mixture of purple and rouge colored part of her left cheek and continued along the length of the jaw, fading before it reached her puffy lips. The lower lip had a dried gash from where Ester had punched her with the key ring.

Arching an eyebrow, she questioned, "Are you sure?"

"You need them more than I do. Besides, Wesley might have snuck in a pain tablet."

"Nurse's pet, that's what you are," she said tartly.

I rattled the cup again. "Do you want it or not. Going once, going twice, going–"

"Okay, yeah, I want it." Licking her lips, she stopped when the tip of her tongue touched the small wound.

"Sorry, I didn't think asking to be checked would trip the behemoth into a hail and brimstone frenzy."

"Ester has always been unpredictable. She even gives Wesley trouble."

Narrowing her gaze in mistrust, she questioned, "Really? It didn't seem like he was holding back this time." She rubbed both forearms. There were finger-sized bruises from where Wesley held her down.

"She reports back to the doctor. If he doesn't comply, he could lose his job."

Irritated, she pulled the threadbare blanket around her like a tee-pee. "He doesn't like me, Emily. I knew I should have stayed asleep."

Her comment made my heart drop into a pool of emptiness. A shadow darted out from Arora's corner to the door. Mistie's hand pointed at the handle. Using the flat of my hand, I motioned for Arora to get back under her blanket.

From the crisscrossed pattern of the window, I could see Kaye watching Arora squirm in pain. Right then, Kaye's hazy reflection distorted into a toxic hatred. Tilting her head at me, Kaye used her chin to motion; someone was coming.

Stepping closer to the window, Kaye gave me a wicked smirk and then looked at the windowsill where I had left the drop of blood. I wasn't interested in the notches anymore, only the placement of the sun. It was hard to tell the time because of the cloud cover, but maybe Ester was coming to take me to the showers.

Teetering on my feet, I overcorrected and grabbed my ribs. While hissing in pain, I thought of a dark place I could shove Ester's baton. Picturing her bloody, beaten, and not breathing caused the corners of my lips to curve up from my 'what if' daydream. From behind me, Kaye and Arora laughed as the reason for my newfound good nature stepped into our little hell.

Ester twirled the key ring, and said, "Time to scrub off the crud."

Gradually, I parted my lips enough to show a hint of teeth. "Yes, I'm ready."

***

Showering alone sucked. The room had an oppressive presence that was always hovering. The spray was lukewarm, but it was a blessing. Most days it was freezing by the time I was allowed to clean myself. Ester must have bumped up my shower time as an apology since I wasn't her direct target.

Moisture added to the air's heaviness making it hard to breathe. Fingers grazed along each rib, pressing certain spots until I found the bone which almost made me pee myself. Frowning, when I came to the conclusion it was possibly bruised and the main reason my lungs weren't working correctly.

Arora was pretending to snore when Ester had ushered me from the cell. Mistie was afraid of the guard and the doctor so she had moved to a safe spot. As the door closed, Kaye glared at me like I had betrayed her for not insisting to Ester she needed a shower too.

I was taking a bit longer than usual since it hurt to move my torso. Picking up the ketchup looking packet that contained a generic shampoo and conditioner, I placed the corner in my mouth and used my teeth to rip it open. I squeezed the contents onto my palm and then used both hands to scrub the white slime into my hair.

Humming a few bars, I recognized the song and froze. Eminem's lyrics faded as Rihanna's voice echoed the chorus and when it reached the part about being crazy…

Ire boiled under my skin making the drops of water sting like hail. "Et Tu, Emily? Of all the songs you could be thinking about," I scolded myself.

The guard cleared her throat to remind me she was still there.

Lightning immediately answered Ester's gesture with a thunderous boom that ricocheted through the shower room. If my skeleton could have jumped out of my skin and ran, my husk would be a puddle on the floor by now. An invisible force popped my ears, and both hands instinctively whipped up to cover them. The caged fluorescent lights above me flickered and buzzed like a nest of angry hornets.

In a controlled panic, the guard asked, "Emily, are you okay?" Her words were muffled and strained, assuming she had fallen and was trying to stand.

Voice shilly-shally, I replied, "Yeah," over the water's sputtering streams.

Another canyon boom echoed and this time the building seemed to tremble in fear. There was an electrical spike in the glass tubes, similar to a photo flash, and then the room fell into a blinding black.

Unmoving, I listened for Ester, wondering if she was going to suddenly appear, and then drag me out of here naked and dripping wet. Picturing it, I slapped a hand over my mouth to make it harder for her to find me in the dark. Using the water's spray to mask my movements, I waited to see what she would do. To my amazement, Ester did the unthinkable.

"Emily, stay where you are, I'll be right back." Her booted footfalls echoed until I heard the exit door's hydraulic pressure protest from the abrupt motion. Then the *ka-shhh* of air as it closed, followed by the handle's click, confirmed she had left.

I was alone.

A constant ticking warned me the backup lights were attempting to draw on enough battery power to come on. When the yellow emergency lights grew brighter, a realization hit me. I was blissfully by myself. No guard, no nurse, no Dr. Reins, and no clingy-needy friends.

Naked and about five feet from my towel, I estimated how long it would take for me to find my clothes and hide. Absentmindedly, my hand found the wall lever for the shower, and with shaky fingers, I turned off the water. Spurring forward, I recalled there was a laundry cart in the strip and search room, on the other side of the wall.

Could this be the opportunity I had dreamt for?

With Ester checking on the unforeseen problem, she had no idea her bad day was about to get worse. And with a nervous intake of air, I whispered, "Thank you, Zeus, for the lightning bolt."

Lights above me blinked in sporadic pulses trying to stay on. This reminded me I had little time to put my plan into action. In between the flashes, I placed a foot on the slippery soap-scum tile. When I took my second step, there was a ping from a buried emotion. It resonated like the peal of a grave bell throughout my soul. And now from one of the plots–I kept within myself–Faith had awakened and was furiously pulling on my heartstrings.

I ignored the distraction. Optimism was the dangerous illusion of an ambiguous promise; whereas pessimism was the cushion that broke your fall when fate decided to let go. Thinking this way helped me plan for the 'what ifs;' when others who believed in fate's control, dotted their 'i's' with little hearts.

I had made it to the corner of the shower area where my towel lay on the seat of a bolted plastic chair. Reaching for the powder-blue towel caused me to whimper when my rib warned I was moving too fast. Frustration burned away some of the discomforts as I wrapped the cloth around me.

Worried, I bit my lower lip. A painful spot throbbed as though I had the side-effects of a new piercing, and I clenched my jaw. Laughing nervously, I said, "That's all I need is a cold sore." My tongue pushed on the annoyance, and I tasted blood. Figuring I must have smacked it and not realized; I pressed on.

Holding my towel tight with one hand I followed the wall with the other. Each row of lights lost their fight for power, and I found myself in darkness again; this time even the emergency lights flickered before fading out. Fumbling for where the wall ended, my foot kicked something hard, and it moved with me. Freaking out by the sudden movement, I overcorrected, and my ankle gave way. I went down without a lumberjack hollering timber. *So much for protecting my ribs,* I thought with disgust.

Coughing, I inhaled a sharp gulp of air. My world had become two-dimensional, with everything outlined in a black permanent marker and colored in shadow. Readjusting my towel, I rolled in the direction to whatever had tripped me. Curiosity needled my resolve and using my free hand, I cautiously patted the floor until… four fingertips grazed stubble.

Recoiling, I blinked and strained to see the figure better. Leaning in closer, the lights hissed to life. Wesley's face was staring at me. His perfectly dead face, with both eyes empty of emotion and parted blue lips. Wild, I dropped my towel and lobster-crawled away to give me some personal space.

The nurse wasn't wearing his typical uniform. Wesley was dressed in a Fallout Boy-band shirt. There were several dark red stains on the front. Eyelids wide from comprehension, I roamed down his torn black jeans, to a pair of muddy black-silver Nikes. *He was dead.*

Hands over my mouth, one of the band's songs began to play in my head. Free falling into a memory, I said,

"You loved Fallout Boy." My fingers were slick, and the smell of rusty pennies made me pull both hands from my mouth. Blood dripped from them. Horror smashed into me as I grasped that the blood was not mine. Unable to contain it, I screamed.

Crying, I yelled, "Get up. Wesley, stop playing."

He didn't move.

"Get up," I shrilled in demand.

Escape plan and dignity forgotten, I lunged forward, clutched his shirt and straddled him. Fiercely shaking my male nurse until his head wobbled, Wesley's expression stayed fixed. Dropping him, I leaned down to listen for breathing.

Hot tears burned a trail to my chin; a few fell from my nose. "Who did this to you? Who did this to you?"

My heart must have taken leave because the erratic pulse running through my veins had ceased. Curling over Wesley until my forehead rested on his, one phrase echoed from within me. *Kaye did this to you.*

Sobbing, I cupped his face. "I love you. Why would she do this?"

My world inverted, as I looked through tears, and past my heaving breasts to his chest. One of my hands was wrapped around the hilt of a knife protruding from the middle of his rib cage. I began to cry harder, when a voice from within begged, *I didn't do this. This isn't me. I love him. This isn't me.*

The shower room door swung open, and Ester stepped through the threshold. The familiar *shhh* the door made seemed appropriate, telling Ester to keep what she was about to witness, our dirty secret. Through stringy hair, I could see her brown eyes widening, taking in the horrific scene.

Just as I turned away from her, hopelessness glued my eyelids shut. I didn't want to see Ester's ugly sneer right before she smacked a patient senseless. Or Wesley's lifeless form beneath me. *How was I going to explain this?*

Boot scuffs made me stiffen as she approached. Praying, I prepared for the first swing of her baton to crack my skull hard enough to send me to wherever Wesley was. Then a hand fell onto my bare shoulder as she leaned in next to my ear. Ester whispered, "What are you doing?"

My eyes flashed open. I was hunched and straddling... no one. I was freezing, and shaking uncontrollably. Wet onyx hair draped over my head from leaning forward. Wanting to dump my guts out right in front of her I started to dry-heave.

Patting my back, while using a mocking motherly tone, she said, "Did the storm scare you? Or are you afraid of the dark?" Sanity drained from my reality as she continued, "It's all right now. The backup generators are working. Come on, let's get you dressed and back to your room."

Traumatized, I said through quivering lips, "There was a dead body here. I saw it!"

Caught off by my blunt outburst, Ester's hand quit moving. "What?"

I didn't want to say his name, as a taboo sense of dread skidded over my skin. Checking my hands, they were clean. Reluctant, I craned my neck slightly to scan the room for Wesley's dead body.

Disbelief made the corners of my eyes dampened. Thoughts scattered, when my reason slipped from random questions, and sporadic statements swam in my mind. *What had just happened? I didn't know my nurse personally. Love, I didn't love him. Wesley had to be alive. Could what I had just witnessed been a premonition?* Nothing was making sense to me. A rumble of thunder made me blink as the guard's demeanor shifted to understanding.

Ester looped one arm under mine to help me off the floor. "Wesley might be right. You are a little off today."

Supporting my weight, she steadied me before I took the first step. "I'll inform the doctor."

Apathetically, I stared at the spot where Wesley was. A powder-blue towel lay crumbled right next to my sanity. Not wanting to make Ester upset, I tried to keep up with her pace as we passed a few metal cabinets before reaching the charcoal painted lockers.

I had stopped taking the drugs Dr. Reins prescribed. Maybe this was a side effect of not taking my morning cocktail. I had tried to go cold-turkey before and ended up in the hospital wing for a few weeks. Arora didn't want me to get in trouble, so she hid them in a hole she had made in the mattress. This way I had them for back-up if the side effects became worse than before.

Ester propped me against my locker. "Your clean clothes are inside. You have five minutes to get dressed, and I'll be back for you then."

Nodding, she left to give me some privacy. It didn't matter to me since I had already walked here in the nude. Facing the ceiling, I inhaled sharply to swallow the pain. Counting to ten, I slowly exhaled to clear my head.

I had seen his lifeless body.

Tasted my fear.

I smelled his blood.

Heard my screams.

I felt the presence of death.

Behind my eyelids, the negative image of Wesley's glazed-over expression had burned into my brain. His lips parted from death's final kiss. The two smears of blood, on either side of his face from where I held his cheeks. Recollecting how the knife's blood-soaked handle felt in my fingers.

A single drop of clarity fell into my pool of madness and the statement I had thought earlier resurfaced.

Why did I believe Kaye had killed him?

***

Muscles sore and stiff, I placed my pillow against my ribs and stretched with care. I curled back up and brought the cushion to my face and moaned. The combination of my internal pain, physical chill, and broken mental balance had me questioning my reality.

Several creaks from the protesting metal made me aware my roommate was moving around. The harsh whisper of hands sliding across her sheet meant Arora was on a mission. It had to be paramount if she was putting that much effort into whatever she was doing.

Body shutting down, I didn't care enough to roll over or ask why. Depression's only positive side effect was fatigue. *Maybe this was why Arora slept so much?*

A long gurgle came from my middle, but I wasn't hungry. *Can you consume your emotions?* I wondered. Absorb servings of pity pie, two or three scoops of 'I-don't-care' and topped with a mound of whipped despair. To my surprise, saliva pooled in my cheek, and I had to swallow to keep from choking.

The smoky shadow of a head poked out from behind the headboard. Hoarse, I croaked, "Hi Mistie."

The gloomy light shining through the window was creating a silhouette of me on the wall. Mistie thinned and moved in a distorted blur to lie down on the shadowed blanket. She wanted me to confide in her, and my heart broke.

Since I was on my side, tears dripped over the nasal bone. I had placed both hands between my cheek and the mattress. They were getting soaked from the waterworks. Snot thinning, I sniffed and used my sheet to dab away the water. Heaving a sigh, I watched Mistie's outline rock slightly; she was trying to be patient.

Taking a moment to collect my thoughts, I said, "I'm never getting out of here." The words sounded final, and it made me cry harder.

"What?" Arora's question was laced in astonishment.

With a one-shoulder shrug, I repeated myself through hiccups and sniffs.

Mistie's head bobbed as airy fingers tried to push a strand of hair behind my ear.

"Don't listen to her," Arora shrieked.

Shocked, I flipped over to stare at my roommate. There was a finger in my face and outrage coloring her pasty complexion. Scared from Arora's outburst, Mistie bolted to the other side of the room and disappeared under the adjacent bed.

"So, you're giving up," my roommate accused.

Tears welled, but I didn't dare blink.

"All you keep talking about is getting us out of here." Flaying me with her words, as both hands whipped around, before placing them on her hips. Arora's reaction made her seem more animated. "Out there—out there—really? Why do you want out so badly? What's wrong with staying here?"

Mouth open, I rocked my head. Words failed me as I sputtered like a drowning frog. Her behavior had me floored. She was passionate over one subject; sleeping. Different positions, and which was the most relaxing. What pills she preferred over others. How her face would brighten when she would reminisce about her bedroom. Explaining to me about the decorations, furniture, and the collection of plush fish toys she slept with. I had a feeling *Finding Nemo* was the reason. I watched her gray-socked feet slowly ambled toward the window.

I sniffed.

Then she did the same.

Standing, I joined her to stare out the glass. Kaye glowered at us like she was expecting us to say something.

The silence began to poison the air in the room, and it spurred Kaye to pace like a caged cat that had woken up from being darted. There was a predatory mien in her smile.

Concerned, I stole a glance at Arora. Sparkles trickled down her chin. In front of us, Kaye's reflection kept moving back and forth, her way of waiting to see what I would do. Since we were having a group shout and share meeting, I decided to go next.

Quietly, I started with, "There was an incident in the showers today."

Kaye didn't stop pacing but hesitated.

Arora looked out the window speckled with raindrops, which I found fitting. A few trailed down her reflection adding to her tears.

Nervous, I reached for my hair and began to comb it with my fingers. Taking a shallow breath, I began to explain. Sharing all the details about the storm, the power outages and how Ester had left me alone in the dark, giving me the opportunity to escape.

Kaye quit pacing and scowled.

Guilt zinged down my spine, as I averted my gaze from Kaye, and focused on Arora. "I wanted to see how far I could get."

"You were going to leave without us?" Arora's eyes held betrayal.

Holding up both hands, I held a long blink, so she wouldn't see my lie when I said, "I would have come back for you if I did."

Bam!

Both of us jumped back as we watched the glass splinter in a web-like fashion from two fist-sized indentations in the window. The whites of Kaye's eyes were hollow and empty. Her fury radiated from the glass surface in front of us.

Arora nodded at Kaye. "Yes, I know she's lying." She turned to face me. "What I want to know is, why you're lying to us now? I thought we were in this together."

Rubbing my knuckles, I could taste regret's rancid bite. *How could I have left them behind?* We were a team, and they had my back, and I had theirs. No matter how annoying, they understood me better than anyone else.

In a gesture of forgiveness, I pleaded. "It was stupid of me to try and leave without you." This was mainly for Arora, but I knew deep down Kaye would force me to bring her along. So, I bit back my distress and acknowledged her too. "I mean, both of you."

Kaye was livid, but at least her eyes were back to normal. My roommate gave me a tremulous smile. It made her seem fragile, and if I had acted differently, she might have shattered. Reassuringly, I tried to return the gesture. I didn't think this discussion was over, especially since I had a few questions for the both of them.

Observing Kaye, with her dark eyes delving into my soul, and her lips progressively curling, I knew this was far, far from over.

***

Exhausted, I fell back onto the mattress. There was a plastic rattle above my head. I cracked an eye to see a clear plastic pill cup. Arora shook it again, and I opened the second one.

Lifting my head, suspiciously I murmured, "What's this?" I held out my hand as she placed it in the middle of my palm.

"Remember, I've been saving them for you." She spun on a heel and within two steps jumped onto her bed. The frame protested from her effort, and she giggled while crawling to the far corner.

I regarded the small pink suppressants. Counting, I was impressed with the amount. "Wow, there's a week's worth in here. How did I manage to do that?" I shook the container.

My astonishment faded to concern. Trying to piece together the last few days made my head hurt. Each moment was smeared in clouds of fog like it didn't exist. I whispered, "Impossible."

A phlegmy rattle came from Arora. "Duh, you gave them to me after you pretended to swallow them. You're lucky Ester doesn't swipe the upper part of your mouth. By the way, Dr. Reins must have upped your dosage because I noticed the milligrams and code on the medications are different than before."

Digging out one of the capsules, I eyed it suspiciously. "I don't recall her telling me she changed it." Frowning, I met Arora's gaze. "Do you remember yesterday?"

She laughed. "Of course, I do. That's a song."

"Come on; I'm serious."

Her laughing stopped. "I am too. It's a song." Arora sounded incredulous. "Um–hello–the Beetles." Then she started humming the tune.

I threw my pillow at her. "Come on. Arora, I need you to think. What did you do yesterday?"

She scrunched her nose in thought. "I slept."

Infuriated, I shot up. "That's a cop-out. What did you have for breakfast?"

She slid down from the wall and pulled her blanket over her head. "Why does it matter? Every day is a paid vacation from reality." Her finger pointed at the window.

Scared, I backed up. "You don't know, do you?"

Her voice was muffled under the covers. "Listen, why poke around the past when the present is right in front of you. Enjoy the now." Flipping the bedding away from her face, she motioned at the cup of prescriptions. "Take one of those, sleep, forget, recharge, and repeat. It's easy. And bonus, you don't have to deal with the three of them." Waving at the door, she continued, "They'll leave you alone if you play their game." Punctuating her advice with a yawn, I realized why I had tried to leave without them.

Then the memory of Wesley's dead expression flashed into my mind. *Was this vision something from my past?* I tested the hunch. "Arora, what is it about my past I'm not supposed to remember?"

She rolled away to face the wall. "Like, how should I know?"

"But you do, don't you?"

Her answer was barely audible. "Maybe?"

With a small ping of hope, I asked, "Can you help me?"

Voice quivering, she answered, "Trust me; you don't want to dig up the past." Sitting up, she scooted her butt to the corner so Kaye couldn't see her. She gave me an earnest expression. "You aren't going to like what you'll find."

"If you help me, I'm sure it'll be okay," I said with confidence.

Becoming somewhat dejected, she uttered, "I'm not your strength. That's Kaye's department."

***

The click of a key made my eyes pop open. Head raised, Ester held the door open for Wesley. Awashed in uncertainty, I thought, *How would he look?* Obviously, he wasn't dead if his cart was rounding the...

A man with raven hair and squinty obsidian eyes glided over the threshold. Panicked, I pushed myself into the far corner of my bed. Pulling my arms tight and clamping my hands over my mouth. I motioned 'no' with my head.

Ester sighed. "Emily, this is your new nurse. He's going to be–"

"Where is Wesley?" I couldn't hide my anxiety.

The stranger addressed Ester, "Is she the–"

"The crazy one, yes." The guard cut him off.

He cleared his throat. "I was going to say special."

My breath caught. Special, he wasn't allowed to think of me that way. Only Wesley thought I was special. I didn't know this guy well enough for him to assume he knew me.

The new male nurse approached me with a cup overflowing with pills. "This will help you forget why Wesley isn't coming back."

Frightened, I yelled, "What are you talking about?"

He shrugged. "You'll have to ask Kaye if you want to know more."

Instantly, she appeared behind him. Seizing his neck with one hand and in the other was a raised knife over his chest.

Mouthing the words, "I'll protect you." She plunged the knife into his chest and then twisted, as he grunted from the pain. Body slack, Kaye released the guy, and he crumbled to the floor. I couldn't take my eyes off of him, and then his head lolled in my direction.

Wesley's face replaced his. I shrieked. "Why? Why? How could you? I loved him. I could never."

Kaye slid her open hand down the blade. With the wish of death sparkling in her irises, I watched in revulsion as the blood ran down her arm. "But, I could."

***

Someone was shaking me and yelling. Then there was a harsh sting that exploded against my cheek. Gasping, tears marred my vision, as I tried to settle down long enough to comprehend what was going on.

Ester was over me, and Wesley had a hold of my ankles. The guard's mass pushed my shoulders into the springs. My nurse released both ankles and removed a vial and sterile syringe from a locked drawer on his cart. Removing the packaging, he plunged the needle into the clear bottle. When he withdrew it, I heard the tapping on the plastic to release the trapped air. Then he picked up a tourniquet and alcohol swab. He nudged Ester to the side so he could reach my arm.

Madly, I skimmed the room for Arora. She was covering her face with a pillow. Resentment rising, I thought, *I defended you, and you're not going to return the favor?*

Using my best in-house voice, I calmly spoke to Wesley. "I'm fine. Really, I'm fine now. I don't need it."

Troubled with whom to believe, he hesitated. I could tell he was battling to accept my previous actions or my words. Lowering the shot, he cocked his head at Ester. "What do you think? I don't want to use it if she is rational."

She grabbed my chin. Invading my personal space, I could see my reflection in her pupils. The twin images of me appeared frantic and petrified. Fear made the lump in my throat expand and difficult to breathe.

Dropping my chin but not letting go of my shoulder she said, "Dr. Reins said if she had a fit to sedate her. It's your call if you want to go against orders." Ester squinted at me. "Her appointment with the doctor is in thirty minutes."

He turned away and softly placed everything on the green medical tray. Voice level, he requested, "Ester, can I have a word with her?"

She straightened, and I rubbed blood back into the area she had held. Gauging her co-worker's demeanor, the guard placed a hand on her baton and drummed four of her fingers. "Sure, I'll be right by the door."

Walking around him, Wesley stopped her by placing a hand on her arm. "Can I have ten minutes with her, alone?"

I was in disbelief. Wesley was asking her to break the rules. *Was he crazy?*

Cheeks red, Ester blew out hard. "You know I can't leave you alone with her."

"I would like to try. I believe I can reach her." The pinch in between his brows relaxed. "Ester, ten minutes, please. You can time me."

She turned on a heel. "If she goes out of her freakin'-ass-mind and kills you, your blood won't be on my hands." Glancing at her watch, she turned to us. "Ten minutes, starting now." Taking the silver seven from her pocket, she fingered the ring and twirled the key, then grabbed the handle to close the door. I didn't hear the lock, which was her way of saying, she was right outside.

Wesley released a profound sigh. "Well, that wasn't as hard as I thought it would be."

I massaged the arm he was going to stick. Skeptical, I kept my jaw locked, figuring it was better to remain silent until he revealed his reason to be alone with us. Bringing my knees toward my chest, I wrapped my arms around both legs and peered at him from over my knee caps.

Arora was still hugging the pillow but tighter than before. Her body shook as though she was crying. Grimacing, I turned my attention back to the male in the room.

Lost in thought, Wesley stood in front of me with an expression that made my heart pause as I pictured him dead. The air in the room was oppressing, and it peaked my anxiety meter to new heights. I wasn't sure if this talk was something we were going to benefit from, but I chewed on the inside of my cheek and waited for the executioner's axe to drop.

"May I sit?" He motioned to the foot of the bed.

I nodded.

Arora whimpered into the cushion. *What was her problem? He wasn't sitting on her bed? She wasn't the focus of his attention.* When the reproofs in my head stopped, another round of inquiries circled. *What if he wants to ask me a question? What if I answer it wrong, would he end up using the needle on me anyway?*

Wesley cleared his throat. "I can see the questions behind your eyes. Emily, just breathe. I need you to keep calm, or there won't be anything I can do to help if you lose control." He crossed his leg and faced me. "Understand?"

Biting my lower lip, I agreed with a head bob.

Pleased, he said, "Good." Then his lips faded into a thin line. "Emily, I'm going to be direct because I think this is the only way to get through to you. I need you to listen. Some things are going to sound a bit unbelievable, but I really need you to keep up with me. We don't have a lot of time here."

Giving him a half shoulder shrug, he continued, "Do you remember the night we met?"

Wide-eyed, I answered, "No."

"During our senior year, we moved in different circles. I knew about you, but you stayed pretty much to yourself. A friend of mine was having a party, and I asked her to invite you as a favor."

I whispered, "Wendi?"

Sparking the correct answer from me spurred him into the rest of his explanation. "We left the party at the same time, and I overheard you giving Wendi the excuse you had to go home and feed your fish." He grinned at his memory. "I introduced myself as we headed to our cars. I found it peculiar how secretive you were, so I challenged your reason for leaving.

"You gave me the cutest smirk and then thanked me for walking out with you. Before getting into your car, you asked if I would like to get a coffee. You were giving me a chance. I was so ecstatic, I agreed."

Narrowing my gaze, I said, "What are you getting at?"

He held up both hands. "Our trust grew, and over time we became friends. Four months later we were dating. At the end of our senior year…" His voice trailed off.

Petrified, but intrigued, I sat up. "What happened at the end of senior year?"

"I asked you to marry me."

Gaping, like a fish out of water. I perused our surroundings. "How did I end up here?"

Worried, he said, "This is where it's going to get hard for you."

"I'm finding most of this unbelievable but continue." I started chewing on a hangnail.

"It was the end of summer, and we were on our last date before heading off to college. Our date didn't end well." He became pale.

"What, did we have a fight," I said sarcastically.

"Yes, we did. Now, looking back it was silly at the time, but you got out of the car and stormed off. I followed to apologize." Raising a hand to his chest, he paused to catch his breath, and then said, "Your pleas echoed through the darkness, and in a panic, I began to search for you." Tears ran along the rims of his eyes.

Breathless, I asked, "Wesley, what happened?"

"There was a group of cloaked men in the woods performing some ritual. I think they might've been deranged or drunk; I'm not sure, but they were definitely evil." He started to sob. "They raped you, and then beat me senseless so I couldn't save you."

I choked on my saliva. "They what?" My temperature rose, and I began to pat my body down to put out the fire. *"What?"* I screeched.

Wesley moved forward and clasped my hands in his. "Look at me, Emily," he said sternly. "It gets worse."

"Worse, how can it get worse?" I tried to pull away from him. "Oh my, are we dead? We're dead, aren't we?"

Leaning in, he sighed. "No, we're not dead."

I relaxed and bowed my head with a relieved sigh.

His words became distant. "No, we're not dead, just me."

Jerking back, I shrieked.

Then I heard the asylums' alarm going off. Ester came crashing into the room. Wesley was trying to shelter me from the guard. Arora yelled at Ester to leave me alone.

Before she got to me, Wesley yanked me closer, so his lips were next to my ear. "Those sadistic bastards gave you a choice. If you killed me, they promised to set you free. I begged you to do it. I loved you. It was the only way I could save you. Even though you kept wailing and reiterating, 'you couldn't.' But when the man with raven hair attacked you with a knife, something happened."

I didn't want to know, but the words were slipping from my mouth before I could stop them. Breathing shallow, I asked, "What? What happened?" Horrific images flipped uncontrollably through my head, and I knew before he even confessed.

"You killed me, Emily Kaye."

The crack of Ester's baton was a blissful godsend.

Epilogue

The alarm's screeching grew louder, branching dream to reality. Lids heavy, I realized they were crusty, probably from me crying in my sleep, again. Debating whether or not it was worth hitting the snooze, I decided to roll out of bed and smack the button to make the annoyance stop.

My head hurt like there wasn't enough room for my brain to think. Sluggish, I made my way into the bathroom. Adjacent to the sinks was the walk-in closet. Picking out my clothes for the day, I hung them up next to the shower so the wrinkles would steam out.

Heading to the dresser, I opened the top drawer and picked out stockings and matching undergarments. Glancing at a picture of a blond man, holding up a girl's hand with short pink hair, they were showing off a ring. I reached over and laid the picture face down. For some reason, I couldn't look at it today. On the back, someone had penned Wes & Kaye with an infinity sign.

Lightning flashed through the bedroom windows; its leftover presence was hard enough to shake the second floor. I raised the blinds to look outside. The rain was turning to hail, which meant I was going to have to hurry and leave early to make my first appointment.

Before walking back into the bathroom, I retrieved my cell from its charger and checked for any messages. Then I placed my phone and undergarments on the counter. I ached all over and my heart fractured in six different emotions. Turning on the faucet, I froze.

Steam clouded the mirror, trying to conceal six sets of eyes staring at me through the reflective surface. I blinked several times as Ester tapped her baton. Arora was yawning in the corner. Kaye's angst was boring a hole in the back of my head. Mistie zipped past and into the shower stall. Emily's presence was the most dominant. She began to cry when Wesley's misty form emerged from the closet and the rest of us gasped in unison.

Clutching my chest, as my mind raced why the seven of us were in this room.

Ozzy's "Crazy Train," interrupted the silence between us. Reaching for several prescriptions, I paused, and then snatched the cell. Locking my gaze with each of them, I proclaimed, "All of you can't come to work today."

Irritated, for not discovering a way to cure myself, I swiped the bar and answered, "Hello. This is Dr. Emily K. Reins, what's on your mind?"

Postpartum

Savannah Rohleder

October 10, 1958

"He's coming!"

"Or she." Edward appeared at my side in an instant.

Pain tightened like a band around my stomach. I couldn't take it. My knees buckled, and I toppled to the awaiting sofa. Panting, begging for the contraction to end, I can't believe centuries of women had managed to survive this. There's no way I would survive. I had to survive.

"I can't do this," I moaned.

"Yes, you can, Eleanor." Edward's warm tone felt like a pinprick of light in the dark, comforting but too small to make much of a difference.

Wiped out from the most recent spasm in my middle, I slumped against the sofa exhausted. I don't know how long had passed when Edward placed a gentle hand on my shoulder.

"I have the bag. Let's cut out for the hospital."

I took my husband's strong hand, and he helped me to my feet, which protested very loudly at being used once more. Stringing my arms through my dark, woolen coat that he held for me, I tried to think positively. I can do this. Soon, I'll meet my baby boy. I was convinced I was having a boy, but Edward thought otherwise.

Another pain stabbed through me and I collapsed onto my husband. He barely caught me. I couldn't breathe while the contraction wreaked havoc on my body. My eyelashes felt wet with tears. I can't do this. I can't do this. I'm gonna die!

Edward dragged me along. I felt like the Raggedy Ann doll I had growing up after the chickens had pecked it to shreds. My insides felt like mush by those very birds I had hated for ruining my favorite toy. My legs felt useless and fumbled with each step. I don't know how Edward got me to the car, but next thing I know, I'm tucked in the back of his Ford. The leather is cold but does nothing to cool my burning skin. The back seat feels too small. I want to lay down, but there isn't enough room.

Suddenly, I felt a gush of fluid rush out of me, almost like I'd peed, but different. I hadn't wet myself since I was little. Heat spread across my face. The embarrassment lasted only seconds before the next pain hit, and I couldn't hold back a loud scream.

Three Weeks Later

Baby Kenneth's wailing woke me up. Exhaustion begged me to roll over and go back to sleep, but my newly discovered mothering instinct screamed louder. My baby needed me, and I would not let him down.

Dim light peeked through the windows. The hands of the clock on my bedside table told me it was the early hours of the morning, not early enough that Edward was still home, but earlier than I liked to rise. A slight chill hung heavy in the air, making me shiver. Crossing my arms to ward off the cold, I stuffed my feet into my soft pink slippers by my bed. This room was always cold. Since fall was in full swing, I couldn't get moving fast enough, and I shuffled out to the hall. Kenneth's nursery was the room to my right, just next to the one I shared with Edward.

Kenneth's crying grew louder, and I rushed to his side. Scooping him up from his crib, I cradled him against me. Right away, my little one opened his mouth in search of food. Chuckling at his appetite that was remarkably similar to his father's, I moved to the simple wooden chair in the corner and sat down. Slipping the white sleeve of my nightgown off my shoulder, I let Kenneth eat.

My mind wandered while he ate. The list of chores had been steadily increasing since I'd given birth. Edward said I should take all the time I needed to recover before worrying about the house, but I didn't feel right about sitting idle while he worked to put food on the table. He never complained about the state of the house, but I knew he'd noticed the things that hadn't gotten done. I'd also seen the dimming of his eyes in disappointment the first few nights when he had to prepare their dinner. I loved him for not complaining, but I wouldn't let another day go by without having his dinner ready for him when he got home.

Kenneth cooed. I smiled, looking down at my beautiful boy. His rosy cheeks and perfectly round face turned up to me. Those clear blue eyes sparkled. I could stare at him all day.

A pungent odor rose to my nose, breaking me out of my thoughts.

"Is it time to change your diaper?"

Grabbing a new one, I set Kenneth on the changing table. Actually, it was just one of the fold-out tables we'd had in the living room with a blanket over the top. Even though we weren't poor by any means, Edward still wanted us to reuse everything possible. He didn't see the point in spending money on something that could work just as good. I didn't see the point in complaining.

Opening Kenneth's used diaper, I wiped him and wrapped the soiled cloth to put in the hamper. The new diaper went on, safety pins securing it, and then his blue and white romper. Picking him up, I headed toward the crib.

Once again, I wanted to get lost staring at my little boy. His black eyes…

That wasn't right.

I blinked, trying to clear my vision.

When I looked down again, Kenneth's eyes were white and vacant. His skin looked like leather. Mouth hanging open, slimy maggots wriggled in and out. His cheeks were hollow. No nose, only a hole. A maggot popped out of an eye. Oozing pus drained down the face. One arm ended above the elbow, the bone visible. Rags hung loosely on the corpse.

A scream ripped out of my mouth. I dropped the horrible thing in my arms. The stench of decay choked me. Darkness and death hung heavy in the air.

Heart racing, I needed to get away from that thing. I needed to find my baby. That was not my baby. What happened to my baby?

Kenneth screamed.

My vision cleared.

A new kind of horror froze the blood in my veins. What had I just done?

I scooped Kenneth up from the crib and cradled him close to my chest. Rocking and bouncing to soothe him, I murmured words of love. I even tried soft shushing. He wouldn't calm down.

"Honey, mommy's got you. Please, stop crying."

Tears stung my own eyes. I couldn't let myself think of what I'd just done.

Kenneth was the priority. Make sure he's alright.

His screaming reached an even higher pitch as I lifted him to look for any damage the fall could have done. I stretched out each of his limbs. They looked fine.

My ears wouldn't soon recover.

I checked his reddened and scrunched head. Was that a bruise? Goodness, tell me that isn't a bruise. A suffocating wave of guilt swept through me.

How could I have let this happen? What kind of mother was I that I could drop my baby? I hurt my son.

I hurt my son!

Sinking to the ground, I couldn't hold back the sob rising in my throat. Kenneth's screams ripped at my heart. It was all my fault.

**

"Is that a bruise? What happened?" Edward turned to me, Kenneth still in his arms.

The warm feeling from moments ago withered in my chest. What could I say? I can't tell him the truth. He would take Kenneth from me. I couldn't let him take away my baby. But what else could I tell him? There is no other excuse for the fall.

"I-" My voice faltered.

I couldn't tell him.

"Ellie?"

"You know I hate that name!" I snapped.

Hurt flashed in his eyes, but I couldn't stop that now.

"What happened, Eleanor?" His voice lacked warmth.

The anger melted to sadness. I still couldn't forgive myself for earlier.

"It was an accident." Tears rushed from my eyes.

"An accident?"

"He slipped out of my arms. I didn't mean to. Ed, you have to believe I wouldn't do anything to hurt Kenny."

Edward wrapped his free arm around my shoulders, and I buried my face in his neck. The sobs shook my whole body. Edward's hand caressed my arm, becoming the soothing balm I'd needed all day.

"Darling, I'm sure Kenneth is fine. No harm was done."

I weakly nodded, still unable to lift my head and face my forgiving husband.

"You seem tired. How about we eat and relax. We don't even need to hand out candy this year if you aren't up for it."

I started. I'd completely forgotten today was Halloween.

"No. I'm fine."

Wiping my face, I lifted my head and patted my hair, making sure everything was in place. Smoothing down the skirt of my day dress, I moved further into the kitchen. At the stove, I checked the pot boiling the peas. It was ready.

"Sit. I'll get our plates ready."

Edward obeyed. I took the few steps required to reach the table at the other end of the kitchen. The simple peach-colored rectangle table easily seated our small family. It wasn't something I would have picked, but it was a present from Edward's parents. Two place settings with plates, silverware we'd received as a wedding gift, and the napkins my older sister had embroidered with simple flowers sat on the table. I grabbed both our plates and pivoted to the stove to fill them.

I froze.

The lids from the pots exploded, boiling water bubbled over. The flames from the stove engulfed the cookware.

The smell of burnt dinner soured the air. The oven popped open. Soot leaked out. Spiders scattered around the kitchen.

The plates slipped from my hands. They shattered at my feet. I jumped at the sound. My knees buckled. Landing on my rear, I scooted as far as I could from the madness in front of me.

Fire licked up the wall. Cockroaches skittered across the floor. A looming figure rose up beside me. I flinched. This can't be happening.

Fear smothered me. I closed my eyes to block everything. I pressed my hands to my ears to block out the screaming. My screaming?

What was happening to me?

"Eleanor?"

Something shook my shoulder. I didn't want to know what it was.

"Eleanor!"

The voice snapped me out of it, and I glanced up at my husband's concerned eyes.

"Eleanor, what is going on?"

I looked around. The kitchen was normal. The only thing out of place was the shattered plates on the floor.

"I... I don't know." My voice sounded odd to my ears, strained. It took too much effort to just say those simple words.

"Maybe you should lay down for a while."

Edward looked at me like any moment I would break. Maybe I would.

***

That evening, I was awoken by the squeals and giggles of happy children. The Halloween festivities must be in full swing. A chorus of "trick or treat's" sounded from somewhere outside and I couldn't help but smile. On a normal year, that would have been enough to keep me waiting at the door to greet the neighborhood kids, but I couldn't muster the strength to move.

The images I'd seen earlier were imprinted on the backs of my eyelids. Every time I blinked, they screamed out at me.

A shadow moved across the wall, and I jerked up. It had moved toward Kenneth's room. What if it wanted to harm him? What if Kenneth was in danger at this very moment? What if they wanted to steal him?

I shoved the sheets off me and raced to the door. In seconds, I stood in Kenneth's nursery. The shadows danced around the crib. I cried out.

They would not get my baby!

I would not let them take him.

Before the shadows could descend, I snatched Kenneth from his bed and pressed him tightly to my breast. The shadows came closer. I dashed from the room. They followed, clogging the hall. Darkness deepened. My feet flew. I burst from the hall to the kitchen. More shadows waited.

I needed to get outside. I needed out of here. It wasn't safe here for Kenneth. I needed to keep him safe.

I reached the side door as a voice called behind me. I couldn't listen. I had to leave.

Racing to the trees at the back of our property, I weaved in and out to find a safe place. Footsteps pounded behind me. I ran faster, running nearly blind in the dusk light. The rhythm of movement closed the gap. I couldn't outrun them. I needed to hide.

Taking a right, I ducked behind a thick trunk. Kenneth whined in my arms. I shushed him.

"Eleanor?"

Edward?

Would he protect us?

"Darling, please come out. You're scaring me."

Edward nearly tripped on me. He stepped on my toes, and I winced in pain.

"Darling, what's going on? Why did you run?"

"I had to save Kenneth. They were coming for him. I had to save our baby."

"Who was coming?"

"They were! I have to keep him safe, Edward. I have to protect him. They were going to take him. I couldn't let them take him from us."

Kenneth started to cry.

Edward reached for him, but I moved so he couldn't take Kenneth.

"It's cold out here. How about we go back inside."

"No! They are waiting for us. Edward, we can't let them take him."

"Darling, you are scaring me. No one is coming for Kenneth."

"Yes, they are!"

Edward raised his hands in surrender. A pleading look passed over his face. "How about I take us somewhere where they can't get Kenneth."

I nodded. We couldn't go back home. They were waiting for us. I could feel them.

Edward helped me to my feet. Once again, he reached for Kenneth, who had finally calmed down, but I couldn't let go of my precious baby boy. Relenting, Edward let me hold our son and led me through the trees. The sounds of delighted children grew louder. Fear sent prickles up my spine the closer we got to the house. Heading to the car, Edward helped me in. I didn't know where he planned on taking us, but I didn't care as long as it wasn't back to the house.

As Edward drove, I relaxed. My eyes drifted shut.

The next thing I know Kenneth was taken from me. I jumped after the hands that stole him. I scratched the arm of the man. He doesn't let go of my baby.

Someone is stealing my baby!

Large hands grab me. I scream and thrash. They pull me farther from Kenneth.

"No! That's my baby! Give me my baby!"

"Ma'am, we are trying to help."

I slap at those harsh hands holding me. I break free for a second. An arm clamps around my waist. I pound my fists into the meaty thing, but it won't free me.

I need to get free!

I scream again. Something pricks my skin. A sharp sting travels up the arm trapped between by body and the unrelenting arm encircling me. I don't care about the pain. I don't care about anything but getting to my son.

The men drag me into the unfamiliar building. The light blinds me. I dig my bare feet into the slick tiled ground, but it does little to stop the giants pulling me. My feet burn. My eyes sting with tears. My arms ache from fighting.

I need to save my son.

They push me through a doorway and drop me on a bare bed. The thin mattress does little to absorb the impact. The springs squeak in protest of moving. One bites into my back.

"Where is my son!" I scream as they scramble out of the room.

I topple off the bed. My legs aren't working right. I need to get out of here. I need to get to Kenneth. I can't let them stop me.

A man stands in the doorway. He looks familiar. My eyes snag on the small form in his arms. My son!

The door slammed. My view of Kenneth is blocked. The lock clicked in an ominous finality. I rammed my body into unyielding wood. I have to get to Kenneth.

"Let me out! Please, let me out! I need to be with my baby! He needs me!"

The door absorbed every one of my frantic blows. It didn't budge.

"Please! I need to be with my baby! Give me back my baby!"

Footsteps echoed through the hall, leaving me. How could they leave me? Why would those monsters take my son?

"Please! Give me my son!"

I kicked till my toes ached. I clawed. My fingernails shredded and bled. I rammed my shoulder into the door.

Nothing worked.

Kenneth needed me! Why wouldn't they listen?

"Help me! Someone! I need to save him! Get me out of here! I need to be with my son!"

Hot tears burned my face. My voice faltered. Only a raspy squawk came out of my throat. No one approached. Slipping down to the icy ground, my body leaked the last of my strength. The chill of the room soaked into me. Dread loomed like a dark cloud. Every part of me hurt. Most of all, the prick on my arm burned fiercely. My eyelids became too heavy to keep open.

What did they do to me?

"Please. I need to be with my son."

The Creep

E.M. Fitch

A dark shadow lives in my closet. In the daylight, he looks like sewn together fabric thrown over a hanger and hung on the coat rack. A hat perches above it on a shelf, giving the shadow a place to hide when the lights come on. He ducks his shadowy head and slips inside the folds of the long, heavy coat. But he's there, watching me.

Especially at night.

"It's just a coat," Michael grumbles. He purses his lips at me, watching me as I eye the closet suspiciously. My brother grunts and rolls back over. I hear the bed springs creak as he turns his back on me.

Creak, creak, creak.

He reaches out and turns out the bedroom light. The room goes black. It's not just a coat. Michael knows that. The dark thing that hangs in our closet moves sometimes. It watches us.

Michael shifts to adjust himself and pulls the covers tight to his ear. His bed is further from the closet than mine. He can turn his back on the door that always slips open, ignore the black coat that hangs in the depths—moving in the non-existent breeze. His feet are already tucked up under his scratchy comforter, even though it's blazing hot in our dark room. I can usually see him—especially in the summertime when the fading light would slant through the crooked blinds in our room—but it is dark tonight. Doesn't matter. I know. Michael never leaves his feet uncovered.

Our mother once told me why.

"Keep your toes covered, Nicky boy," she had crooned, her breath sickly sweet and warm. "He might just come."

"Who, Ma?" I remember asking. The yellow light that hung from a cord over the kitchen table gave her skin a waxy look like she was a poorly rendered statue in that museum Michael once snuck me into. Carved Frankenstein monsters, vampires, and witches all cackling over bubbling pots, and Ma, smoking a cigarette in the yellow light of the kitchen, propped up against a nicked oak table with round burn marks dotting the surface.

When she finally answered, her words slurred. "The Creep in the Closet," she said. "He wants to eat your toes."

Michael had told her to shut her mouth and yanked me back. Her teeth snapped together, clanking. *Clank, clank, clank!* The noise echoed and followed us as Michael dragged me into our bedroom. Through the door he slammed shut, we could hear her laugh and then hiss out an angry tune.

"He's a dirty Creep, and he wants to eat your toes. Nom, nom, nom! Feed him tasty toes!"

She kept going, an ongoing chorus of high-pitched squealing interspersed with cackling laughter, a modern day witch sitting in a yellow spotlight. Her song mingled with the clink of glass bottles, the squeak of the linoleum floor as she shifted her weight, and the occasional clacking of teeth. It was her very own incantation.

Like she was calling him.

That song still plays in my nightmares.

"Nom, nom, nom," it hisses. *"Feed him tasty toes."*

It's hot tonight. I only have the one comforter, no sheet, no small blanket. Only the comforter. It's thin; the cotton bunches in places and I can never get it to even out. Still, I'm sweating and itchy. My pillow's damp when I move my head. I can feel the sweat bead on my forehead and trickle into my hair.

Gross. I feel gross. I hate always feeling so gross.

My clothes are folded nicely on the shelf Michael and I had improvised out of the old milk crates we found. We zip-tied them together—red, orange, and blue—in a wobbly stack. My crates are blue; Michael's are orange and red. My stack of clothes is there, waiting for me. Not clean, but folded. At least they look nice. They might smell a little, but they wouldn't be all wrinkly when I went to school tomorrow.

Behind the stack of milk crates, in a secret hole in the corner of the baseboards that even Michael doesn't know about, my little blue pills are piling up. He wants me to take them but I hate it. It makes me sleep harder than before and I don't want to sleep hard, not when the shadow in the closet is watching, not when the Creep could come at any moment.

A trickle of sweat runs by my eye and I swipe at it, trying to ignore the sting. I can't hear anything from the living room. I don't know if Ma is alone or not. I hope she is. The men that sometimes come, they scare me.

That's whose coat it probably is, some man who came to see Ma and never came back. It's weird that she didn't try to sell it or something. It's dark black and long, like something out of the old movies Michael and I sometimes watch. The hat that sits on the shelf above it could have belonged to one of those old guys, too. Michael called it something once, a fedora, I think.

"Look, Ma," I mouth into the scratchy comforter. I imagine I'm pulling that hat low over one eye, glaring out from beneath it. "I'm on top o' the world."

In my head, I sound hard and gangster, like in those old tough guy movies where they wear dark hats and darker coats, afraid of no one and nothing. I'm not, though. I'm a kid in a dark room, afraid if I poke my toes out from under a blanket the Creep will come and nibble them off.

"Nick, go to sleep," Michael hisses. I grit my teeth. I hate it when he hears me acting stupid.

I close my eyes, start counting in my head. Not sheep or something stupid like that, just numbers, breaths, a soft repetition to get me settled. One of my teachers taught me that once.

The closet door creaks open. My eyes fly wide and I burrow under my comforter. Michael grunts. Sleep's already taken him. He sleeps like the dead because he takes *his* pills. He won't wake 'til morning. I bet his toes are safely tucked, though. I'm sure they are, even if I can't see them in the dark.

Mine squirm at the end of the bed. I kick a bit and wrap the end of the comforter around my sweaty feet.

Gross.

The closet creaks again. I don't want to look, but I do.

"It's just the coat, just the coat, just the coat." No matter how many times I whisper it, it never feels true.

The dark shadow that wavers in the depths of the closet seems to stare at me. His limbs are long and bulky; his torso flares out at the hips. His neck is thick. I can't see a face. It's covered by the hat. But it's so dark in that closet it'd be hard to see features anyway.

Not that there are features. It's a coat. Just a coat and hat. Michael tells me it is. But when Michael's asleep, it doesn't always behave like just a coat and hat.

The tune starts again and it's hard to tell, is it Ma through the door? Or me? Or the Creep that hums?

Nom, nom, nom! Feed him tasty toes.

The words echo in my skull, beating into the sides. First, it's Ma's voice, sickly sweet, then his. I hate that I know his voice so well. But I do. He skulks around my bed at night, poking at the covers, a dark fluid shadow.

"Nom, nom, nom," he always hisses. Just like tonight.

I hate to whimper. I sound like such a baby. But I do sometimes, quietly in the dark, especially when he sings. His voice is more of a rasp, like the Creep has to force breath to wheeze through his throat.

My feet twist in the scratchy comforter, tease a knotted ball of cotton. My whole body prickles with sweat, the air under the comforter is dank and heavy. I try to convince myself he's just a hat and coat. But Michael must know, just as I do, that he's more than that. Why else would my brother's feet be all twisted up in his blanket?

The closet creaks again and this time the door flies open and bangs into the wall. The coat wavers and shifts, the Creep filling out the empty fabric, pulling the hat over his eyes just as I imagined I would do. He falls to the floor, out of my sight. The humming shifts to words, they vibrate through the small space of the hot room.

Nom, nom, nom...

"Michael," I whine. It's no use. He never hears once he's asleep. Damn pills.

I'm a dirty Creep, and I want to eat your toes...

My chest aches with anger. I don't want to be afraid. I'm sick of it. Michael's feet are wrapped up tight. The room is hot and dirty and small, and I don't want to be stuck in it anymore. I'm sick to death of sweaty feet and smelly clothes.

I kick at the blankets again. My toes poke out. He hums louder, hungrier.

Nom, nom, nom!

The air is cool at the end of the bed. It licks up my legs. Even with the Creep crawling on the floor, it's refreshing. Worth it.

Screw him! And screw Ma and Michael and everyone else that lets the Creep paw around my room.

The mattress depresses, just a small dip at the end like someone has sunk their claws in the fabric and is trying to pull themselves up. The rush of breath on my skin is hot, worse than with the covers. The hairs prickle all over my body. For a split second, I think about yanking the comforter down, covering my feet.

The thought comes as the claw does. Hot as fire, his grip wraps around my ankle, anchoring me to the bed. His claws are sharp, worse than fingernails, more like needles. They pop through my skin easily like pins stuck in a pin cushion.

Pop, pop, pop.

I call for Michael, my voice rising in an embarrassing pitch. He's gonna be pissed if I wake him up again, I'm sure of it. But he doesn't wake. He snorts a bit and falls silent.

Feed me tasty toes!

I can't move my ankle. I'm up now, trying to pull myself away, yanking at my leg. His grip is fire and steel, unyielding. His breath is hot on my foot. Still, I can't see his face! Just a shadow, a hot, breathing shadow at the end of my bed about to gnaw off my toes.

"Michael!" I wail. I throw my pillow at him and he mutters, telling me under his breath to go back to sleep. The tongue is wet fire, burning on my pinky toe. With a *pop* it's gone. I can feel the bone pull free, the quick tear of skin.

Nom, nom, nom, he hisses, the words a bit garbled now. *Feed me—*

"Michael!"

"What, Nick?" Michael finally yells. He throws off his covers and flips on the light. I blink into the sudden, stark light. The bare bulb above me hisses and whines. Michael stands in the middle of the room. A sweat stain marks the dingy tee shirt he sleeps in and looks like a fist mark on his chest. His mouth pops open as he looks at me.

"Geez! What'd you do?"

Me? ME? My chest is rising and falling, hard, urgent breaths fill my lungs. The Creep is gone. My eyes flit to the closet and though the door wavers at my gaze, the coat hangs innocently empty. The hat is dusty on the shelf.

The bottom of my sheet is stained a vivid red.

"Ma is gonna freak, Nick," Michael murmurs, rushing to the foot of my bed and balling up the already stained sheet against the stub where my pinky toe once was. "You gotta stop doing this. They're gonna take you away again."

"It wasn't me, Mikey, it was—"

"Cut the crap, Nick!" Michael hisses. "Shit. I can't get this to stop."

The blood stain grows, but I don't worry about that, it'll stop eventually. Michael presses the fabric hard to my foot, it hurts but I don't flinch. It's the Creep that's watching that draws my attention. I glare at the closet door, my teeth grit as I force air through my nose. I hate him.

"Put that down, will 'ya?" Michael asks, nodding toward my clenched fist. The steak knife I grip is bloody and I want to smack myself for not using it on the Creep. I forgot I took it to bed with me. In a quiet voice, one I'm not used to hearing from my big brother, Michael asks, "Nicky, where's the toe?"

**

Michael tells Ma and the doctor at the clinic that maybe it's rats. I'm shot full of some kind of medicine, and they send me on my way. Michael warned me not to tell them about the Creep. They wouldn't believe me anyway. Sometimes I think even Michael don't believe me. But he does know it isn't rats. Rats wouldn't take off a toe, not clean as that. But something took my toe away. Michael couldn't find it. Not even in the blaring light of day.

The next night, Michael makes me take the blue pill in front of him. It's no big deal; he's made me do it before. It's tiny, easy to hide between my teeth and my lips, easy to spit out afterward and shove in my hidey-hole when Michael goes to brush his teeth.

I tie the closet shut. It probably won't stop the Creep. Michael tucks me in all around, tucks my comforter so far up my legs I'm almost sitting on it. He tells me to stay put; he tells me to leave it tucked.

I probably will. But my gaze falls to the creaking closet door, and my grip tightens on the knife I stole back from the kitchen drawer. It's hidden in my fist under the pillow. I probably will keep my feet tucked.

Then again, maybe I won't.

Blind Justice

Jaidis Shaw

"This would be easier if you would just hold still," he said.

Amanda struggled against the ropes that were cutting into her raw, bleeding wrists. She could feel her kidnapper tugging on the ropes, removing what little slack she had managed to gain over the last several hours.

"Please just let me go! You don't have to do this," she pleaded, tears streaming from underneath the stained blindfold.

"Of course I do. You left me no choice after you rejected me the way you did. Did you really think I would just let you lie to me like that?" Heavy footsteps paced back and forth, rubbing a path in the dust covered floor.

"Rejected you? I don't even know you! You've made a mistake."

"Mistake? Oh no, I remember quite vividly when you looked me in the eyes and told me that you couldn't go out with me because you were babysitting. You think you're clever, don't you? You think you can just lie to me in order to get out of a date? I followed you. You didn't have to babysit tonight, did you?"

"What? No I..." Amanda paused as she suddenly remembered why the voice speaking to her sounded familiar. "Steve? I didn't lie to you! I swear! One of the children got sick, and the parents canceled. I promise I didn't lie. Why are you doing this to me?" A new stream of tears began to fall, splattering on Amanda's torn, dirty sundress.

"Lies!" Steve stopped his pacing and stared down at the fragile girl whimpering before him. *She should have just said yes. I can't turn back now,* Steve thought to himself. Tenderly removing the tear stained blindfold and tossing it aside, Steve caressed Amanda's swollen cheek. "I didn't want to do this you know. I really thought we had something special. But you know that I can't just let you go. You'll go tell the police and then what would happen to me?"

"No. I won't tell anyone I swear! I'll do whatever you want; say whatever you want me to say. Just please let me go. I'll give you their number so you can call them. They will confirm that I am telling you the truth."

Reaching into his pocket, Steve pulled out a cold pair of rose pruners. Amanda struggled against her tight restraints in terror, glancing around the dim room in an attempt to find salvation. Anything that would help her make it through this alive. "Please don't make this any harder than it needs to be. Everyone must pay the price for their misdoings and the time has come for you to pay for yours." After placing a gentle kiss upon her salty forehead, Steve grabbed Amanda's face in a firm grip, forcing her to stop her constant writhing. Bracing himself for what he must do, Steve inserted the clippers and in one smooth movement, stopped Amanda from telling any more lies.

***

Molly sat at her vanity, sunlight streaming through her locks of golden hair. Being careful not to knock anything out of place, she searched for the Mocha Kiss lipstick that she just adored. She couldn't remember how it looked upon her lips, but she knew at one point in time it looked marvelous. Funny how one's life can change in the blink of an eye. In Molly's case, it was the not blinking that changed her life forever. If only she had thought to close her eyes instead of looking at the car racing straight for her on that rainy night, maybe she would still be able to look at her Mocha Kissed lips. Molly never knew that a windshield could shatter like that. When she woke up in darkness at the hospital, she realized the sudden impact that windshield had on her future.

Finding the familiar tube, she applied the last of her makeup and stood up, smoothing down her skirt. "What do you think, Zeus? Do I look okay?" Zeus, her loyal German Shepherd, barked his agreement and rubbed against Molly's leg. Running her hand through his thick fur, Molly knew that Zeus would never lead her in the wrong direction. Molly never needed a pet before her accident, nor did she have the time for one. After several insistent nudges from her doctors, Molly finally agreed to give Zeus a chance. Grasping the lead collar, Molly followed alongside Zeus as they headed for the door. Hearing the faint music that had started to play beside the door, Molly headed over to the table, running her hand along the smooth varnish until she found her cell phone. "Molly Kenway," she said as she put the phone to her ear.

"Ms. Kenway, this is Sheriff Tillons. I was wondering if perhaps you were available today to go over some new leads in a case we have been having some difficulties with?" Sheriff Tillons was a good man. Over worked, under paid and always stressed to the limits, but he was the heart of the town and was respected by many.

"I suppose I can come in for a little while. I can be there in about fifteen minutes if I walk. Is that okay?"

"I can send a car to pick you up if you like Ms. Kenway. You know I worry about you when you go walking around town."

"I can take care of myself, John. You know that. I'll see you in a little bit." Molly flipped her cell phone shut before he could protest further. Grabbing her purse from the side table and throwing her phone into its cluttered depth, Molly let Zeus lead her out of the apartment and into the steady flow of the city.

Pulling her purse strap up further on her shoulder, Molly started her slow yet steady pace down Madison Avenue. The sun's warm rays caressed her skin, and she instinctively reached up to make sure her sunglasses were in place. It was a nervous habit she had picked up after losing her eyesight in an attempt to hide the scarring around her eyes that remained. In truth, she couldn't even say what her eyes looked like as she had no way of knowing, but her mind kept telling her that her eyes were an awful sight. When alone, she would often trace the jagged ridges that surrounded her eyes. Molly pulled to the left and Zeus followed her lead. The people at the shelter where Molly was first assigned Zeus said that he would need to be told where to go. Over time she learned how to guide him, and how to give cues and commands. Zeus seemed like he knew where Molly wanted to go and they worked in unison to arrive where they needed to be. People flowed past Molly on both sides, never hesitating in their daily stride. She often felt like she was moving in slow motion as the rest of the world rushed by, going about their daily business without even noticing her. That feeling would soon be shoved aside as someone bumped into her, as they always did, knocking her slightly off balance before continuing on their self-involved mission to be somewhere. A siren wailed in the distance. Behind her, a shrill whistle to call a taxi could be heard. A man somewhere to Molly's right was humming an unrecognizable tune. Never abandoning her, the sounds of the city were always there to remind Molly that she was never alone.

The sun's warmth disappeared behind the ever-growing buildings. It was a sure sign that she was getting closer to the police station. Like a memory etched into her brain, the shadows that cast their chill upon her skin always let her know when she was amongst the tallest buildings in the concrete jungle she called home. Halting at her side, Zeus nuzzled Molly's hand as he pushed it against the hand rail that lined the steps leading into the police station. Step by careful step she made her way into the building, leaving the rush of people and her insecurities behind her.

***

"What do you mean it's no longer in my jurisdiction? All of the murders have been in my jurisdiction," Sheriff Tillons exclaimed as he pointed to a wall of victim photos.

"I mean that you are no longer in control. From here on out the FBI will be handling this case. We will need to review all of your files," Agent Simon Goode said. He was trying to keep his irritation from making him say something he would later regret. He really didn't like playing hardball with the sheriff, but he had orders to follow. "There have already been two murders, and you have nothing to go on. We believe that the same killer is responsible for two other cases with the same M.O. that are indeed out of your jurisdiction. How many more lives are you willing to sacrifice before you admit that you need our help?"

"We have everything under control. In fact, I've called in a Psychological Profiler to examine these cases and give us an idea of who we're dealing with. I'm confident that she will be able to help shed some light on the case."

"You really think that bringing in a profiler is going to help break this case? We're dealing with a serial killer. Plain and simple. Have you taken a look at those photos?" Simon pointed toward the wall that held the pictures of the victims. "The latest victim was only twenty-three. She had so much life left, and it was taken from her too soon. I'm taking this case from you now. Do I need to remind you that you have no choice in this matter? Would you like to see my badge again?"

"I would love to see your badge," Molly said as she walked into the room with confidence. She wasn't sure what she'd walked into, but she could feel the tension.

Simon whirled around to face the voice that threatened his authority. Slightly stunned to see a woman standing tall before him, he quickly regained his composure before she could notice.

"Does this help? Can you see it now?" Simon asked as he thrust his badge in her face, trying to assert his dominance. It always worked for him, always made the person standing before him back down just enough to let him take over. Of course, those people were always male. He had never met a woman with the nerve to test his authority before. Molly stood before him without so much as flinching.

"No, not really. Maybe if you hold it a little bit closer I'll be able to see it. Though I would suggest you slowly pull your hand away from my face and take a step or two back before you're unable to hold your badge." Molly had always had a sarcastic personality, and after the accident, it seemed only to get worse. Putting this man in his place made Molly feel confident and in control.

"Excuse me?" Simon had already taken another step forward before he heard the growl that rumbled from the large Shepherd's jaws standing guard at Molly's side. "What the...who let that dog in here?" Simon asked as he backed away, glancing around for the nearest protection. He had always had an underlying fear of dogs, especially large dogs that could rip his throat out without a moment's notice.

"I told you to back away. Zeus doesn't like people who are threatening. Especially when they are threatening me." Molly reached down and patted the large dog's head, reassuring him that his threat had been heard loud and clear. "As I said, I would love to see your badge. Then again, I'd love to be able to see anything these days." Without another word, Molly walked past Simon in the sheriff's direction. John was always easy to pinpoint, even in a room full of other officers. She thought the world of him but he always bathed in his aftershave.

"John, you know it's not good to get your blood pressure so high. You better calm down before that vein in your forehead decides to burst," Molly teased as she held her arms open, patiently waiting for John to claim his hug.

"Molly, dear, you know me so well. I really wish you would have let me send a car for you. Did you have any trouble on the walk here?" John asked after giving Molly a gentle bear hug. He always had a tender spot for Molly, thinking of her as the daughter he never had. She was once a confident woman that didn't need anyone to take care of her and could do anything she set her mind too. But that time had passed, and John knew that just under the surface, threatening to explode without a moment's notice, Molly was struggling to keep afloat in the darkness.

"Oh stop it. You know I can handle walking a few blocks. It's not like I was alone, I had Zeus with me."

"I know. You can take care of yourself. Speaking of taking care of yourself, you know that you, well your dog, just threatened an FBI agent, right?" John asked, struggling to hide the smile that was working its way across his lips.

"We did not threaten him. He shouldn't have put his hand in my face. So what was it that you wanted me to go over?"

"Well, I wanted you to read over a recent case. We are having a little difficulty in figuring some things out, and we are hoping that you will be able to shed some light on the kind of person we are dealing with. We haven't had time to convert the files to Braille yet, so I'm afraid you'll have to listen to them."

"You know that I'm always willing to help out when I can. Have you cleared it with the agent walking this way who is about to try and take your case again?" Molly asked, grabbing onto Zeus's lead collar and turning to face the man as he moved toward them.

"I apologize for the incident earlier, ma'am. I shouldn't have acted that way. My name is Agent Simon Goode, and you must be the profiler that the sheriff was telling me about," Simon said as he instinctively held out his hand for a handshake.

"If you're wanting a handshake, I can't see it Mr. Goode, and yes I am. My name is Miss Kenway, but you can call me Molly."

"Oh," Simon said, and he rushed to put his hand to his side, "Please, call me Simon. Do you think you will be able to help with this case? I mean, it's nothing against you, but how can you review this case if you're blind?"

"You don't have to be able to see in order to put the pieces together. In fact, I like to think that being blind gives me the advantage because I'm not looking for obvious clues. I'm able to start with a blank slate; envision the scenes as they really happened, not what they appear to be. The same goes for finding what makes the criminal's mind operate the way it does. I can offer some insight into this case if I'm given the chance."

"Okay, fine. Take a look...oh...umm...sorry. Just let me know what you find out. Sheriff, you don't mind if I stick around for a bit, do you? Although I do have the authority to shut you out of this investigation, I would like to try to work together first," Simon said, still gazing at the interesting woman standing before him.

"Of course, Simon. I'm going to help Molly get set up in the conference room and then we can all go over the case in say...ten minutes?" John put his arm protectively around Molly's shoulders, leading her away from the staring police officers.

Ten minutes later everyone was pacing in the stuffy conference room. Simon walked into the room with his head held high, carrying some yellow case folders. Pulling out a chair across from Molly, he let the folders drop to the worn table. Stealing a quick glance in Molly's direction, he wished that he could sit near her and he would have if not for the large dog that was determined to get in his way. He didn't know what it was about her, but he found her fascinating and yearned to learn more. Molly sat patiently with her hands folded in her lap, waiting for the testosterone in the room to settle down. She would never be able to understand why men were always in a constant competition with each other, always trying to be the alpha in every situation. She didn't have to be able to see to feel the power struggle swirling around her.

"Shall we get started?" Simon asked. "I'll start off with the cases I brought with me. We have reason to believe that the suspect responsible for the murders in your city may be the same suspect in ours. First off we have Stacy Mingler." Simon held up a photograph of a young woman standing on a track field. Silence filled the room as everyone waited for Simon to continue. Molly reached out to the table, slowly moving her hands along the worn finish until she found the cup of water before her. After taking a sip to soothe the itch in her throat, she eased the cup back down without spilling a drop. The last thing she needed was to look incompetent in front of everyone.

"We believe Ms. Mingler was the first victim. She was twenty-two years old, five feet eleven inches tall, one hundred and fifty-two pounds. She was last seen by her teammates during a last minute practice the night before a big competition. When she didn't show up for the competition, her parents got worried and called it in. Her body was found two days later in a wooded area in the park. Although neat, it looks like a crime of anger. Her legs were severed from the rest of her body. No evidence was found that can give us any implication of who did it." Simon paused momentarily to catch his breath.

"There is no evidence? No hair or fibers, no fingerprints, nothing at all?" Molly asked, patronizing Simon.

"It appears this murder was well planned and organized. We are dealing with someone who knows what we look for, though I guess that would be your job to determine." Simon was offended that Molly would think of him as simple. He wasn't sure if it was because she was trying to overcompensate for her blindness, or if she was just that arrogant. It seemed as though they both had something to prove. "Continuing on...the second victim is Anthony Piers," Simon said as he shuffled through the file to find the victim's photograph. "A nineteen-year-old baseball pitcher, six foot three inches, two hundred and seventeen pounds. He was last seen leaving an after party alone. Mr. Piers was found four days later in a back street alley across town from where the party took place. The autopsy shows that blunt force trauma to the head is the cause of death and that his right arm was removed post mortem. Again, no significant evidence implicating a suspect. There was a cloth fiber found, but we have nothing to compare it too." Simon glanced toward Molly, expecting to see her condescending expression but she was just sitting there with a slight smile upon her lips. Just then the conference room door opened, startling Simon. A young deputy hesitated a brief moment and then hurried over to Molly.

"You're late, Matthew," John said, breaking the silence in the room.

"I'm sorry, sir. It won't happen again." Matthew bowed his head in shame. He had never been good at standing up for himself, especially to authority figures.

"Yes, well I've heard that phrase before, and I'm sure I'll hear it again." John stood and cleared his throat. "Do you have anything else to add, Simon?"

"That is all we have. You can go over your cases now." Simon sat back in his chair and focused his attention across the table. Matthew had leaned in and was whispering in Molly's ear. Her face didn't betray a reaction to what he was saying.

"Right, so you've all heard the new cases that Simon discussed. I'll go over what we know so that Molly can be clued in. First up is Kayle Sinders. Twenty-six-year-old female, five feet five inches tall and one hundred and twenty pounds. Her family said she was trying to break into the entertainment business and often traveled to singing auditions across the country. She disappeared after having a class with her vocal instructor and was reported missing forty-eight hours later. Her body was found on the bank of a river just east of the city. An autopsy showed that both carotid arteries and the jugular vein were severed, which killed her instantly." John paused and took a long gulp of water from the glass before him. Clearing his throat, he began again, "It seems as though this was planned out and executed with expert proficiency. Her blood toxins report showed high levels of chloroform."

"No other evidence was found," Molly stated in confidence. She already knew the answer. The one thing that linked these cases together so far was the lack of usable evidence.

"That is correct, Molly. That is why I am hoping that you will be able to give us something to go on. Our most recent victim was identified this morning as nineteen-year-old Amanda Garssen." The sheriff held up a senior high school photo of a young woman. "She was found yesterday after her parents reported her missing. They claim she was supposed to babysit the night she disappeared. We interviewed the family she was to babysit for, and they said that she did arrive as originally scheduled, but they had to cancel their plans at the last minute because one of their children got sick. They offered to give Miss Garssen a ride home, but she said that she would just walk back. We believe that she was abducted on her way home. Her body was found on a wooded trail just outside of the city. An autopsy is scheduled for later this afternoon to pinpoint the exact cause of death. She was badly beaten, with multiple lacerations, and was missing her tongue."

"Her tongue?" Molly was surprised as this case was different from the previous ones she had heard. "Was there any evidence?"

"Actually, yes. We did find a sample of semen on the victim which suggests that she may have been raped prior to her death. That is our best clue as to who our suspect is." The sheriff couldn't help but feel confident that he had a better handle on this case than Simon. After all, he was the only one so far with any usable evidence. Simon finished writing his notes and addressed Molly before the sheriff could beat him to it.

"Molly, do you have any thoughts on these cases? Any glimpse as to who we are dealing with?"

"Of course. Up until the last victim, all of the cases were linked by their lack of evidence—"

A phone in the room rang loudly, startling Molly and breaking her concentration.

"I'm so sorry!" Simon said, removing his cell phone from his pocket. Several moments passed before he hung up. "That was the mayor. There is a press conference taking place in about five minutes in front of the station. I'm sorry Molly, but you have to finish your profiling to the media."

"What! Isn't there someone else that can do it? John, you know I don't do press conferences." Molly stood in a panic, bumping the table and spilling the glass of water before her. If there was one thing she resented more than being blind, it was having to stand before a crowd of perfect reporters, having to sense their pity as they looked upon her like she was a fragile creature, nothing but damaged goods.

"Okay everyone, I think we're done here. Go prepare for the conference please," John said, ushering the other officers from the room. After everyone but Simon left, John walked to Molly and grabbed her sweaty palms. "Molly, I know you don't like talking to crowds. Hell, I don't even like it. But when the mayor calls, he expects things to be done. The public will want to hear your findings first hand, not passed on through someone else. Most of the reporters don't even know that you are blind. You can leave Zeus off stage, and I will walk you up there. It's sunny outside, and I guarantee you that they won't even second guess your sunglasses." John did his best to settle the nerves that raged through Molly. Simon took a tender step closer to her side and placed his hand on her shoulder.

"Would it help if I went up there with you? I know we don't know each other, but sometimes it helps to have people supporting you." Simon hesitated before removing his hand from her shoulder. He didn't know how to feel about Molly, but there was something under her tough exterior. Something that screamed to fit in and be seen for who she was rather than the person people believed her to be.

"There is no way I can get out of this, is there?" Molly asked John in earnest.

"I'm afraid not. It will be over before you know it." John did his best to send her a reassuring smile. Taking several deep breaths, Molly wanted nothing more in that moment than for the conference to be over. Taking hold of Zeus's lead collar, she followed her trusted companion toward the pack of perfection waiting for her. Stopping a safe distance away from the reporters, she knelt down to Zeus and scratched playfully behind his ears.

"I won't be gone long, okay? I'll be fine...you'll see." Standing up and smoothing down her skirt, she gave Zeus a final stay command and held out her hand for the sheriff. Grasping his hand tightly, she walked close to John, trying to seem as normal as possible. Coming to an abrupt halt, John stood in front of the podium as the murmuring voices slowed to a hushed silence.

"Good morning. My name is John Tillons and as most of you already know, I am the sheriff of this fine city. You have all heard by now about the recent homicides that took place. We have reason to believe that these homicides were committed by the same suspect as two cases in another jurisdiction. We have brought in a psychological profiler whom we believe will be able to give us a better look at the kind of suspect we are dealing with. I'd like to introduce Ms. Molly Kenway." Gently pulling Molly to the left, John guided Molly's hand to the podium standing in front of her before stepping back a few steps.

"Thank you, Sheriff Tillons. Good morning everyone. After comparing the cases given to me, I believe I have enough information to make an accurate profile of our suspect. It appears the suspect took his time in committing the perfect crime. Starting out in an organized fashion, he selected victims based on their skills or area of expertise. This suggests that our suspect is envious of perfection and popularity. He longs for companionship, to have what has been denied to him. He is someone who most likely did not have a good childhood or has been rejected throughout life. Most likely an outsider, someone who doesn't fit in with society, our suspect is easily angered and may have a prior criminal background. However, he has become impulsive and disorganized in his attempt to become perfect. We are currently following up on new leads, and I am certain that our suspect will be apprehended soon. That is all at this time."

"Ms. Kenway! Do you believe—"

"Is the town safe?"

"Can you tell us about the—"

The crowd surged to life with the hopes of having their questions selected and answered first, all yearning to be the first to report on the recent homicides. Molly stumbled back as the unexpected assault of questions hit her like a cannon. Tripping on darkness in her rush to flee, Simon was suddenly there, saving Molly by catching her in his protective embrace.

"Quiet down please!" The sheriff moved in to take control of the situation. "There will be no questions answered today. We have given you all of the details that we can share at this time. Thank you for coming." John turned from the microphone to see Molly standing right next to Simon. He hated that Molly had been forced to speak to the reporters and he felt guilty for not warning her about possible questions. Taking her hand in his, he led her to comfortable safety while Simon was left looking after the woman he was now determined to protect.

***

"Disorganized? She thinks that I'm disorganized! How can she get up there and claim she knows me? Doesn't she see that she has it all wrong?" Steve paced back and forth in the dim lighting. His life was spiraling out of control before his eyes. Had he left evidence behind? He had been careful to clean up after himself, removing everything he thought would be incriminating. He even made sure to wait and dispose of the used condom until after he was home so there would be no semen linking him to the crime. Steve couldn't remember even though flashes of that night tormented his dreams. "It was all Amanda's fault you know. If she had just told me the truth, I wouldn't be in this mess now. And neither would you." Steve looked down at the beaten body lying on the floor. Matthew hadn't even noticed Steve following him home from the press conference. How could he have noticed anything else but his seething jealousy of that stranger holding Molly? Matthew had abruptly left the conference before he made a fool of himself. He knew Molly would never feel the same way he did, but he refused to see another man take his place. Now all he wanted was to return to the conference, even if Simon was throwing himself on Molly. It was better than being here, although he wasn't quite sure where that was. Cringing as his assailant crouched before him, Matthew wasn't sure what to expect next.

***

"What do you mean Matthew is missing?" Molly stopped stroking Zeus's sleek fur and tried to slow the thumping of her racing heart. When John called to tell her that Simon was on his way to pick her up, she knew that there was something he was not telling her. She expected there to be a new development, but she never thought that Matthew would be involved.

"He hasn't been into work in days. Nobody has heard from him since the conference. Someone said they saw him rushing from the conference after your speech but didn't think anything of it. He always acts strange around you." John did not know what he should tell Molly. He remembered a brief relationship between Molly and Matthew, but it faded out just as quickly as it had started. The sheriff was pretty sure it had something to do with Molly's pride. Not wanting a man in her life to pity her; take care of her. In a way, Molly was right about Matthew. He was still young and wanted so desperately to fix the broken. The terror of reality had yet to hit Matthew and open his eyes to the cruelty lurking, just waiting for the right time to strike. The door to the office flew open, startling Molly from her shocked silence. A young deputy rushed in, carrying a package with shaking hands.

"This was found sitting on the front steps. It's addressed to Ms. Kenway."

"Why would it be left here for her? May I open it, Molly?" John walked over and examined the box. There was nothing out of the ordinary: just a simple brown box with Molly's name scribbled on the top. Taking out a pocket knife, John carefully slit the tape that held the box closed, allowing the flaps to pop open. Inside was another box, this time wrapped in a giant red bow.

"Molly, there is another package inside. Do you mind if I open it for you?"

"Please do. It's not like I can see what it is anyway," Molly replied in a shaky voice. Her gut was screaming that something was wrong and her gut had yet to let her down.

John tugged the red bow off of the package and lifted the tissue paper off of the top. Inside, sitting in a small puddle of blood, was a severed hand. Dropping the tissue paper, John jumped back from the box.

"What the—"

"What is it?" Molly asked, hoping that she was wrong and that it was just a normal package. Simon walked over to the box and took a look inside, flinching at the bloody carnage. Reaching inside the box, he pulled on a small white envelope that was tucked against the side of the box.

"Here's a note for Molly," Simon said, glancing up at the sheriff who stood by the open window trying to breathe in some fresh air.

"Well, what does it say?" Molly grabbed Zeus's collar and allowed Zeus to lead her toward the box.

Simon hesitated, not sure if he should read it to her or not. Casting a desperate glance the sheriff's way, he waited for some sort of signal. John gave a brief nod, knowing that Molly wouldn't let them get away with not reading it to her. "It says 'Meet me at 6:00PM at 173 Chestnut Parkway. Be alone.' Do you know that address?"

"That's Matthew's address. What time is it?"

Simon glanced at the worn-down clock ticking loudly on the far wall. "It's only 2:15PM. That gives us a little time to organize how this is going to work."

"What else is in the box? I smell blood." A nauseating flood filled Molly's stomach. The sickly sweet scent of blood normally did not affect her but knowing that it may belong to someone she cared about churned her stomach. Simon smiled an amused grin. He knew that the timing was inappropriate, but he just could not get over how incredible Molly was. She had no way of seeing what was in the box and yet she knew there was blood. He was such a fool to have felt pity for Molly when he first met her. Standing before him was a capable woman who didn't have to rely on anyone to survive. Maybe he didn't need to protect her after all.

"I asked what else was in the box, Simon," Molly said with urgency. Startling Simon from his stupor, he hesitated before telling her the truth.

"There's a human hand in the box. It appears to be masculine, but we will have it sent to forensics for analysis."

"No need for that. It belongs to Matthew," Molly stated.

"How can you be so sure?"

"Seriously? Who else could it belong to?" Molly said, trying to hide the irritation in her voice. "John, you know I am going to his house so please don't argue with me, but I will allow you to drop me off a couple blocks away."

"Molly, you know that I can't let you go there alone." John released a troubled sigh. "I also know that you won't budge until I change my mind." He wished there was a way to convince Molly not to go, but if he tried talking her out of it, she would just become more determined to go. Why did she have to be so set on proving herself? There had to be some way of talking her out of going. "What about Zeus? The note says to come alone, and there is a good chance that whomever is behind this doesn't know you're blind."

"What about him? He has to come with me. It isn't like I can just stroll in there without him. It has been forever since I was over at Matthew's house and I barely remember the layout. I'm just gonna have to take my chances."

"Molly, I don't think it is a good idea for you to go. What if we sent an undercover officer in your place? There are a few women here that could easily pass for you." John wiped the sweat that was forming on his brow. There had to be a way to pull this off.

"Actually, I'll tell you what. I will let an officer go in the house first, but I will be there just in case something happens. I do have a feeling the Zeus will be a hindrance. Is that a fair compromise?"

"Wait. Did you just agree with me? I thought for sure you would fight until death to get your way." John stumbled and put a hand on the nearby table while a devilish grin spread across his face. "I think I need to sit down," John joked.

"I'd like to stop by my house first though if that's okay while you guys finalize the plans. Will someone drive me?"

"Do you think that is a good idea? What if this guy knows where you live?"

"I doubt he does. If he did, he would have sent the package there instead. He probably didn't know where else to send it and figured it would have a better chance of reaching me if he sent it here." John pondered Molly's idea briefly but could not find any reason to believe otherwise.

"I'll drive you." Simon took a few hesitant steps toward Molly. There was no way he was letting her out of his sight. "Sheriff Tillons is capable of finishing the plans, and he can run it by me before we get there." Simon placed his hand on Molly's shoulder, hoping that she wouldn't feel awkward by the tender touch.

"Thank You." Molly placed a tentative touch on Simon's cold hand before removing his hand from her shoulder. She thought about the path her life could have taken before the accident before her world was plunged in darkness. There was still a part of her buried deep inside that longed for the simple things in life; even if it was just a small part. A life-long companion. A house she could turn into a home. Maybe even children. Those dreams always had a bad habit of trying to rush to the surface if she let her guard down for even an instant. Simon seemed like a suitable companion, and there was a part of her that was attracted to him. She could feel his desire radiating from him every time he was near. No matter how many times she kept telling herself, she couldn't deny her attraction to him. But she didn't have time to let anyone close to her. It was only a matter of time before he began to see her the way everyone else did; like she was a precious china doll that needed to be locked away for fear of breaking. The familiar rage began to surface, tugging at Molly's thoughts, giving her the clarity she needed to focus on reality.

"So are we meeting back here or near Matthew's house?" Molly asked, anxious to get moving.

"I say we meet back here about 5:00PM and then head to Matthew's together. I'll drop you off and then be back to pick you up around ten till five."

"Sounds good to me. John, I guess I'll see you later," Molly said as she patted Zeus's head in reassurance that they would be leaving soon. Leading the way, Simon headed for the door, glancing back briefly to make sure Molly and Zeus were following. His stomach was flipping cartwheels as the thought of being alone with Molly raced through his mind. Pushing the station's heavy front door open, a moist breeze caressed his skin, sending goose bumps racing across his body.

"Smells like rain," Molly stated. She loved listening to the rain; feeling the smooth wetness slide down her skin. As much as she wished she could curl up in her apartment window seat and listen to the rain's soothing melody on the window pane, she knew that rain would only decrease her hearing. She needed to be alert if she was going to succeed in finding the man responsible for kidnapping Matthew.

"I hope the rain holds off." Simon cast a worried look toward the darkening sky. "Who knows what we will find at Matthew's house and I don't want the rain ruining any possible evidence." Placing a hand on Molly's lower back, he escorted her toward his car. "You can ride in front, but

I'm afraid Zeus has to go in the backseat. Will he be okay with that?" Simon had no idea if Zeus would allow himself to be separated from Molly but he hoped for the best.

"I'm sure he will allow it just this once," Molly said as a smile crossed her face.

"That's a relief," Simon joked although instant relief flooded through him. Simon opened his passenger side door for Molly, taking hold of Zeus's lead collar while she slid into the leather seat. "Okay boy, your turn." Simon opened the door and put Zeus in the car, scratching behind his ears as a reward. "Good boy."

***

Steve paced the room in nervous anticipation. His plan had to work. He was counting on the police to keep Molly away from that low-life's house. If everything worked like it was supposed to, she would be taken to her house for safekeeping while they went to the meeting place. They might even try sending in an undercover officer in her place. He had seen all the shows on TV about how these types of things worked. Steve glanced at his watch which now read 3:27PM. Should he call her now or wait a little longer? With a nervous glance he looked out the broken window. He had to move fast if he was going to beat the impending storm. There wasn't any power in the abandoned warehouse, and if it got much darker, he wouldn't be able to see. There was a little kerosene left in the lantern that he had taken there the same night as Amanda. He tried calculating how much longer the kerosene would last but he had no idea how to answer such an equation. He would just have to take his chances and hope that the rain would hold off. Taking another quick peek at his watch, he decided it was now or never. He pulled the cell phone from his pocket and dialed Molly's number with steady fingers.

***

Molly was glad to be back in her apartment. She had expected the car ride with Simon to be awkward, but it was surprisingly comfortable. Simon had tried to spark conversation a couple of times, expressing his worry over the thick clouds that were now covering the city in a dark shadow or sharing his thoughts on how brave he thought she was because she wasn't scared of anything. She knew that he was trying to flirt with her and maybe if they had met at another time, another place, things could have been different. Focusing on what she needed to do, Molly headed for her bedroom as Zeus went to his water bowl, sliding her hands along her walls as a guide. Reaching her bedroom wall, she slid her hand up and flipped the light switch out of habit. Not that it really mattered but just going through the motions helped balance her sense of normalcy. Making her way through the room toward the closet, she knelt on the hardwood floor and moved the plush rug that covered the floor to the side. Searching for the familiar coolness of the metal latch, she opened it, exposing her hiding place beneath. She knew where everything was located like a map etched into her memory. Lifting the leather duffle bag from its resting place, Molly unzipped the bag in search of her folding pocket knife. She only carried it on special occasions and this seemed as good a time as any. When placed in the waistband of her jeans, hugging her lower back, it was undetectable unless a thorough search was performed. She first began carrying the knife for protection after she lost her eyesight. The feel of the cold steel helped give her a sense of security. Before long, she had grown comfortable in her abilities to take care of herself, and now the knife spent most of its time in the cool darkness under her closet floorboards. Checking that the knife was secured, Molly replaced the bag and covered all traces of her secret hiding place. After exchanging her favorite red pumps for a practical pair of worn tennis shoes, Molly gave a shrill whistle for Zeus, listening for his soft footsteps as they padded down the hallway.

"You ready, Zeus?" Molly ran her steady hand through the slick fur on his back. Soft music began to play from her jean pocket. Molly quickly flipped her cell phone open. "Molly Kenway."

"Well hello there, Molly," a deep voice hissed into the phone.

"Who is this?" Standing alert, Molly's gut began to turn.

"I think you already know who it is. Did you like the present I sent for you?" A sinister laugh sent a shiver down Molly's spine.

"Why did you have to take Matthew? He hasn't done anything to deserve what you did to him." Molly was trying to stay calm, but the familiar rage was beginning to build.

"Oh, was that his name? Matthew? I didn't even think to ask him. How terribly rude of me. Forgive me if my actions were, what was the word you used, disorganized? Yes, I believe that was the way you phrased it."

"Just get to the point. What do you want? I know that meeting place is probably just a decoy." Zeus began to rub against Molly's leg, sensing the tenseness that was building around her like a ticking bomb.

"So smart. Too bad we couldn't have met under different circumstances. You're going to meet me at the warehouse on Sumter Street in thirty minutes. I don't think I need to remind you to come alone, do I?" Steve couldn't believe that he was actually talking to Molly. His plan was working just as he planned and soon his nightmare would be over and he could get back to his life.

"Fine. See you then." Molly hung up the phone before he could get in another word. A plan was brewing in the back of her mind and soon she would know if she could pull it off. "Come on, Zeus. We've got an appointment to keep." Molly and Zeus left the apartment as rain began to come down. Pedestrians darted under building overhangs to avoid the downpour's assault. Thunder cracked overhead, making Molly flinch. Lightning never bothered her as she had no way to see it, but the thunder that followed unnerved her because she was unable to tell when it was about to occur. Molly decided against walking in this weather and hailed a cab instead. Soon she would be at the warehouse and be able to face the man responsible for Matthew's pain.

***

The rain leaked through the holes in the roof, creating puddles on the rotten floor. "I really wish the rain would have held off," Steve said into the silence as he knelt by the glowing kerosene lantern. Lightning flashed, making Steve raise a hand in front of his eyes. When the dimness returned, he mentally reviewed his plan again, looking for anything that could go wrong. A streak of yellow caught his eye through the slotted window as a taxi pulled down the dirt road. Ready or not, he had to put his plan into motion. He could taste freedom on the wet breeze that rushed through the window as more lightning flashed overhead. Making sure that the lantern was out of sight, he made his way toward the door, waiting for his prey to fall into his trap.

***

"Is this enough?" Molly asked the taxi driver as she took a folded bill from her pocket. She knew that a twenty-dollar bill would be enough, but she was trying to take her time, planning out last minute details of her plan.

"That is more than enough. Let me get your change," the bald man said, reaching for his change compartment.

"Keep it. Thanks!" Molly opened the door, letting Zeus jump to the muddy ground below. The tires crunched over gravel as the taxi drove away, leaving Molly no way of escape. Not that she had intended on trying to run in the first place. A low growl crept from Zeus's throat as he sensed the danger ahead. "It's okay boy. We have been in worse situations than this before." Zeus took a tentative step toward the door with watchful eyes. "Here goes nothing," Molly said as she stepped through the doorway. A sudden pain erupted from her skull as she collapsed into the darkness.

***

"I knew she wouldn't stay at home," Simon said as he watched the blinking red dot move on the tracking device's control panel. He was only glad that Zeus allowed him to slip the discreet black box on his collar while putting him in the back of his car. He knew that Molly would never agree to him waiting at her house and so he knew he would just have to follow her. He thought about trying to drop the device in Molly's purse but knew that it would be a long shot. The only thing that was guaranteed to be with her at all times was Zeus. A brief twinge of guilt crossed Simon's mind, knowing how upset Molly would be if she knew that he was following her. Weighing the odds, Simon preferred to take his chances rather than risk not knowing her whereabouts. Turning his windshield wipers to their highest setting, he raced in Molly's direction, hoping that she knew what she was doing and could handle herself until he could get there.

***

Molly awoke as a rush of cold water splashed on her face. The throbbing in her head was an instant reminder of what occurred as she arrived at the warehouse. A brief wave of panic washed over her as the rope dug into her wrists, pulling a hiss from her lips.

"It's about time you woke up. I didn't think I hit you that hard," Steve said, standing over his prey in excitement. "I thought I told you to come alone. That includes your dog."

"He needed to go for a walk. Where is he?"

"Oh, he's around here somewhere. Not that it really matters." A clap of thunder roared through the room, making Molly flinch. "You're not scared are you, sweetheart?" Steve trailed his calloused hand along Molly's cheek, his excitement growing with each passing moment.

"Hardly." Molly turned her head in disgust. She needed to get in control of the situation and fast before her temper boiled to the surface. "Where's Matthew?"

"His house of course. It wouldn't be nice of me to not reward the police for their trouble of going there. Just think of all the hard work and planning they did to organize it." Molly gave a sarcastic sigh, growing impatient with his childish behavior.

"I bet you think you're so smart, don't you? The cream of the crop."

"On the contrary. I just want this whole nightmare to be over with. If it hadn't been for that liar Amanda, we wouldn't be here right now."

"Amanda Garssen?" Molly asked.

Steve stopped pacing at the question. "So you're familiar with her case?"

"You mean to tell me that you're responsible for her murder?" Molly couldn't believe that the coward before her had the nerve to kill someone.

"I had no choice. She lied to me. All I wanted was to take her on a date, but I just wasn't good enough for her. She couldn't even think of a believable lie, just spouted some nonsense about having to babysit. I'm just as good as any other guy, and I deserve a chance too." Steve clenched his fists in anger.

"What a dumbass. Sometimes when a girl rejects you, it's for a good reason. I've heard all about Amanda's case. She did have to babysit that night. The parents let her know after she was there that they had to cancel and offered her a ride home but she refused and said she'd walk."

"That's a lie!" Steve lashed out, slamming his fist into Molly's face, sending her glasses crashing to the floor. The urge to hit her again was strong, but he refrained. For now.

Pain throbbed through Molly's skull, and the scent of blood tainted the air, but she refused to show any emotion. "If you say so."

"We're getting off topic. The point of the matter is that you are the one responsible for this mess. Why did you have to trash talk me like that to the media? You made me look like a joke to everyone!" A fist slammed into Molly's face again.

"I wouldn't suggest you do that again."

"I don't think you are in any position to tell me what to do." Arrogance swirled around Steve as lightning flashed overhead. "What was Matthew to you anyway?"

"That is none of your business!" Molly seethed.

"He sure was dedicated to you. No matter what I did, he just wouldn't break. Did you know that it is a lot harder to cut off a human hand than it looks on TV?"

"You shouldn't believe everything you see on TV." Molly wrapped her fingers around the cold steel that clung to her back. If she was going to get out of this, it needed to be now.

"Boy was he a trooper, though. He put up one hell of a fight. The hand was the final straw you know? Once that was gone, he just couldn't keep the information that I wanted to himself anymore. He did try to get me to reconsider my plans, though. Thought he had me fooled when he said you were blind and should leave you alone. Can you believe that?"

"So the truth comes out. You're not as smart as you think you are."

"What does that mean?"

"He was telling the truth, moron. If he caved into the pain as you say he did, why would he bother telling a lie?"

"Because he was weak and pathetic. That's why! You wouldn't be working for the police if you were blind."

"Take a look for yourself if you don't believe me." Molly sat motionless, knowing that he would be curious enough to look. Cautious footsteps stopped in front of her, the stench of his hot breath on her face. She could feel his stare drilling into her core. Lightning flashed on her face, highlighting the scars that marred her fair skin as Steve reached a tentative hand to her face.

"You are blind aren't you? He was telling the—"

Molly seized the moment, pushing the steel of her blade into the soft flesh of his stomach. Thunder crashed in the distance, but Molly barely noticed over the adrenaline pulsing through her veins. Steve slid to his knees, looking at the blood oozing between his fingers as he tried to make sense of what just happened.

Molly scooted her foot along the floor looking for obstacles, the frayed rope still dangling from her wrists.

Giving a shrill whistle, she hoped that Zeus would be able to hear her from wherever he was.

"Yes, he was telling the truth. Maybe you should have listened to him." Molly concentrated on Steve's labored breathing, making sure of his location. "You want to know a secret?" Molly boasted. "The police actually think that you are responsible for multiple murders. It's absurd really, thinking that someone like you could pull off the perfection of the other crimes."

"What are you talking about? I've only killed once before," Steve muttered as pain raced through his body with each breath.

"I'm surprised you had the balls to kill someone at all. You're too sloppy, too dumb. But do you really want to know how I know that you didn't kill the others?" Molly waited for some sort of acknowledgment but heard none. "Because I did."

Steve flinched as thunder startled him and the pain surged through him again. "What do you mean? You're blind! You don't have the ability to harm anyone."

"Wow! You're really asking that question now? Why doesn't anyone ever think that I could be a threat?" Molly seethed with anger as her emotions flowed to the surface. "That is the problem with people today. Staring down at people with disabilities. I am just as good as anyone else. Those other victims, they didn't consider me a threat either. Do you know the victims I'm talking about? You should, after all, since you're being blamed for them." Molly let a snicker escape her lips.

"I don't know what you're talking about." Steve stood up, gritting his teeth against the pain.

"You better stay put," Molly warned, raising the knife in Steve's direction. "I'm more than capable of taking care of myself. Just ask Stacy, Anthony or even that little singer...what was her name? Gayle? Kayle? Something like that. They thought that they were perfect, much better than a poor blind woman. They won't be making that mistake again. Oh, and you know what? It's only hard to sever limbs if you're using the wrong tools." Molly smiled, remembering the adrenaline that coursed through her body as she detached Stacy's legs with skilled efficiency.

"If you think I am going to go down for your crimes, you better think again." Steve leaped at Molly, knocking her off balance as the knife crashed to the floor nearby. Thunder echoed through the empty building as their bodies thudded to the floor. Using his heavyweight to his advantage, Steve wrapped his hands around her throat as he pinned her to the floor. Molly smashed her knee into his groin with all the force she could muster. She knew she had found her mark as he fell to his side, an agonizing moan escaping his throat. Crawling on her hands and knees, Molly searched the darkness for the knife. It has to be here somewhere.

"You are going to regret that!" Steve yelled as he stood up, hissing with pain as his muscles straightened. "Don't even bother looking for your knife. You aren't even close." A growl erupted from the darkness and before Steve could turn around, a sharp pair of teeth tore into his flesh. Zeus shook his head back and forth as blood spilled from the corner of his mouth. Steve slammed his fist into the dog's massive head, screaming as the teeth ripped from his thigh. Molly heard a thud as Zeus's body collapsed to the floor with a whimper.

"I hope you didn't think your dog was going to save you," Steve said as he leaned over to pick the knife up from the floor. "Now it's your turn." Steve limped toward Molly, a look of defiance crossing his face. Panic bolted through Molly as she backpedaled across the slippery floor. Bumping into a wall, Molly had nowhere else to turn. Step by heavy step, Steve inched closer. He looked down at the frightened woman cowering before him. "How does it feel to be on this end of the blade? I only wish that I could look into your eyes as the blood drains from your body, taking your life with it." Lightning flashed behind Steve as he raised the knife above his head, preparing to administer the final blow.

"Freeze!" Simon bolted into the room, popping off two rounds before Steve had time to react. The knife crashed to the ground as Steve's lifeless body crumpled to the floor. "Molly! Are you okay?"

Relief washed over Molly as she heard Simon's voice. "Simon? How did you find me?"

"I put a tracking device on Zeus's collar." Simon rushed over to Molly, appraising her for damage.

"You what? How long have you been here?"

"I'm sorry I couldn't get here sooner. The rain made it near impossible to drive in. I never should have left you alone."

"Where's Zeus?"

"Uh..." Simon spotted Zeus a few feet away. "Here, I will take you to him." Simon wrapped his arm around Molly as he helped her stand, leading the way to her loyal companion. Molly knelt at Zeus's side, running her hand through his fur with care. Zeus gave a low whimper and licked Molly's hand. Police sirens wailed in the background as help began to arrive. "Everything is going to be okay now, Molly. I've got you." Simon squeezed Molly in relief, happy that the woman who had stolen his heart was safe.

Obsession

M L Sparrow

This story is written in UK English

Jeffrey Martin watched his girlfriend strut down the catwalk. Modelling a skin-tight red dress, she was absolutely stunning and she knew it, as did all the men in the audience watching her with wide-eyed rapture.

He focused on her through the lens of his camera and clicked away. By the time she had disappeared back behind the heavy curtain separating the backstage area from the seeking eyes of the audience, he had at least a hundred photos. He would sift through them that evening whilst she was busy at the after-party she was duty-bound to attend, although Jeff knew she would prefer to spend her time with him, cuddled up in front of the television.

With that in mind, he drove home alone that evening. Radio playing in the background, he approached the big, elegant white house surrounded by wrought iron gates with a long gravel drive leading up to it. Out of habit, Jeff parked his little Renault on the street and entered the property from the back.

Inside, he removed his shoes and stowed them in the hall closet, catching a whiff of perfume from her coats as he ran a hand along them. Wandering through the stylishly furnished house, feet sinking into the plush carpets, he smiled at the evidence of their life together; the mix of male and female clothes in the wardrobe, the toothbrushes standing side by side in the ensuite bathroom, thrillers and romance novels mingling on the bookshelves.

In the kitchen, a tiny dog yapped wildly at him when he walked in. Crouching down beside the cage, where the well-groomed Yorkie with a pink ribbon atop its head was confined until it's owner returned, he pulled the latch across with a gentle *snick* and swung the door open.

The dog was still wary of him - he'd only moved in permanently a few days ago – and it refused to come out. Jeff reached into the cage to get it, but the animal nipped at his fingers with sharp little teeth. Yanking his hand back, he shoved to his feet and left the kitchen.

It was getting late, so he headed upstairs to bed.

***

Maria Santiago teetered up the front steps in her sky-high heels, silently cursing her stylist for talking her into them. But then, pain was beauty, and she knew she'd looked beautiful today. Even a little drunk, she was still perfectly made up; the amount of hairspray in her dark locks meant they'd stayed in place as she danced the night away at the exclusive, celebrity-only party she'd attended after the shoot.

Kicking off the heels once she was inside, she wiggled her toes into the thick carpet and proceeded to strip right down to her underwear right there in the hallway, carelessly leaving her dress on the floor.

Lou-Lou ran up to her yapping wildly and turning in tight circles. Delighted by the welcome, she scooped her Yorkie into her arms and covered her furred face in kisses, which the creature eagerly returned. It would mess up her makeup, but there was no one to impress here. This was her private space, her home, her sanctuary. Only Lou-Lou and her fiancé had total access.

Flicking on the living room light, she walked over to the large bay window and struck a pose as the limo passed through the gates at the end of the drive. If the driver glanced, back he would see her standing there in her lacy red underwear, pet in hand, with a winning smile. The world regularly saw her wearing next to nothing, so what was a little more exposure?

Once the limo had disappeared down the private street, she moved away from the window and turned the lights back off, plunging the large house into darkness. Too wobbly to tackle the stairs, she fell asleep on the sofa, pulling the blanket hung over the back around her body.

***

Waking early the next morning, he realized that he was alone and frowned in disappointment. Jealousy swelled inside him as he entertained the idea that perhaps she had stayed out last night with another man. She was beautiful enough to charm any man she wanted, all it would take was a tilt of those ruby red lips, or a glance from eyes the colour of rich, dark chocolate.

Anger was simmering beneath his skin as he got ready for work, washing his blond hair and scrubbing his teeth, before headed downstairs. It all dissolved, however, when he beheld her curled up on the sofa, the weak morning sunlight reaching across the carpet towards her.

She must have decided to sleep in the living room so as not to wake him.

Creeping closer, he gazed down at her. Gently, Jeff traced the elegant curve of her jaw with the very tips of his fingers and her eyelashes fluttered. Holding his breath, he backed away, not wanting to wake her. Instead of opening her eyes, though, she uttered a soft, sleepy sound and rolled over.

Woken by her movement, the dog's eyes immediately zoned in on him, and it began to growl low in the back of its throat, lips folding back to reveal a mouth full of glistening white teeth. The dog probably had better dental care than he did.

Quickly, he retrieved his shoes and left.

Thankfully, there was no headache to contend with when she woke the next morning. Well, morning was stretching it a little since it was long past midday. Uncurling her long legs, she stretched her arms above her head and blinked at the bright sunlight streaming through the windows.

Padding upstairs, Lou-Lou at her heels, she disappeared into her bedroom to use the ensuite. She didn't notice anything straight away, but once she was showered and her head had cleared, she walked back into her bedroom and realized that something felt off.

Glancing around, Maria frowned. The bed looked like it had been slept in, however the maid didn't come until tomorrow so it was hard to tell. The thing that was really bothering her was the smell.

It was her fiancé's cologne, she realized, and it was fresh.

Confused, she poked her head into the walk-in-wardrobe to see if his suitcase was there; maybe he'd come home from his work trip earlier than expected. It wasn't there. She glanced around to see if anything else was amiss, before lifting the landline off the bedside table.

"Hi, babe," she greeted when his deep voice came on the line, "did you come home last night?"

"Maria," he sighed, "have you been drinking again? You know I'm not coming home until late tonight."

"I know, I remember." Switching the phone to loudspeaker so that she could pull on some clothes, she glanced around uneasily. "I think someone was in the house last night."

Another tired, put-upon sigh. "You went to the after-party last night, didn't you? I told you to stop snorting that stuff; it makes you paranoid." She could imagine him shaking his head and running a hand through his thick black hair. "I can't keep living like this, Maria, we need to talk when I get home."

Having heard all of this before, she just rolled her eyes; he may threaten to leave her, but he'd never actually do it. He loved her too much. And anyway, it wasn't as if she was addicted to the packets of white powder her friend, fellow model Larissa Krane, gave her occasionally. But he was right, the drugs did make her paranoid, so maybe she *was* imagining things.

No longer concerned, she ended the conversation and made her way downstairs for a cup of coffee, already planning to spend the rest of the day lounging by the pool. Her agent was always banging on about the fact that sunlight would damage her skin and make her age prematurely, but she didn't care. She planned to retire in a few years anyway.

In the end, she dozed off on the lounger by the pool, completely uncovered to the blistering California sun, only to be woken a few hours later by a shadow passing over her. Lifting a hand to shade her eyes, she squinted up at the figure looming over her. For a moment her heart jumped before she recognised the man.

"Enrique? What are you doing home?" She glanced around, wondering if she'd slept the entire day away, which did sometimes happen, but the sun was still high in the sky.

Sitting at the end of her lounger, her fiancé ran a hand down one smooth, sun-warmed leg. "I was worried about you. I started to think, 'What if there really was someone in the house?' I'd never forgive myself if anything happened to you, so I got on the first flight home."

Sitting up, she smiled slowly. "I knew you loved me," she purred, running a hand up his chest and sliding it inside the collar of his crisp white shirt to caress hard muscles.

"I always love you," he said, eyes suddenly hot with hunger as they raked over her naked body.

Leaning in close, breasts bouncing, she whispered in his ear, "Show me."

***

After a hard day's work Jeff was looking forward to coming home and relaxing with Maria. *Maybe they could go out for dinner*, he thought as he parked the car and wandered around the back of the house. He'd forgotten his keys so he climbed over the fence, cutting his hand on the spikes at the top in the process.

Swearing to himself, he studied the bloody gash as he walked towards the house. Heavy panting and feminine moans, the slap of skin on skin, made him look up and stop dead. He flushed red with anger. His girlfriend was being attacked; crying out, she tried to push the man away, scratching him with her long nails.

Overwhelmed with rage, he charged towards the pair. Tackling the man, they tumbled to the hard ground. Maria screamed. They grappled; the intruder was bigger, but Jeff had the element of surprise and pure fury on his side. Gripping handfuls of hair, he smashed the man's head against the pave stones, again and again, until his opponent went limp. He sat back on his heels and watched bright red blood pooling around them and running into the gaps between the slabs.

Silence reigned for a long moment before Maria started shrieking. "You killed him! You killed him, you bastard."

Clambering to his feet, he wiped his stained hands on his jeans. "It's okay, you're safe. Calm down. He can't hurt you anymore."

Face stricken, she backed away from him. "S-stay away from me."

"Maria, wait…"

Twisting around, she dashed towards the house. He took off after her.

Long legs carrying her across the lawn, she reached the house seconds before him, slamming the back door shut and fumbling with the lock. "I'm calling the cops," she cried, snatching up the phone on the counter and dialing with trembling hands.

"Don't do that, baby. I saved you." Frustrated, he tried to reason with her, but she wasn't listening. Spying an open window, he hoisted himself through it and fell awkwardly onto the tiled floor. Maria fled the room.

Her dog, the annoying little rat, suddenly darted into the room and flew at him, a ball of fur and rage and snapping teeth. It sank its teeth into his ankle and refused to let go. Yelling in pain, Jeff tried to shake it off to no avail. Blood stained his pant leg, dripping onto the floor. Desperate, he stooped down and grabbed a handful of fur, yanking the creature off and feeling his skin rip in the process. He flung the dog away, heard it yelp as it hit the wall and caught a glimpse of it lying motionless as he rushed from the room, following her upstairs.

Locked in her safe room, the heavy metal door shut firmly against the intruder, Maria lifted her hands to her face and sank to the floor, salty tears streaming down her face. Enrique was dead, she knew he was. There was so much blood. She could still see his open eyes staring blankly up at the sky. Bile rose and she unloaded the contents of her stomach. The acidic burning in her throat only made her cry harder.

How had that psycho gotten into her house?

Goosebumps prickled her arms and she began to shake.

Suddenly, the phone in her hand rang and she almost jumped out of her skin. Fumbling with the devise, she pressed the green button and held it to her ear.

"Miss Santiago, the intruder has been apprehended and removed from your property. There are officers outside your safe-room door and it's safe for you to come out."

Shakily pushing to her feet, she cautiously opened the door. Peering through the crack, she saw two men in black uniforms with gold stars pinned to their chests.

"Ma'am," one of them spoke to her softly, "are you all right?"

She nodded, accepting the blanket the other officer pulled from the bed and handed to her, only then realizing she was completely naked.

"Enrique," she rasped, "my fiancé, is he... is he alive?"

The look on the man's face confirmed her worst fears. Seconds later her vision went black.

***

For three years Jeff had been confined to this white-walled building with a bunch of nut-jobs and frumpy nurses. All because he'd been defending the woman of his dreams. He still couldn't understand why Maria had lied to the police; she had told them that he was an intruder, that her attacker was her fiancé and that he'd killed the other man in cold blood before chasing after her. Maybe she'd been confused by all the questions, or maybe she was just scared of the media attention it would garner if anyone were to find out she was dating a humble gas station attendant from Kentucky. Either way, he would find out soon enough.

With only three days left until his release, he was jittery with anticipation.

He'd been forced to spend the last few years denying his love for the beautiful, fiery Latino model to the slew of doctors, nurses and other specialists who questioned him. He'd even gone so far as to claim that he had never been her boyfriend, that he had been stalking her since they met one day when he filled her car with gas. Obsessed, he'd broken into her home, terrorized her and murdered her boyfriend. Not to mention her dog, which he did feel mildly guilty about. However, none of that was true. He'd had to tell them what they wanted to hear so that he could get back to her.

In three days he'd get the chance to explain and to hear her explanation.

In three days they would be reunited.

Lauren

Jacqueline E. Smith

"It wasn't your fault, Sean."

"It was an accident."

"A terrible tragedy. She was so young."

"How are you? Are you doing okay?"

"Please don't blame yourself. It wasn't your fault."

It wasn't your fault.

It wasn't your fault.

But it *was* his fault.

His fault for not paying attention. His fault for driving too fast. His fault for asking her to join him that day, for being late to pick her up, for choosing that moment to take his eyes off the road, to look at her, to see the pain in her eyes. He needed to see the pain because he knew it would torment him. As well it should. He was the reason it was there.

But the pain was only there for a moment. One brief, fleeting moment. Then it was gone, eviscerated by the sudden and disorienting impact of the crash.

Then *she* was gone. She'd loved him. And he'd killed her.

Everyone—the doctors, his mom, her sister, their friends—insisted over and over again that it wasn't his fault. They reminded him that it was an accident. They urged him to forgive himself.

"You know that if Beth were still here, she would have already forgiven you."

But he knew the truth. That while these grieving loved ones were assuring him that they didn't blame him, that he had no reason to feel guilty, they were all thinking the same thing: *Thank God it wasn't me.* They wouldn't know how to live with themselves. No one in their right mind would know how to live with themselves. Yet somehow, they expected him to. And maybe if he'd only killed her, he would have eventually learned to adapt. But he'd betrayed her and he'd broken her. And for that, he could never forgive himself.

It had happened the night before the accident. He'd been out drinking with a few of his buddies. They'd planned on making it an early night. He'd just closed out his tab and was in the process of pulling his jacket on when she approached him. He recognized her immediately.

"Lauren," he'd whispered.

"Hey, Sean," she'd smiled at him.

For Sean Behrens, Lauren Crawley was the one that got away. They began dating their sophomore year of college and had only broken up because she had been offered a job out of state. They tried to make the long distance work. More than once, Sean had even considered buying a ring, hopping on an airplane, and proposing to her. He could have done it. Packed up his life in small town Denison, Texas and made the move to big city Chicago. But something always held him back, insisted that he wouldn't belong there, that she had moved on and so should he. And so he did. Fifteen years later, he was happily engaged to Beth Sullivan.

But he never told Lauren that.

He knew he shouldn't have offered to buy her a drink. But he truly believed that he could keep the evening platonic. After all, he loved Beth. She was bright, beautiful, sweet, funny. Beth was the woman he was going to marry. Lauren was a woman he hadn't seen in over a decade. Surely no harm would come from him buying her one drink.

But one drink quickly became two drinks. Two became three. And innocent conversations about their respective lives rapidly evolved into sentimental reminiscences, and Sean found himself regretting his decision to ever let her go. And by the time he finished his last drink of the night, he'd already invited her back to his place for the night.

Drunk as he'd been, Sean remembered every moment of their passionate reunion: how smooth her skin had felt next to his, the soft glow of moonlight reflecting in her pale blue eyes, the faint scent of lilac in her golden hair... And not once, not *once* had he thought of Beth. It was only as Lauren was kissing him awake the next morning that he realized what he'd done.

"What's the matter?" Lauren had asked him.

"Lauren..." he'd muttered, his own heart aching at the thought of breaking hers. "I have a fiancée."

At first, she looked like she hadn't heard him correctly. "What?"

"I'm getting married. Her name is Beth. I'm supposed to pick her up this morning. We're... we're going to meet with the florist."

"I don't believe this."

"Lauren, I'm sorry. I—"

"*Don't* talk to me."

And with that, she scooped up her clothes, dressed, and stormed out the door. Sean didn't try to follow her.

He hadn't known how he was supposed to face Beth. She knew him better than anyone. One look was all she'd need to know that something was tormenting him.

Sure enough, she had no sooner climbed into the passenger seat of his car before she asked, "Is everything okay? You look terrible."

"I'm fine," he lied. "I just... didn't sleep very well last night."

But of course, he'd ended up confessing everything to her anyway, mere seconds before the car accident that had claimed her life. In his thirty-seven years, Sean Behrens had come to regret many things, but he would never regret anything so much as his decision to tell Beth the truth in *that* moment. If he'd waited a second longer, she could have died peacefully, still believing that her fiancé was a good man who would never, ever hurt her. Instead, the last thing she experienced was the sting of betrayal, the shattering of everything she'd come to trust. And his last memory of her would forever be the look of utter devastation on her beautiful face.

It was his fault. Everything was his fault.

The funeral was torture. More than once, Sean had to excuse himself to the restroom to dry heave. He didn't have enough in his system to throw up, but his body was still rebelling against him.

The third time he emerged from the restroom, he saw her. Standing there near the church's entrance, in a simple black dress, her blonde hair tied up in an elegant bun. He blinked, bewildered. It couldn't be her. It didn't make any sense. But it was her.

Lauren.

Curiously, cautiously, he approached her.

"What are you doing here?" he asked.

"I heard about what happened. I wanted to make sure you were okay."

"Are you serious? No, I'm not okay," he snapped. He knew his anger was misdirected, but he couldn't help but feel that she'd crossed a line by showing up at Beth's funeral. He knew she was angry with him, but this was downright inappropriate. "Listen, you can't be here."

"Why not?" she asked, looking perplexed.

"You know damn well why not."

"You weren't so quick to kick me out of your bed the other night. And I certainly shouldn't have been there." Then she reached out and straightened his tie. "Listen. I know this is a troubling time for you. You're feeling guilty and confused. But look on the positive side."

"What are you talking about? There is no positive side."

"Of course there is. Now that Beth is dead, you and I can be together."

Sean was so horrified by her suggestion that he found himself rendered speechless. But before he could come to his senses, his brother, Kevin, called out to him.

"Sean, it's almost over."

"Get out," Sean hissed at Lauren before turning on his heel and walking back to the sanctuary.

"I'll see you soon, baby," she bid him. Sean bit his tongue, determined not to acknowledge her again. Thankfully, Kevin had already disappeared back into the church.

***

In the days that followed, Sean spent countless hours sitting in the cemetery, atop the fresh mound of brown earth that covered Beth's casket. He spoke to her in a hushed voice, almost as one might murmur a prayer in a quiet cathedral. He apologized profusely, begged her forgiveness, proclaimed his love for her over and over and over again. But nothing he said or did brought him a moment's peace. He was broken.

On the fourth day, as he stood to leave, he noticed the woman watching him from just beyond the trees that lined the perimeter of the graveyard. Lauren had returned.

"Are you following me?" he demanded.

"I'm checking on you," she corrected him. "I'm worried about you."

"It's not your place to worry about me."

"Of course it is. I care about you, Sean."

"If you really care about me, then stay away from me."

"But why?"

"*You have to ask?*" Sean yelled. He'd never seen this side of Lauren before. The Lauren he knew was kind, gentle, understanding. This Lauren was clingy, childish, possibly even a little deranged.

"Please don't push me away, Sean. You shouldn't be alone right now."

"I'm not alone." That was a bold-faced lie. He'd pushed everyone away. He didn't deserve the showering of love and forgiveness that the rest of his friends and family had bestowed upon him. They should have been condemning him.

"Sean, why don't you let me take you home—"

"*No.*"

"I don't think you know what you're saying."

"I know *exactly* what I'm saying. Get out of here, Lauren. I don't want to see you again." When she didn't budge, he yelled, "GO!"

"Oh, darling," she sighed. But finally, she did as he asked. Sean heaved a sigh of relief as he watched her walk away, but the sensation was short-lived. He couldn't shake the feeling that she would be back. And sooner rather than later.

He was right.

She appeared again a few nights later. It was around nine o'clock in the evening and Sean had just settled into his makeshift bed on the couch. He hadn't been able to sleep in his own bed since his night with Lauren. It felt dirty to him now. So he'd been spending his nights on the couch, watching mindless sitcoms on TV until the early hours of the morning. He resisted sleep because when he slept, he dreamt of Beth and woke up with a cold, hollow pain in his gut.

That night, he had just turned off all the lights in his living room when a dark, shadowed figure passed swiftly and soundless by the window. He nearly jumped out of his skin before he caught a second glance and realized it was Lauren, dressed in a white, flowing nightgown and pacing around his backyard, completely barefoot.

Ignore her, he told himself. *Ignore her and she'll go away.*

But when he looked again, she was standing at his back door, staring inside. She'd seen him. And she knew he'd seen her.

"Let me in, Sean."

"No!" he declared, rising up off the couch and storming over to the door. "I don't know what the hell you're thinking, prowling around here like a damn stalker, but if you aren't out of my yard and off my property in thirty seconds, I'm calling the cops."

"Please, just open the door. Let me talk to you."

"Don't you get it, Lauren? I am *done* talking to you. The other night was a mistake. You know it and I know it. Now I just want to forget it."

"You *can't* forget it, Sean. Don't you see that? And it's because we're supposed to be together. This is destiny."

"This is not destiny. This is a nightmare. Now get out of here!"

Lauren simply started at him with those wide, blue eyes.

"You're not going to call the police," she stated.

"The hell I'm not! Why wouldn't I? I've got a crazy person standing on my back porch!"

"If you call the police, they'll want to know the whole story. And the last thing you want is for people knowing that you were in bed with another woman the night before you killed your precious fiancée. This is a small town, after all. Once one person knows, everyone knows."

He didn't want to admit it to her, but she was right. Heaving a reluctant sigh, he unlocked the door and let her in.

"Listen, Lauren. I'm sorry I've been so short with you. I know that what happened between us isn't fair to you. But... you've got to understand that I can't be with you."

"Why not? I know you want me."

"I've already told you, the other night was a mistake. And yes, I admit it. I did want you. You were my first love and I'll always have feelings for you. But we will *never* be together. I need you to accept that."

But it was as though Lauren hadn't even heard him, as though she'd gone into some sort of trance. Without a word, she closed the space between them and reached up to stroke his face.

"I know you want me," she repeated, her voice barely a whisper.

"Lauren," Sean said, drawing in a shaky breath. "You need to leave."

"I know you want me."

"Stop it."

"You want me."

"*Stop saying that*. I *don't* want you! I want Beth!"

141

"But Beth is dead. And you killed her," Lauren reminded him gently. "You killed her so that we could be together."

"No! No!" Sean screamed, fighting back tears.

"There, there, baby. Please don't be upset. I love you, too."

"I do *not* love you," Sean hissed. "Get out of here, Lauren. And please, if you care about me at all, please do not come back."

Lauren looked at him with sad, pitiful eyes.

"Very well, Sean. I'll stay away."

He wasn't reassured.

A few days later, Sean ventured into town. It was his first real outing since the accident. He'd wanted to avoid any places that might remind him of his time with Beth, any people who may have known her and who wanted to know how he was doing. But he needed a break from the monotony of grieving inside his own home or at her graveside. Even if it was a brief trip to the local brewery, a few moments in the real world would hopefully do him at least a little bit of good.

It did. When he returned home, he felt, for the first time since the accident, that he was able to see through the haze of depression and guilt that had blanketed his very being since the moment he found out that Beth was gone. He still had a long way to go, but it was enough to give him the slightest sense of hope. And best of all, he hadn't seen nor heard from Lauren. He was so encouraged, in fact, that when Kevin called him and asked if he could take him to dinner the following evening, he gladly accepted.

***

"So, how are you doing?" Kevin asked once they were seated. "I know, that's probably a stupid question and you're sick to death of hearing it. But you're my brother. I have to ask."

"I'm not okay. I don't know if I'll ever really be okay again. But... I think I'll eventually learn to get by. I guess I'll have to."

"Look, man. I can't even begin to imagine what you're going through right now. I just want you to know that I'm here for you. If you need anything at all, if you need to talk, you know you can call me."

In that moment, Sean almost confessed everything. After all, if he couldn't trust his brother with his innermost demons, who could he trust? And yet, just as he'd opened his mouth to speak, a beautiful girl with long blonde hair walked into the diner and took a seat on the opposite side of the room.

"Oh, you've got to be kidding me," Sean muttered.

"What?" Kevin asked.

"Just..." Sean sighed. "It's nothing."

"Are you sure? You know, if you need to talk to someone, or maybe even go see a psychiatrist, there's no shame."

"I said it's nothing!" Sean snapped, turning half the heads in the diner, including Lauren's. She didn't look at all surprised to see him. In fact, the moment he caught her eye, she sent him a spine-chilling half-smile, like he should have known that she wouldn't stay away for very long.

Fighting every impulse to confront her, Sean remained seated, but he could feel the weight of her gaze smothering him for the remainder of the night. After he and Kevin finally paid their checks, Sean excused himself to the restroom so that he could slip out the back door. He didn't want to pass Lauren. He didn't want to give her the opportunity to reach out to him.

As it turned out, though, she didn't need it. The next day, when he stopped by the local farmer's market, she was there. Later that week, when he stopped by the florist to buy fresh roses for Beth's grave, she was standing just outside the window. He found no refuge at home, because every night, she would sit beneath the magnolia tree in his backyard and run her fingers through the grass while she waited for him to approach her.

Perhaps this was her sick, twisted way of seeking revenge. Maybe she didn't want him at all. She just wanted him to suffer for the pain he'd caused her. It wouldn't make much sense, but it made more sense than accepting that the woman he thought he'd loved so many years ago had completely lost her mind. Whatever her intentions, it was getting harder and harder to ignore her, and sooner or later, others were going to start catching on as well.

Almost as though she had read his thoughts, Lauren stood and walked to the back door.

"How long are we going to do this, Sean?" she called.

Sean didn't respond. Instead, he leaned up against the hallway wall, slid to the floor, and pulled his knees to his chest. He squeezed his eyes shut and covered his ears with his hands.

"Go away. Please just go away," he murmured.

"You don't want that, baby." Her voice startled him. He glared up at her.

"No. No. How did you get in here?" he demanded.

"Your spare key. The one you keep under the brick, remember?"

"How did you know about that?"

"Oh, darling. We're going to spend the rest of our lives together. I should know where you keep your spare key."

"Stop it! *Stop* saying that! We are *never* going to be together because you—"

But then, Sean noticed something that stunned him into silence. He couldn't think. He could barely breathe. He could only stare, light-headed and horrified, at the diamond ring glittering from Lauren's third finger.

Beth's ring.

"Lauren," he murmured, trying to calm his staggering heart. "Where did you get that?"

"What are you talking about, baby?"

"That ring! Where did you get that ring?"

"You don't like it?"

"That is *Beth's engagement ring!*" he screamed, lunging for her hand. But she managed to slip away.

"Not anymore."

"How did you get that?" Sean demanded.

"Why should it matter? She's not using it anymore." Then she sighed. "It really was a lovely viewing, wasn't it? She looked so... peaceful."

Sean's blood ran cold and his heart dropped to the pit of his stomach as he realized what she was telling him.

"*You bitch,*" he hissed.

"Now, now, Sean. It's such a beautiful ring. What a shame it would have been for it to be buried six feet down. Besides, I think most people would agree it looks much better on my finger than it ever did on hers."

"You're sick, you know that? You're *sick*. I'm calling the police," he announced, whipping out his smart phone.

"Are you sure you want to do that?" Lauren wondered. "By the time they get here, I'll have gone. And it will be long enough to tell people the truth: that you wanted Beth dead so that you could be with me. Why else would you give me her ring?"

"*I never gave you that ring*. You stole it! You stole it out of a dead woman's coffin!" Now, Sean was livid. "You've been planning this, haven't you? Since the moment you spotted me in that bar!" Then, something even more terrible dawned on him. "How did you know I would be there that night?"

"Oh, Sean..."

"You knew... Because you've been following me! You knew I was getting married. You knew about Beth. You knew *everything*!" It took every ounce of concentration and control he possessed to keep from dissolving into a full-blown panic attack. "I bet you drugged my drink that night! You did, didn't you?! That's why I took you home! That's why I was stupid enough to... Oh, my *God...*"

"Sean, please, you're being irrational—" Lauren tried to reach out to him, but he slapped her away.

"No! Don't touch me! I'm calling the cops." With trembling fingers, he dialed 911 and held his phone up to his ear.

"911. What's your emergency?"

"Hello. This is Sean Behrens. I'm at 3213 Hillcrest Rd. And I need to report a robbery and a stalker."

"You'll regret this," Lauren sighed. Then she turned and fled.

When Officers Pike and Linley arrived at the scene moments later, Sean described in vivid detail his last encounter with Lauren. He recounted every instance of stalking, every confrontation. Finally, he confessed to their night of passion.

"But I think she drugged me. This woman... She's crazy. The lengths she's gone to... I never thought it could happen to me. How anyone could become that obsessed... She even stole my fiancée's ring. Right out of her casket. You've got to find this woman. You've got to lock her away, or at least get me a restraining order."

"We'll do all we can, Sean. You have our word on that," Officer Andrew Pike assured him. "We just need a few more details for our report. This woman, what did you say her name was?"

"Lauren. Lauren Crawley. She just moved here from Chicago, but to tell you the truth, I don't know how long she's been back."

"Lauren Crawley?" Officer Patricia Linley asked. "That's impossible."

"Why?" Sean asked, his heart pounding with dread. Had Lauren already planted her twisted story? Spread her phony alibi? "Why is it impossible?"

"Sean... My God, I thought you knew."

"What?"

"Lauren died in the accident, Sean. The same one that killed Beth."

"H-How... What? No. That's... That's not right. She - she wasn't there. Beth and I were alone."

"That's true. But that accident occurred because you collided with another car. And Lauren was driving that car. I know this is a lot to take in..."

But her voice had faded to barely an echo in Sean's mind. What she was telling him wasn't real. It wasn't.

It couldn't be...

"Goodbye, Sean."

Verity Incognito

James William Peercy

A shadow caught Tom's eye. It passed over the pavement and lifted the end of a metal bar. The bar raked across the cement alley.

"Mike, behind us!"

Tom dodged. The shadow missed him. Bits of cement exploded where the bar struck the ground. He grappled with the arm that held the weapon, but the shadow's free hand thrust him away. Though the person appeared to be Tom's same height, the darkness hid the details in a blurry light. Before he could regroup, the shadow lifted the bar and struck the back of his friend.

He dove toward the ghostly apparition, slamming into it. As they collided, he felt bone-snapping pressure as something gave against his elbow. Before he could grab onto the shadow, it escaped into the depths of the alley.

In slow motion, Tom's friend fell forward. Not a sound left his lips. The metal bar stuck out of Mike's back on the same side as his heart. In the glow of the streetlights, his body slammed down face forward against the ground. The bar vibrated. Like a flag on a battlefield, it gave evidence of who had won the war.

Liquid flowed, pooling around the unmoving body. Tom fell to his knees, his eyes wide in disbelief, "Mike, come on man! It's not that bad! It can't be! Oh, God! Mike!"

A loud metal clank sounded from the blackness of the alley. The person dared him to follow. Tom's lungs heaved as four emotions collided: anger, guilt, fear, and the desire for revenge.

"Help me," Tom screamed out at the top of his lungs. His hands pressed down against Mike's ripped shirt, trying to keep the liquid from flowing. "What's wrong with you people?" His eyes swept those nearest to him. People attacked each other in ones and twos only to turn on those they had just helped. A void danced in their eyes. "Somebody call the police!" His eyes dropped to stare at his friend's body. "Mike," he pleaded, "show me you're alive."

His friend did not respond. He grabbed Mike's wrist but felt no beat beneath his two fingers. Slowly, he pulled back, turning his own palms toward himself.

The red on his hands sent a cold chill through his heart. It taunted him with a reality just out of reach. His gaze caught sight of a shiny lid from a tin can leaning against the brick alley wall. In the wind, it wobbled. From the distorted image, he caught his own expression.

The eyes were soulless too. The life was gone. As he watched, his skin visibly paled. Words stabbed up from his subconscious, "What's wrong with me?"

A siren jerked him from his thoughts. With it, the screaming of others roared into his conscious mind. For an instant, he could not remember where he was. His head darted around, looking for clues to his location.

He sat beside a downtown movie theater. The name of the show, *Twisted Assassin*, stood brightly out on the marquee. Moonlight glimmered off the dark metallic letters. Across the street, illuminating the windows of an apartment complex, red and blue lights flashed.

People were running, striking, and killing. Police barricades had been established two blocks out while law enforcement stood outside the barrier, holding shields and weapons. He spotted not only his friend, Mike, lying in front of him, but the body of the girl they had flirted with inside. His thoughts grew confused as if something spun them away. *What was her name? Alethea?*

Not far from her, a schoolmate they had known since grade school crumpled next to the theater's windows. Inside the building through the clear glass, he saw the guy who had served popcorn unmoving against one of the movie doors. Those were just the ones he recognized. In shock, he whispered, "What is going on?"

The clang of metal on metal resumed, drawing his attention. As his mind focused back upon the incident, he realized Mike's murderer was there. The feeling returned to his body. His heart pounded harder. As his pulse soared, his nose flared. Something gripped him in its tight embrace, took the desire for revenge, and powered it up a thousand fold. With jaw set, he rose slowly and leaped into the darkness.

A thundering of feet echoed from the street behind. More screams filled his head, distorting his ability to think. It wasn't right. Something wasn't right. His steps slowed. In an attempt to clear his head, he shook it from side to side.

Darkness encircled him as he slipped from the lamplight beyond the moon's glow. His eyes lost their acuity, forcing him to slow even more. With each step, the anger morphed trying to guide him back to logic, but something else was there. It urged him to be out of control.

A large green dumpster emerged from the shadows. The wooden fence behind it shifted as if someone ducked away.

The clanging grew louder. He could see the image of a person crouching down beside the trash receptacle. Why did they beat on its side?

A tingle traveled up his spine. Flickers of movement drew his attention. What if there were more? What if they were waiting?

Too late, they crept up on every side. Garbage cans shifted, and paper boxes pushed away. They blocked the path out of the alley. There was no turning back.

Mike's unmoving body flashed before his eyes. His hand brushed his elbow. Rage from a place he did not understand rippled through him. These people intended to kill him. There could be no doubt. Whoever they had been in their past, nothing sane drove them now.

The words 'nothing sane' reverberated inside his skull. With eyes set, Tom dove at the shadow beside the dumpster.

Brightness swept by him. Flashlight beams struck the sides of the alley. From the brick walls, shouts of police officers echoed. Those behind him scattered as if the light itself had caused their demise.

The shadow he chased slithered through a hole in the wooden fence. Steel clanged against the side of the dumpster. The source of the sound hung from the trash receptacle's opening, blowing in the wind.

A male voice called, "Stop! Halt!"

Tom hesitated. Even through the rage that tried to overtake him, he knew to obey the law. He fought his emotions, grabbing with all his might, but the reasoning behind it simply slipped through his fingers.

A separate urging loomed in encouraging him forward. If he stopped now, Mike's killer would get away. His adrenaline soared, shoving the thoughts of all else into his mind's distorted corners. Ignoring the calls of the officer, he ducked into the hole.

The rough wooden edges scrapped him. They caught his shirt and pulled threads from his clothes. How the person he chased could have moved through so smoothly was beyond what he could understand.

His bloody hands decorated the edges all around his escape as bits of dirt and debris stuck to his fingers. A gunshot thundered behind him. In the moonlight, pieces of glass glistened like knives as he dragged himself through.

Pain stabbed him. His elbow, was it broken? Just as he pulled out of sight of the opening, a ray of light shot through the hole, illuminating the edges. With heart in his throat, he refused to breathe, biting back the pain from his arm. The beam came closer, sweeping over his trail. All at once, the light winked out.

He gasped for breath to feed his starving lungs. His eyes fought to see which way the fleeing apparition had gone.

Crates stacked on both sides. Those at the back had tarp coverings. The coverings formed small alcoves that a body might crawl into. He had stumbled into a den of shadows.

A whimper left his throat, not out of fear but discomfort. Though still sharp, the ache in his elbow tried to abate. It was probably a bruise, perhaps from his collision with Mike's murderer. His ears listened as the sounds beyond the fence became even more muffled. Everyone had moved to the front of the alley, and soon, if not already, Mike's body would be taken away.

The memory angered him. He would find that person and make him pay. The voice in his head said so.

Shadows loomed like ghostly specters, but it was nothing like the alley he had just crawled from. His body swayed slightly as he staggered to his feet. He had crossed a barrier, broken an obstacle. It did not make sense. Behind him was death, he knew that. Yet here, there was something else. The very thoughts sent quivers up his spine. Why?

He grabbed hold of a metal pole used to help support a bar above his head. The coolness of its touch reminded him of the trouble he was truly in. The blood on his hands and clothes, his fingerprints on Mike's body, all of these things rolled through his brain as the adrenaline continued to seep away. In his mind, a girl's voice whispered from an unexpected recess, "What if they think it was you?"

"It wasn't me," his voice mumbled as if accused before a judge. "It wasn't me!"

His head whipped toward the shadows as a movement caught his attention. Two eyes met his, but the darkness swallowed them up.

He crept closer, watching to see if these eyes belonged to a person or a creature. After moving a few feet in the general direction, he deepened his voice and demanded, "Which way did they go?"

Nothing stirred. Like the spirit who had killed his best friend, could the eyes have fled too? As if a pin pricked him on the elbow, he flinched.

Tom inched nearer. The wind caught a piece of material and flipped it. Newspapers rustled. Nothing else moved. His voice became threatening, "Tell me. I know you're there."

With each moment, his vision adjusted to the semi-darkness. Though crates did cast shadows of speckled configuration, the moonlight was enough to give this world a glow.

"Tell me."

The wind paused, and in that moment of stillness, smells wafted around him. Mold, mildew and rotted wood lay heavy among the crates. Feces stank from a corner where a disconnected toilet stood. When the breeze picked up again, it carried with it urine and sweat. The abruptness of the combination caused a momentary retch.

Before Tom's gaze, an old worn blanket slipped down from the top of a wrinkled-faced man. His bald head caught the moonlight. His long ashen beard glowed faintly. The man's words were barely audible, "Go away."

Tom stepped closer. "You were there," he pointed at the man. "I know you saw them."

A high-pitched cackle came from Tom's right as he felt something brush his arm. Tom jerked.

Crates squeaked. Someone ran between them. Boards jumped, but no one appeared. From behind a stack of wood ten feet away, the same high-pitched voice returned in a sarcastic whisper, piercing him to the core, "Verity saw you."

"This is not about me," his chin rose, zeroing in on the source of the voice's location. "I need to find the person that killed my friend." A gasp escaped his lips as his arm throbbed.

The female voice teased him, "Verity watched you from the fence."

Tom glanced over at the man, but his gaze snapped back to the crates. "You were the one watching? You are Verity?"

The cackled laugh returned. "You've been a bad boy."

The pain in his elbow returned with a vengeance. He drew it in and cupped it with his other hand. "Why do you say that?"

A girl stepped out from behind the crates. Her tattered dress held dark red stains. Her brown hair seemed familiar, but a fog had drifted over that section of his mind.

"Do I know you?" The more he studied her, the more he was certain he had seen her before. The clothes triggered a memory he could not touch. The face's shape teased him. The eyes danced with a shine that spoke of intelligence, despite the presentation of her words.

She tapped a finger on the side of her nose. "Verity knows. Verity knows her own kind." With a cackle, she skipped off down the line of crates. The female voice of before whispered into Tom's thoughts, *Follow her.*

Tom hesitated, but a glance at the old man showed he had already pulled the cover back over his face. "Wait!" He struggled to keep up. Ahead, the girl turned and vanished out of sight. "Talk to me! Tell me who killed my friend." He inhaled quickly and tried to ignore the pain that rippled up his arm.

The crates became long narrow hallways of speckled bright and dark patches. The fence behind him disappeared as the darkness swallowed it up. Small murky corridors extended between the crates. At the spot he had seen her step from sight, he turned and stopped.

A man, one and half times Tom's own height, tapped an old water pipe into the palm of his free hand. "You don't belong here, boy," the male voice cut from the darkness. The man's eyes bore into Tom. "Who do you think you're looking for?"

Shuffling came from around the other crates. With every heartbeat in Tom's chest, the noise grew louder. His voice remained steady, but his fingers had started to twitch. "The murderer of my friend."

An old woman stepped from the darkness. In her hands was a rusty pick with dried black stains on the handle. "We aren't killers," she shook her head quickly.

A rat stuck its nose out from under a nearby crate. The woman's eyes lit up. Faster than Tom could see her move, the pick descended, stabbed through it, and held it up for all to see. "We don't kill." With a strange light in her eyes, she bit off the leg of the rodent as the creature screamed.

Tom shook. His elbow ached. All the bravado, the adrenaline, the feelings of revenge drained out of him. What was he doing here? What would make him lose his logic and dive into this world of madness? His lungs heaved so fast he barely got out the words, "I—I—" He tried to back up but slammed into the body of another. A strange heckled laugh echoed about him as his eyes looked up to see a toothless grin. Tom's voice shook, "I just want to go home."

A fist came from nowhere and collided against his jaw. A bright sequence of lights flashed with the hit, and he fell toward the center of those that surrounded him. As he struck the floor, he heard Verity's words, "You are home."

***

Faces hovered in the obscurity of his mind. Images morphed and faded. Voices spoke with broken sentences in languages he could not comprehend. His mind caught something familiar. Recognition ignited. They were words he could understand. In a monotone voice, he heard, "Tom, wake up. You're safe now."

Tom knew that voice. He blinked but shut his eyes tightly. Bright blinding light made him cringe.

A hard table stretched out beneath him. Loose leather straps held his ankles and wrists. He had the distinct impression that if he tried to get up that looseness would become much tighter. "Where—am I?"

"You are safe, Tom. This is all that matters."

He squinted, but the bright lights focused on him so intently, he could not see beyond them. "Why am I here?"

"So, you do not remember?"

Murmurs came from others behind the brightness. By their tone, this was what they wanted to hear.

He closed his eyes tightly, "Remember what?"

The voice answered amiably, "Why you were trying to kill your friend."

His heart thudded as the mere idea drove him to the point of hysteria. His elbow ached. He reached to grip it with his palm, but the restraints kept him from it. For the first time, Tom realized there were wired probes connected to his head and chest.

A second quieter voice came from beyond the light. "He's telling the truth. He really doesn't know. See how he's drawn toward his elbow each time the act is mentioned? The memory block is working. I'd say the test was a success."

The ticking of pencil lead against metal came from the darkness. A third voice barked. "Take him out. We need to talk."

Two men stepped into the brightness followed by a man wearing a white coat. One by one, the man in white removed tape from each of the probes and laid the devices carefully beside Tom.

The voice of the man was friendly and assuring, yet Tom's pulse soared when he saw him. "Tom, we're going to remove your tethers. If you cooperate, there will be no need to restrain you again. Do you understand?"

At the phrase, 'do you understand,' something clicked. Tom's mind became focused and sharp. The strangeness of the table and manacles slipped from his thoughts. His body relaxed. In a faraway voice, he answered, "Yes."

"Good." The man stepped back, nodding at the two with him. The closer they came, the more Tom could see their military uniforms. One came to the head of the table, the other to his feet. They loosened the straps that held him. With Tom's hands and feet free, he sat up slowly and put his legs over the side.

"Excellent Tom. You're doing just fine. You must cease fighting against your programming. It is driving you mad. Do you understand?"

His body relaxed again, and he hesitated only briefly before nodding. Despite the use of the phrase, 'do you understand,' he fought against accepting the words.

A frown crossed the face of the doctor as he continued, "For now, I need you to go with your keepers."

Slipping from the top of the table, Tom felt his feet touch the floor. A cold sting sent a shiver up his spine as the bottom of his souls connected. He blinked as the memory of his hand clutching the pole came vividly back.

The doctor noticed the second anomaly too and fished, "Tom, are you okay?" The man pointed down. "Please, use your slippers. Do you understand?"

A strange clarity filled Tom's mind as he realized what the doctor had done. Every time he heard the key phrase, the command suppressed his conscious thoughts. Now that he saw it for what it was, he clung to them in a death grip.

With a nod, Tom lifted each foot and pressed them into the footwear. His two keepers waited. Every person watched. He could feel their eyes even beyond the lights. Once ready, one of the guards led him toward a vertical rectangle in the darkness. It outlined a door. The second keeper followed at Tom's rear.

Above the door, a red light turned on. Methodically, the door opened toward them. As it did, a glow came from beyond its borders. Like a sickly sun hanging in the sky, it burned dull yellow.

A room was here. In one corner was a bed. Beside it was a wooden dresser completely mismatched.

Tom remembered the dresser. The bed was familiar too. On the bed, his clothes lay neatly stacked. When the door shut behind him, he appeared alone.

Moving toward the clothes, he touched the top of the pile. They smelled clean and felt real. Why would he think they weren't? The last he remembered, he had been knocked to the ground. He touched his chin to find a bruise. Surely from a hit like that, there should be some mark.

His eyes glanced to the dresser but saw no mirror. Instead, the wall to his right had one built-in.

He advanced toward it. The hit had been right across the jaw, yet no discoloration showed upon his face. How could that be?

His attention dropped to his hands. There was no red stain. Where could the blood have gone?

As his mind tried to shift through the confusion, the logical side stepped in. Of course, there was no blood. His clothes had been washed, his body had been cleaned, and somehow, he existed here, wherever here was.

No. Yes. The focus he had attained through his revelation of the doctor's phrase started to fade. The more he concentrated on the event in the alley, the less sure he became. Why could he not remember? What happened before that?

He squinted at the image of himself in the mirror. For a brief instant, there was red upon his palms. The panic of before grew at the corners of his mind, but somehow it made the memories sharper.

He clung to the scene, despite the fear that soared in his heart. With gulps of air, he watched his pupils dilate, but he refused to let go. Before that—what happened before that? All he could remember was chasing the murderer of his friend Mike.

A throbbing surged through his elbow. His jaw tightened. His head shook. He hung onto the image for dear life.

Like a soap bubble, something popped. Pictures dropped into a line and moved toward him. Slowly at first, they marched with legs and feet until they hurried so fast the images formed a video feed.

The movie was unclear, but features did begin to make sense. They had, he and Mike had, watched a movie. Or—or started—to. That's right. They had gone to the opening of *Twisted Assassin*. In general, he didn't like horror movies. However, his friend had talked him into it so he could meet—Alethea. That's right. She was the same girl he had seen dead not far from Mike's own body.

Convulsions hit him. Pain pierced his arm. With one hand clutching the wall, he hunkered over struggling to stay upright. It sickened him: the blood, the violence, and the senseless death of so many people. Why had it happened?

Breathe, he told himself. Gradually, the air helped the panic though it did not entirely go away. It was during the movie that—why couldn't he remember? Tom stared at his own face as it studied the mirror. It moved when he didn't.

The cackle of Verity's voice echoed around him. "That's right, Tom. You went to the movie and?"

"And?" He could not take his eyes off his own image while it morphed into another's.

Verity's face appeared. "Remember. Start from the beginning."

Sluggishly, his mind played back the events of the night. Mike had introduced him to Alethea before they had left the lobby. The beautiful smile on her face had captured him. The tilt of her head, the life in her eyes, and the cheerfulness of her manner stole his heart. When she spoke, he completely forgot about the movie.

Movie. Theater. Death. The smile that had taken his lips faded. He jumped at the stab of pain that lanced through his arm. He stared in horror at the death of his friend and the death of Alethea.

Verity's voice cut through the image. It was strong now and clear. "Tom, what happened next?" Her vision stared at him.

His eyes centered on the mirror. "Mike," he swallowed, fighting to keep the death scene at bay while the pain subsided to a dull ache. "Mike elbowed me."

The event returned. Tom felt the elbow hit his side. Alethea giggled. Mike rolled his eyes, "Come on, man. Let's go see the movie. You can flirt with her after the show."

Tom grinned unwilling to take his eyes off the girl, "You'll still be here? Right?" The happy emotions gave him strength. The scene gained depth.

"Of course, silly," she flipped her hair over her shoulder. "After all, this is where I work."

His eyes darted to the shirt she wore and caught the theater's logo. His face blushed.

Her voice lit up in laughter, teasing him to stay. "You better get going. The previews are over."

Mike had started down the hall. Tom rushed to catch him. As they found their auditorium number above the correct doors, Tom followed Mike inside.

The sound struck him oddly. It reached into his mind and shook him to his soul. It was haunting. A crescendo of screams played within a melody. Before the door had closed behind him, Tom was already on edge.

The scene showed a forest. Shadows wavered. The slow creep of something unseen slithered from tree to tree heading toward a group at a campfire. Tom half-turned toward Mike unable to completely pull his eyes from the screen, "Why are we watching this?"

161

"Shh," his friend waved him away.

The memories faded. Tom was back in his room staring at nothing even though the mirror was directly in front.

The image of Verity watched, daring him to continue. "What happened next?"

"I—I looked back on the screen, and suddenly it was over. We—we rose. All of us." Tom swallowed as an unnerving tingle raised the hairs on his arms. Confusion filled his mind, "We stood up and walked out."

A smirk crossed Verity's lips. "Surely you remember what happened next?"

He had seen that smirk before, but the realization did not stop the agony that cut through his elbow as he tried to latch onto the memories. Something did not want him to know. When the words of the doctor in the white coat echoed back, he renewed his effort. He had to beat this. He had to get it out of his head. "A—"

"Barrier exists," the voice of Verity soothed him.

He knew her voice, and yet, he could not place why. Quizzically, his eyebrows crossed. "Yes."

"But you know how to get through, don't you? You know about the hole."

The hole in the fence—the hole he had to struggle through. Her voice teased him, taunted him, and drove him to push on. His eyebrows relaxed. "Yes." His body crouched down emulating the process by which he had climbed through the wooden fence. "Why is it so hard?"

"Because they don't want you to know. Because they hid it from you. We are the same, you and I. I saw it in your eyes."

Dread rose from the bottom of Tom's feet. The ghostly apparition that had picked up the metal bar waved before his eyes. It wore his face.

The terror crawled up his skin, filling him with fear. "I don't want to know what happened. I don't want to know what I did."

"Tom, let go."

"No."

"Tom, it wasn't real. Not yet."

"No!"

"Tom—"

His voice screamed at the mirror, "Leave me alone!" He fled backward and bumped into the bed. Without climbing, he leaped in and pulled the covers around him. "Leave me alone. I don't want to know!"

Verity appeared sitting on the bed beside him. "Why not?"

He jumped, shifting as far from her as possible.

Her eyes drew him in, "Don't you want to save your friends?"

Tom's voice shook, "Mike and Alethea?"

"That's right, Tom. If you don't remember, how can you save them?" She reached out a palm. "I'll be right there."

With trembling hands, he took hers. He was certain she would vanish. After all, she could not be real. Yet, the hand remained solid beneath his. It was warm to the touch, and he caught that same smile Alethea had given him before he had entered the show.

The shaking steadied. His resolve returned. "Alright, I'm ready."

Her grip tightened. "What happened next?"

"Words, sounds," his eyes widened. "Commands? Why would they do this? How did they get inside my brain?"

Pointedly, Verity pushed him again, "Who?"

"Oh my God," Tom swallowed, seeing things only in his mind. "They want me to kill my friends!"

"Who?"

Tom stared in disbelief. Sweat started down the sides of his face. "What are they trying to prove?"

Verity's voice grew more persistent. "Who, Tom? You must remember who."

An image flickered into his mind. A van, nondescript uniforms, and a government badge flashed into existence. "They offered money to help our families in exchange for testing."

As he gained strength to continue, her voice softened, "What was it about?"

His grip tightened on hers. "They told us it was safe. They promised us we would be okay."

Her voice soothed him. She did not let go. "Think it through. Remember. What were they trying to do?"

His face lost all expression. He spoke as if reading from a textbook. "Mind control. They used the movie to tap into our subconscious. The fear triggers an emotional buildup. Pleasure or pain will work. It allows their commands to pass into our subconscious minds. It is used to make us forget, to remember, to do whatever they want us to do anytime and anywhere."

The hand that held his vanished. The bed and dresser were gone. Tom sat in the chair of the movie theater gazing at the screen of the film they had come to see.

Was it real? Had it ever happened? The musical crescendo rose and fell. With a final scream, the movie ended, and the house lights gradually came on.

Mike stood up and turned to Tom. "Told ya you would like it." He slapped Tom on the shoulder and led the way out.

Tom hurried after. Never in his life had he been more relieved to exit a theater.

They walked from the hallway to the lobby. Before passing outside, Alethea met them as they waited for the line to thin. She grinned at Tom, "I'm off now. Care to walk me home?"

Shoving the movie from his mind, a grin spread across his face, "Sure!"

"Wait outside," her face glowed. "I'll get my bag."

With a twirl, she spun around. He blinked. From the back, she looked just like Verity, but that was only a dream.

The line had thinned. He and Mike pressed against the door's bar and stepped out into the night. The moon had risen. With a bright glow, the streetlamps shone. Mike pointed to the corner of the theater. "Let's wait there."

A cold shiver went down Tom's spine. "Mike, I don't think that's a good idea."

"Oh really? You mean one horror movie turns you into a scaredy-cat?" He pushed Tom toward the corner.

Irritation filled Tom's voice, "No." With a glance back, Tom saw the boy who made the popcorn wave goodbye to Alethea. She spotted Tom watching, smiled brightly, and started in his direction. "I just don't want to take any chances."

"Wuss," Mike teased but caught the direction Tom was looking and turned to watch Alethea himself. The popcorn boy's head jerked toward the inner theater doors. Unbelief rolled across his face.

A shadow caught Tom's eye. It passed over the pavement and lifted the end of a metal bar. The bar raked across the cement alley.

"Mike, behind us!"

Gethen

Liz Butcher

This story is written in UK English

1888 – Whitechapel, England

It was a wonderful time to be alive. At least, it was for an entity like Gethen. Darkness and depravity hung above the town, as thick and ominous as the black smog that filled the lungs of the mortals on the streets.

Gethen loved lurking through the dirty streets at night, gleefully watching people spilling out of the numerous taverns and into the shadows, where drunken moans rose and fell, and coins clinked as they fell into expectant hands. Though he remained invisible to the mortal realm, it hardly mattered. The people were so wrapped up in their own despair and their futile attempts at survival that they wouldn't have noticed him anyway.

The thoughts wafting on the evening air as the crooked, the desperate and the violent all walked past him tempted him to come out and play. Yet he resisted the urge, knowing that while it would be fun, oh so fun, to join the

166

playground before him, the pleasure would be short lived and inevitably he'd feel disappointed. No, it was far better to wait. Gethen knew in a place, at a time like this, someone special would come along—and it would be sooner rather than later. He preferred a damaged mind. Burdened, dark and pitiful, easy to mould to his evil will. The unstable ones were always easier to tip over the edge– half the time, they didn't even notice his influence.

Gethen had waited less than a week when he came across his chosen one. Usually, he would call the ones he chose to inhabit his victims. But not this one. The thoughts that spilt out from this human's mind as he watched the nightlife before him sent shivers of pleasure up and down Gethen's spine. They even shared the same penchant for lurking in the shadows, observers rather than participants.

Over the course of three nights, Gethen allowed himself to move closer and closer to his intended target. The closer he got, the more enraptured he became with the heady scent of twisted hatred that emanated from the man. It was going to be an honour to occupy such a mortal. And so he did.

Then the fun really began. Gethen didn't make him do anything he didn't want to do, not really. He simply gave him the strength to act upon the thoughts and impulses that haunted him every night. The two of them together was like a merging of souls. They completed each other. And so, one of the most fearsome creatures to ever walk the streets of London was born. A creature Gethen fondly recalled as, "Ripper."

Together they had created a den of fear in the heart of London, luring the women from their corners and their alleys with nothing but a false promise and a charming smile. Then they were both in their blissful element. So evil was his host that Gethen needed to do very little. More often than not, he could sit back and appreciate the horror as it unfolded in front of him.

Gethen relished in their handiwork as they crouched over their victims, methodically cutting, slicing. So precise, so perfect. Their own exhibition of macabre art – left out on display for the world to bear witness.

At least, until the damned priest.

Unfortunately for Gethen, while he was aware that a man of his host's social standing would have an extensive circle of friends and acquaintances of impressive sorts, he hadn't been privy to the knowledge that one of them was a priest. Perhaps in his enjoyment of this host, he had become lax. If he'd taken full control of his host, the priest would never have suspected a thing. But, alas, this wasn't the case, and somehow, between his rests between victims, or his time spent conjuring up the gory details of the next, the priest had realised that the gentleman—his friend—wasn't entirely himself. What he didn't realise was that he was more himself now than he ever had been. He just had someone else with him.

The priest, with his devout belief, was convinced that if his friend could be exorcised, then he could be saved. But from the moment it started, Gethen could feel the rage within his host–a rage that rivalled his own. It was then that Gethen let out a laugh so evil it turned the priest's hair white – his host didn't want to be saved! He was enjoying his role as a deranged-yet-methodical serial killer. Gethen's laughter died away as the realisation sank in, and with it, the knowledge that the host had lost some of his charm. Gethen liked his hosts to fight him; he enjoyed the corruption, the breaking of their souls. Yet, he'd been so caught up with the horrific charm of this host that he'd been blinded to the fact that he was evil enough in his own right. When he thought about it, he wondered how much of their heinous activities could be attributed to his own demonic power, and how much to the pure evil of his host's soul.

His ego bruised—his heart would be a little broken too if he'd had one—he sneered as the priest through every chant, every prayer, every dash of holy water that was flung at him. Gethen was done. He was leaving on his own terms, not because some priest had ruined all his fun.

So Gethen returned to hibernation. All the strength he had gained from his ventures had been diminished by the ferocity of the priest's attacks against him. He was weak, tired, dismayed. So instead of searching for a new host, Gethen decided he would sleep and regain his strength until a new host drew him out of the darkness and into the mayhem that was possession.

2016 – Brisbane, Australia

Gethen stirred, the first tugs on his consciousness so faint they didn't register straight away. A sadness wafted by him, lingering, like the scent of an enticing perfume long after the wearer had passed. At first, he didn't realise what it was, his mind sluggish as his subconscious tried to keep him weighed down in the darkness. Too weak to fight it, Gethen allowed himself to be pulled back under.

He was unsure how much time passed before it happened again. It was stronger the second time, and he was unsure if it was the sadness itself that had intensified as he regained his consciousness. Though he still found himself surrounded by darkness, he felt his senses tingling in anticipation of his return. Gethen knew it wouldn't be easy. While he had no idea how many years, decades had passed since he was forced into hibernation, he knew he was little more than a mist that hovered, barely existing in the ether of the world. Something deep within him recognised the potential in the owner of the sadness; it had the power to make him strong again, to make him whole and return him to his glory.

He knew he had to be patient. It would take time to regain his consciousness in full, to become an independent entity once more, rather than this listless, formless, pitiful version of himself. Fortunately, the owner of the sadness returned periodically, and he found himself looking forward to the encounters. Each time, he felt the energy run through him like an electrical surge, leaving him a little stronger, a little more present. Excitement seized him as he caught his first glimpse of the mortal responsible for his resurrection. They were just quick flashes in his mind's eye, but they thrilled him.

A young woman, her vision partially obscured by dark hair that hung in her face as she walked. She didn't need to see where she was going; she had walked the same way a hundred times before. Barely registering the light drizzle that fell from the heavy grey clouds above, she hunched her shoulders upwards and shoved her hands deep into the pockets of her jacket. Mena. He caught her name; as it fluttered from her mind so softly, he had to listen to it for a second time. As he hovered in the limbo between her world and his, it was hard for Gethen to determine their location when her gaze didn't move from the ground directly beneath her feet. Her peripheral vision, however, gave away hints of stone. They varied in shape, height, and colour, and some were quite worse for wear. A shiver enveloped him at his realisation.

They were in a cemetery.

Gleefully, he watched her as she stopped, finally lifting her gaze to stare at the matching headstones.

Anthony & Katrine Stuart
1960 - 2015
Loving parents
Taken too soon

Together, always

Now he knew the source of the sadness, why it was so fresh, so raw. Gethen had found his ticket back. He didn't know why this girl or why now and frankly, he didn't care. She was in mourning, her grief bound tightly to her like a shroud—and she was exactly what he needed.

As the weeks came and went, Gethen strengthened to the point where he could detect the girl the moment she stepped through the cemetery gates. As he became giddy off her grief, he forced himself to focus, to learn as much about her as possible in the time they were near each other. He'd already decided she would be his next host. Sure, she certainly didn't possess the same...appetites...that his previous host had, but all the better. He wanted someone he could break and mould into his own vision. This time, he wanted to ensure he was the only one in control. Fortunately, the girl was an open book; she had no defences up. It was as though she'd already given up; life had already defeated her. Gethen was slightly annoyed that he wouldn't have the pleasure of wearing her down completely, but he also knew he had to take what he could get—and her grief only seemed to intensify with each encounter.

As he grew stronger, he was able to push himself into her mind, sifting through her thoughts to find what he needed. By the way that she scratched at her head, he could tell she could sense him, which was surprising. Though she would never in a million years guess the cause of the itch. Once he dug under the grief, he found something else that excited him. She was alone. In every sense of the word. Her parents were the only living family she'd had. While she'd had close friends, one by one they had dwindled away over the course of the year as their attempts to console her, to have her live her life again, failed.

171

Mena went about her mourning ritual, kneeling at the foot of her parent's graves and staring blankly at their headstones as tears streamed down her face. She absently played with the grass beside her. Gethen got as close as he dared, not wanting to spook her, and tried to take form. It took all of his concentration, but gradually he felt himself evolve from the apathetic shapeless thing he was into an actual being. With pride, he watched as the dark smoke that he had become bound and wrapped around itself, forming long legs, a lean torso topped with broad shoulders that lengthened out to his outstretched arms, and of course, finally, his head. Though his vision was hazy as a result of his transformation, he revelled in seeing the world again for himself. He lowered his head back skywards, arms outstretched, and a shudder ran through him. He grinned a smoky grin that reached from one side of his face to the other. Gethen let out a howl, certain it would not be heard across the mortal plane. To his surprise, Mena turned, her expression first scattered and then fearful. As he watched, she scanned her surroundings, looking skittish. Amazed at her natural perception of his realm, Gethen took it as a sign he'd found the right host. Not wanting to miss his window of opportunity, he drew as much energy as he could muster into his being. As he fixed a steely gaze upon his target, he dove towards her, merging them into one.

Mena grasped her head in her hands, overcome with an intense pain as though a white hot needle had been shoved through her temples. It was gone almost as quickly as it had started. Leaning forwards, she braced herself with her hands in the grass; her head left ringing as though she had sustained a blow. Feeling a wetness on her hand, she stared at it a moment before realising it was blood. Mena forced herself to sit up as she touched her fingers to her nose, pulling them back to find it bleeding. With nothing else on her, Mena wiped her face with the back of her jacket sleeve

172

before staggering to her feet. Saying a hurried goodbye to her parents, she shoved her hands back into her pockets and fled the cemetery.

***

Mena fumbled, dropping her keys in her rush to get inside. Forcing herself to take a deep breath, she tried the lock a second time. She sighed with relief as she pushed the door open, closing it firmly behind her. She took a moment to calm herself; there was an odd comfort to having her back pressed against the hard surface. After a few deep breaths, she stepped forward into the small and modest apartment, shaking her head as she reprimanded herself for getting spooked. She'd spent so much time at the cemetery since the death of her parents, Mena was stumped as to why the place had gotten to her today. Perhaps her nerves were a little more on edge, as it was the anniversary of their death, yet even still, she felt childish.

Mena walked into the living room, yawning. She plonked herself on the couch, heavy with the weight of her grief. All she wanted was to curl up in bed and sleep the day away, safe from the pain and the sadness. Instead, she looked down at the laptop on the coffee table, knowing she was behind in her writing. Her next deadline was looming. Mena knew she was fooling herself, trying to distract herself with her writing when all she could think about was her parents and how alone she felt.

After staring at the screen for half an hour, Mena was satisfied with her persistence and closed her laptop to curl up on the couch. Certain that it was a step up from going to bed at ten o'clock in the morning, she closed her leaden eyes and fell into a dreamless sleep.

***

Gethen opened his eyes, blinking in quick succession as he focused. It felt good to see through human eyes again. As he sat up, he surveyed his surroundings, most of which were completely foreign to him. In fact, there was very little at all that resembled his previous mortal habitation. Gethen got to his feet, surprised at how natural his movements felt. Looking down at his long and slim, yet curvaceous body, he found himself amused that he now possessed a female, especially one far lighter in clothing than he'd previously been used to. Scanning the room, he hunted for a sign of the year, but to no avail.

"Never mind," he said aloud. "There's plenty of time." Drawn to the thick, closed drapes, Gethen hurried over, hoping for a glimpse of the world. Instead, he was disappointed to find the window overlooked a garden, overgrown and neglected, barely holding onto dear life. Although he found it far more appealing than the excesses of floral displays he'd been exposed to at the cemetery, it did little to hold his interest. As he moved through the room, he was surprised to find a narrow hallway with other rooms branching off it. Mouth agape, he strolled from room to room, running his fingers along the clean, albeit dusty walls and furniture. For one person to have so much space all to themselves, they must surely be rich. Or had things changed that much in his absence? During his last possession, people would cram together in a single room, sharing the bed, the floor, whatever they could find. Though his prior host had been a well-to-do man, he hadn't expected such fortune in a female host.

Gethen stepped into the bathroom, unable to withhold a gleeful laugh as he viewed his host completely for the first time. Running his hands slowly over her body, he turned this way and that in admiration. As he coaxed his fingers through her long and messy black hair, Gethen grabbed a handful of strands and inhaled deeply; his eyes rolled back blissfully as he enjoyed the heady scent. Gethen removed her clothing, deciding to leave the undergarments on as he fondled the delicate lace; it felt nice to his touch. Leaving the clothes on the floor, he walked back through to the lounge room where he noticed an unmistakable bottle of wine on the adjoining kitchen bench. Wine was wine, regardless of the century; he ignored the dirty glass and took a thirsty gulp from the bottle. He relished the warmth as it spread down the back of his throat and through his chest.

Carrying the bottle with him, Gethen strolled back over to the couch and sat down, legs comfortably apart, resting his arms on his thighs. It was then that he felt her stir, and knew he would be cast aside soon. He was not yet strong enough to dominate her consciousness. Finishing off the last of the wine in one long, delightful guzzle, he placed the empty bottle on the coffee table in front of him. He laid on the comfortable couch, allowing his head to fall back against the cushion. His hands rested at his sides. A self-satisfied smirk swept across his face as the darkness pulled him back under.

***

Mena yawned. She slowly opened her eyes, while stretching out her arms. She sat up with a start, her eyes darting down at herself, to the couch, around the room, and back again.

What the hell? She thought to herself, panic stirring deep within her stomach as she realised she was in her underwear. Jumping to her feet, she scanned the room for her clothes, tossing cushions to the floor in her search. A clatter from behind her caused her to jump and she turned to find the knocked over wine bottle on the coffee table.

Mena could do nothing but stare at it for a moment or two, knowing full well that it hadn't been there when she'd gone to sleep.

She remembered clearly only having one glass from it the evening before, forcing herself to leave it in the kitchen to prevent temptation. The horrible feeling she'd had at the cemetery returned so fiercely she felt as though she'd been punched in the solar plexus. Stumbling over the cushions strewn across the floor, Mena ran into the hallway, desperate to find her clothes and her mobile phone, which was tucked away in her jacket pocket. She stopped short when she saw light streaming into the hall from her bedroom. Hesitating, her heart pounding, she looked back towards the lounge room before taking a deep breath and walking into her room. The light came from her ensuite. Tiptoeing soundlessly on the carpet, she strained her ears for any sounds. She was fearful of an intruder, but her hands were tied. Unable to call anyone until she located her mobile, she hugged the wall as she neared the doorway. When she couldn't detect any movement, Mena took a hesitant step into the bathroom. Her elation to find the room empty was swiftly replaced by dismay as she saw her clothes strewn across the tiles. At the sound of her phone ringing, she dove to the ground and grabbed her mobile out of the jacket, relieved to find it was her best friend, Rosalin.

"Hello?"

"Mena! Hi! I didn't expect you to pick up. You haven't answered or returned my calls in ages. I just, I know what today is, and I wanted to see how you're holding up."

"Actually, is there any chance you could come over? Now?"

"Um. Sure," Rosalin replied, unable to hide the surprise in her voice. "Are you okay?"

"I just don't want to be alone right now."

Only once Rosalin promised she'd come straight over did Mena feel her fear begin to shift, just a little. She sat on the cold bathroom tiles, her heart still pounding in her chest as she stared at her clothes. According to the time on her phone, she'd only been asleep about half an hour. Had she sleep walked? It didn't seem likely as she'd never done so before, at least not to her knowledge. Then there was that ever-pervading sensation that she wasn't alone. Despite its brief hiatus upon returning home, the feeling was back stronger than before – so much so that she was afraid to leave her spot against the bathroom wall. Without taking her gaze off the vacant doorway, Mena grabbed her clothes one by one as she slowly redressed herself. Once she was done, she sat there with her knees pulled up to her chin, her arms wrapped around them, and her phone gripped firmly in her hand, as she waited for Rosalin to arrive. She tried to keep herself distracted, tried to think of anything other than what had happened and how, tried to ignore the tingle that ran up her spine and the winding up of her flight instinct. All her senses ran on high alert.

Finally, after what felt like an eternity, Mena heard the tentative knock at the front door. Taking a deep breath, she pushed herself up off the floor and ran to the front door, yanking it open to see a bewildered Rosalin.

"Uh, hey. I got here as soon as I could."

Finding her mouth too dry to speak, Mena gave her friend a nod of gratitude as she stepped back to allow her through. Wrapping her arms around herself, she led Rosalin into the living room. Mena curled up as tightly as she could into the corner of the chair, her knees pulled up and making her feel less exposed. She watched as Rosalin sat tentatively at the other end of the couch, her eyes lingering on the empty bottle of wine. She turned to her friend.

"It's been ages, Mena. How are you holding up?"

Mena opened her mouth briefly before closing it again. She felt hot tears start to sting her dry eyes and she feared if she started to talk she would burst into tears. Her nerves were on edge and her emotions ran high.

"How about I make us some tea first." After more than two decades of friendship, Rosalin could read her friend like a book, and she knew Mena needed a moment to get herself together.

As she waited, Mena forced herself to take a deep breath. She wanted to tell herself that everything was fine, that she'd imagined it, but as she stared at the empty bottle of wine on the table, she knew there was something very wrong.

"Okay, here we go. Take this." Rosalin waited for Mena to drink some tea before she continued. "I know today is a hard day for you, sweetie, but I have to say, you look like a deer caught in headlights. Has something happened?"

Mena avoided eye contact as she tried to think of the words to explain what had happened. The anxiety won over and she blurted it out in a single manic ramble. For a moment, there was silence. This time, it was Rosalin who avoided eye contact as she leant over to place her mug on the coffee table. Clearing her throat softly, she fidgeted with her hands. "Mena, you've gone through a lot lately. Maybe the anniversary of your parents' passing has affected you more than you realised. I don't want to upset you, but I really just think it's a case of your emotions running high. You've over-indulged in some wine, you got undressed, and then you decided for some reason to crash out on the couch. There really isn't any other explanation."

Mena wiped the hot tears from her eyes with the back of her hand. "I can see how you could think that; it certainly looks that way. But I'm telling you, I haven't had any wine—it's still morning, for crying out loud. I also specifically remember lying down on the couch fully clothed. Yes, I'm emotional; it's the anniversary of my parents' deaths and it marks the end of the crappiest year of my life. But I'm telling you, something's happened. I feel on edge, like I've been watched, or even worse, like someone else has been in here."

"So you're saying that during your short nap, someone snuck in, finished your bottle of wine, took off your clothes, and dumped them on the floor in the bathroom before propping you up on the couch. Why? As if you would have stayed asleep if someone had tried to move you around. There isn't any sign of forced entry. It just doesn't make any sense, Mena."

Mena put her head on her knees. It sounded so logical—could she really have done all that without even knowing? The theory didn't ring true to her. She felt emotionally and physically drained.

"Look, I think maybe you've kept to yourself for too long. Being alone may not be the best thing for you right now. How about I crash here for a couple of days? Just until you've caught up on some rest and are feeling a bit more like yourself?"

Mena nodded, instantly feeling some of her anxiety dissipate at the thought of having someone else around. It didn't take much coaxing for Rosalin to convince Mena to lie down while she ducked home to gather some of her things. Walking into the ensuite, Mena splashed water on her tired face. She took a moment to enjoy the sensation of the cool water on her skin. As she wiped her face, she gave a yelp at her reflection. For a split second, she could have sworn she'd seen someone else staring back at her. Leaning in closer, Mena stared hard at her reflection looking for any hint of anything untoward. Nothing. "I'm losing my mind…" With a sigh, she turned the light off and flopped down on her bed, telling herself it was all in her head. Even as she felt an exhausted sleep take over, she didn't believe it.

***

Gethen awoke with an evil smile and languidly stretched himself out. Strength was returning to him faster than he expected and he felt amazing. The energy of having a host was like electricity surging directly into his being, invigorating and igniting him. It wasn't the same as having your own body to inhabit and control…it was better.

As he got up, he pondered how to up the stakes. It'd taken no time at all for his host's emotional stability to fold, not that he'd found much strength there to begin with. The first hurdle was easily overcome; now it was time for some fun.

Gethen strolled into the ensuite, lingering in the doorway as he flicked the light off and on.

Light on, Mena's face.

Light off, Gethen's face.

Light on, Mena's face.

Light off, Gethen's face.

Light on, Gethen's face.

He held it there, feeling the strain of his manifestation; it had been centuries since he had gazed at his own reflection. His skin was a pallid grey, marred in places by large black festering pustules. His eyes were bloodshot with black irises, and white puss wept from them. Sparse and straggly hair framed his face. As he grinned to himself, his jaw distended like a snake's, showing two rows of pointy, razor sharp teeth, blackened by age and decay, dripping with viscous saliva.

"Oh you are magnificent…" he declared before his reflection flickered and he lost a hold of it.

Content, for now, he decided he wanted to have some fun. His eyes fell upon the razor that hung in the shower. Grabbing it, he broke the blade out of the plastic casing and held it up for inspection. He heard the front door open, followed by quiet footsteps and the sound of a large bag sweeping against the wall, and then the door closed again. Gethen smirked to himself; the friend was likely hoping Mena was still fast asleep.

Technically, she was.

He listened intently, waiting for Rosalin to make her way into the living room. Lingering in the doorway, he fondled the razor blade, until he heard the sounds of raucous laughter and cheering. He stepped out into the hallway. With slow, purposeful footsteps, Gethen walked towards the living room, scratching the razor along the wall as he went.

"Mena?" Rosalin called out.

Gethen stepped into the living room and was greeted by a look of confusion; Rosalin paused, an apple halfway to her mouth.

"Mena, are you okay? You look…"

"I'm fine." Gethen cut her off in a voice that was both Mena's melodic feminine voice and his own deep, gravelly one. He could feel himself getting stronger. There was an energy in the room that he hadn't noticed before. It seemed to come from a variety of strange objects, in particular from the large rectangle that appeared to house the laughing and cheering people.

Rosalin's mouth fell open as the apple fell from her hand. Holding her stunned gaze, Gethen took a couple of staggered steps forward before raising his arm out in front of him. "How did you get those people in there, and why are they so loud?"

Rosalin looked to the television before turning back to her friend. At first, she thought it was a joke, but she saw the seriousness on her face. "Um. You mean the television? Uh, sorry if it was too loud; I didn't mean to wake you. That was just the volume when I turned it on." Hastily, she grabbed the remote and shut it off. Stunned by their sudden disappearance, Gethen stood in front of the television, which was now nothing more than a large black screen. As he ran his hands over the smooth glass, he felt a zap followed by a pleasant tingle in his hands; the energy he'd drawn strength from pierced him directly. Better still, he could see his reflection in the screen, and he was thrilled to see his host looking worse for wear. It was time to have some real fun.

Turning on his heel, he faced Rosalin. He held out his arm, palm facing upwards, held the razor blade firmly with his other hand, and slashed it across his exposed wrist.

Rosalin yelped and jumped to her feet, her hands clamped over her mouth.

Without hesitation, Gethen slashed again, this time about an inch above the first cut. They were ragged cuts on account of the dull blade, but they were still deep, and he enjoyed the warmth of the blood as it welled and spilt over, rapidly dripping onto the cream carpet below him.

"Mena! Stop!" Rosalin looked like a deer caught in headlights; she frantically looked around the room for something to stem the bleeding. Dashing into the kitchen, she grabbed two tea towels that hung on the oven door before running back to where Gethen stood with the arm still outstretched; he grinned at his handiwork. He ignored her as she tightly wrapped the towels around the cuts, and he pondered the soft skin in the crook of his host's elbow. It looked like a wonderful spot for a third incision. Before he could raise the blade, Rosalin was pulling him into the kitchen. He vaguely heard her screams for more towels as the ones already around his arm turned a beautiful shade of crimson. It ignited him, awakening the final piece of himself.

"Where's my phone? I'm calling an ambulance!"

Before Rosalin could take another step, Gethen pinned her up against the kitchen cupboard, pressing the blade into the skin of her neck. He could feel her heart pounding fiercely against her chest; it caused a surge of excitement to course through him. Looking into her eyes, he watched a multitude of emotions flicker within them: from shock to panic, to fear, and back to shock again.

"Call anybody, and I'll slit your throat from ear to ear." He hissed down at her. Satisfied by the tremor that ran up and down her body, he lowered the blade, releasing her and stepping back. Rosalin didn't move; she pressed herself against the cupboard, trying to further the distance between them. Gethen smirked at her as he backed away. "Now, now. Why so scared? We're the very best of friends, are we not?"

Rosalin didn't answer. Instead, with a few quick blinks, a tear fell from each eye. With his head tilted to the side, Gethen watched the tears run over her smooth cheeks before continuing down her face and disappearing under her jaw. His gaze continued to her throat. Her beautifully elegant throat. He imagined wrapping his hands around it and squeezing, feeling her struggle beneath his fingertips. Then, just before she lost consciousness, he would slash the razor blade across her neck in one magnificent stroke. The thought alone was almost more than he could stand.

As if somehow able to see his wicked thoughts, Rosalin let out a whimper. Wanting to take advantage of her fear, Gethen opened his mouth for a sinister taunt, but instead, he found himself overcome with dizziness. Staggering backwards, he clutched at the counter top behind him, trying to regain his balance. Weakness overcame him as he realised the hold he had on his host was slipping. He cursed himself for allowing his eagerness to regain a foothold in the mortal world to overlook caution. No entity could take full hold of their host so soon; he'd been foolish to act so quickly. Stumbling out of the kitchen and back into the hall, he could only hope, as he felt himself fading, that he'd scared Rosalin enough to buy himself time to regenerate.

***

Mena opened her eyes, noticing straight away that the room didn't look right. When she placed her hand beside her head to sit up, she was surprised to feel carpet. With a start, she looked around. While she was in her bedroom, she'd somehow ended up on the floor rather than on her bed. Placing weight on her other hand to push herself up off the floor, she screamed in agony; pain seared up her arm. Shocked, Mena looked down to see it swathed in the blood-soaked towels. All she could do was stare at it as a mixture of anxiety and fear spread through her. She knew she'd fallen asleep on the bed, intact and uninjured.

"What is happening to me?" she cried, frustration welling within her before she released it in a bellow that bounced off the bedroom walls. As the sound faded away, leaving her panting on the floor, another sound broke through. Mena strained her ears and tried to place it. Was someone crying? Realising it was Rosalin, she awkwardly got to her feet. She clasped her injured arm to her chest as she staggered into the hallway in search of her friend.

Rosalin sat on the floor of the kitchen, her head buried in her arms, her arms folded over her pulled up knees. Mena hesitated. She wanted to know why her friend was crying but had a sinking feeling that she was somehow to blame. Like before, she had no recollection of what had happened.

"Rosalin?"

Her friend looked up at her, startled fear freezing her features. "Get away from me!" she screeched, her voice choked with tears as she scuttled away.

"Please, Rosalin. I can see you're upset, but my arm is killing me, and I have no idea why!"

"You're crazy; you know that?" Rosalin hissed as she got to her feet. "Is the only reason you asked me to come over so you would have someone bear witness to your crazed suicide attempt? Am I some kind of hostage now?"

It took Mena a few moments to process the words. Part of her tried to make sense of them, while the other part of her wanted to hide, to remain oblivious to what was happening.

"Well? Aren't you going to say something? Don't just stand there, answer me!"

"I...I don't know what to say," Mena replied, her voice shaking. "All I remember is falling asleep on my bed when you left to get your things. Next thing I know, I'm lying on the floor of my room, injured, and I can hear you sobbing out here." She took a step towards her friend, her good arm outstretched as she reached out to comfort her. Rosalin slapped her hand away. "Don't you touch me. Don't you dare come near me. I honestly don't know why I haven't called the cops already, but I will."

"Cops? What? Rosalin, please, can you just tell me what happened?"

Rosalin stared at her friend, part dubious and part fearful. "You really don't remember anything?"

Mena shook her head, pleading. "No. I swear. I have no idea what is happening to me!" Her heart pounded as she waited for Rosalin to decide whether she was telling the truth or not. A terror like nothing she'd ever felt before gripped her tightly, cementing her to the spot.

After what felt like an eternity, Rosalin recounted what happened, her voice breaking as she relived the violence against her. Mena gasped, the air rushing out of her lungs. She wanted to say that it was crazy, that it wasn't possible, but all she had to do was acknowledge the pain in her arm to know Rosalin spoke the truth.

Mena opened her mouth, before closing it again, unable to comprehend what was happening. As hot tears rolled down her face, she grabbed the towels around her arm and ripped them off. She washed the remaining blood away under the tap, wanting to see the damage for herself.

"What the hell..." she heard Rosalin whisper beside her. Mena could only shake her head. The wounds were all but healed. It was clear where they'd been, but all that remained were two dark lines like heavy scratches.

"I don't understand? I was in agony. I couldn't have imagined that? Could I? Are you sure I cut myself as badly as you thought?"

"Take a look at the blood-stained towels, or the blood all over your clothes, or even the floor in both here and the living room, if you want to be sure..." Rosalin stated, bending down to inspect Mena's arm herself.

Pulling her arm away, Mena walked into the lounge room. She curled up on the couch. "Maybe you should have called someone," she said with a sob. "I don't know what's happening to me. Everything was fine when I woke up this morning, and now I feel like I'm losing my mind."

After a moment's hesitation, Rosalin curled up beside her friend, "Honestly, I wanted to. But you scared the hell out of me, Mena. You actually threatened me. I was too afraid to do anything. After you left the kitchen, I'd thought I'd gathered up enough bravery to leave. When I saw that you had passed out on the floor of your room, I thought I was safe to run and then call someone to help you from the safety of my locked car. But as I tried to sneak past your bedroom, you let out the most god-awful sound; I swear it was like you growled at me. I was so freaked out by that point that all I could think to do was return to the mess in the kitchen and cry."

"It wasn't me; you have to know that!"

"I...I want to believe you. I mean, you have to understand, it was your mouth moving, and your hand pressing the blade against my throat, but I want to believe that you would never hurt me. Something serious is going on with you, and I say this out of love and respect for our friendship, but this past year has been hard on you. I think we need to get you some help. You're clearly not yourself."

"You think I've gone mad?"

"Look at yourself. You're losing time, behaving strangely, acting violently towards yourself and others. There's no other logical explanation. I think the past year has taken its toll, and you're in the midst of a full-blown breakdown."

Mena was silent as numerous thoughts bounced around her head. Rosalin made sense, yet something told her that it wasn't right. She sincerely believed there had to be another explanation. There was no way she was responsible for her behaviour. Getting up from the couch, she walked over to the window, pulling the curtain back to look out at the evening as it darkened the skies. The fading daylight felt ominous to Mena. Her eyes darted around, and she scanned the yard, feeling more and more on edge. The silence between her and Rosalin grew heavy, and she knew it would persist until she responded. Looking down at her arm, Mena sighed.

"You know, truth be known, as terrified as this all makes me, I also feel better than I have since my parents died. I feel like a weight has been lifted, like I'm not so burdened by my grief."

Rosalin took a moment, running her fingers along the couch cushion before answering. "I think that simply supports my theory that you're undergoing some kind of psychotic break. Everything you've been carrying around with you is finally being released."

"I just don't think so. I don't feel like I'm mentally unstable—and yes, I know that's what crazy people probably say, but it's just all too sudden. It's like I just completely disappear for a while, and when I come back, something has happened. It's like I'm possessed."

Rosalin scoffed at the idea. "Possession? You're clutching at straws now. You've always said you never believed in any of that rubbish, and you're not even religious! Now you want to tell me that you woke up this morning and some deranged evil spirit just happened to jump you? I'm pretty sure it doesn't work that way."

"How do you explain my arm? I should be dead by now after those gashes, but instead, it's like nothing even happened. It would explain why I have no recollection of doing any of these things. You know, at the cemetery this morning something weird happened, I had this god-awful pain in my head…"

"Stop it! Stop it right now!" Rosalin yelled as she jumped to her feet. "You're sick Mena, and I don't know how long it's been going on for – I shouldn't have ignored you when you pushed us all away. I wasn't here for you then, but I am here for you now. I am going to get you some help." As she pulled her mobile from her pocket, Mena stepped away from the window. She pleaded with her. "Please, don't! It's been a long day, and I'm exhausted. Can we sleep on it? Please? If you still insist in the morning that I need help, then I won't fight you on it. Just give me tonight to get my head around it?"

Mena held her breath as she watched her friend struggle with a decision. She wasn't game to say anything further in her defence. After what felt like an eternity, Rosalin finally spoke, reaching around to place her mobile in her back pocket. "Fine. Just tonight. But I suggest you get some sleep, because I will be making some calls in the morning. I suggest we both just go to bed; I have a feeling tomorrow is going to be a long day."

Mena nodded, not wanting to rock the boat further. She headed off to her room. Closing the bedroom door, she leant against it, her heart pounding. She knew she wasn't crazy. She couldn't be. Listening intently, she waited until she heard the click of the spare room door closing before she dashed into the bathroom. Turning on the light, she leant against the sink, closing the gap between herself and her reflection. She stared into her own eyes, unsure of what she was looking for, but certain there had to be something, some kind of sign that she wasn't crazy, that she wasn't in the midst of a psychotic break. Concentrating fiercely, she thought she saw a shadow pass over her expression. She frowned as she scanned her surrounds through the mirror. Fixing her gaze back on herself, she stared. After a few moments, her reflection began to flicker. She held her breath as she watched another reflection take her place. With a screech, she pushed herself away from the hideous face before falling back onto the tiles. She quickly clamped her hands across her mouth, not wanting to disturb Rosalin. It was matter of seconds before the knock came from her bedroom door.

"Mena? Is everything alright?"

"Yeah, I'm fine, it was just a spider, sorry!" she called out in reply. She could tell by the lack of movement that Rosalin still stood outside her room. Mena willed her to move on. Her heart thudded painfully against her chest, the sound seeming to bounce off the tiles, closing in on her, making it hard to hear anything else. When she finally heard the click of the door, she let out a shaky exhale.

She'd been unaware she was holding her breath. Scurrying across the floor, she grabbed onto the sink and slowly pulled herself up, unsure of what she would see in the mirror. Once again the horrific face came into view; she placed her hand in her mouth to stop herself from screaming. An uncontrollable tremor ran through her. She raised her hand to her face. Her reflection did the same. While her face felt like her own under her fingertips, the face in the mirror was not. It was like nothing she'd ever seen before. Hideous and festering, he smiled at her with a large set of sharp teeth, dripping with a viscous substance. Gagging, she looked away. She took a minute to regain herself. As she looked back, it seemed to be laughing at her.

"Who are you?" she hissed, as she once again leaned towards the mirror, trying to avoid looking beyond the monsters' bloodshot eyes.

"I am Gethen," the creature replied, his voice a hiss within her mind.

"How did you find me? What do you want?"

"I've been watching you for a year, every time you visited your parents. Your grief strengthened me each time I saw you, until today, when you dragged your broken soul into the cemetery, giving me the last boost of energy I needed in order to take you. Mena, you're off to a wonderful start as a host…"

"Host?" She felt her stomach convulse as one of the pustules on his face burst and he wiped the vile puss with his finger before sliding it into his mouth, wetly sucking it. Realising she had her finger in her own mouth, Mena yanked her hand away, appalled at the ease in which he controlled her.

"Tsk, tsk, Mena. That was rude. You can't fight it. If I have this much control of you already, it won't take long at all before I stamp you out and take full possession of your body."

Before she could answer, a searing pain shot through her skull, causing her to fall to her knees. Clutching at her head, she sobbed for the pain to stop, not managing more than a whisper. Then everything went black.

***

Gethen picked himself up off the floor, noticing right away that he felt stronger. Yet as he walked out of the bathroom and through the bedroom, he could feel her fighting him. It was as though she was pounding against her confinement and it left him with a queasy, unnerved feeling. While it concerned him that she could fight back now that she was aware of him, he knew that she could only weaken as he grew stronger.

As he walked into the kitchen, his host's blood still smeared across the tiles, Gethen pulled the largest knife out of the wooden block. Holding it up, he inspected the blade. Satisfied, he strode towards the spare room and pressed his ear against the door. He listened for any movement. When he heard nothing, he opened the door slowly and peered in, allowing his eyes to adjust to the darkness. Rosalin lay under the covers, already fast asleep, her hair splayed out over her pillow. With barely audible footsteps, Gethen moved towards the bed and sat gently on the edge, careful not to wake her. He paused, making sure she wouldn't stir, before burying his face in her hair and inhaling deeply. Moving on to her neck, he trailed his nose along the graceful line from her ear down to her collarbone. She still smelled of the days' perfume, a pleasant citrus smell. He pulled back as she twitched in her sleep, pushing the comforter back as she did so. Gethen smiled to himself; it was as though she knew what he was thinking—she was offering herself up as a willing victim, he was sure of it.

Raising the knife, he hovered it over her chest as he considered where he wanted to plunge it first. It wasn't going to be a slash and gash job, no. He'd learned a lot about the artistry of a truly macabre murder from his previous host, and he planned to do his skills justice. As he slowly lowered the blade, relishing the feel of the knife in his hands, the power he felt running through him, he was overcome by a ringing in his ears, and his vision blurred. It felt like he'd been hit in the head with a ferocious blow. He tumbled off the edge of the bed and onto the floor, his grip on the knife faltering as it dropped soundlessly onto the carpet beside him. Gethen writhed in pain, clutching at his head. It was then that he heard her. He let out a furious hiss as he grabbed the knife and scurried out of the room on all fours, not wanting to alert his victim.

"Give me my body back!" The screech of his host sounded like nails on a chalkboard within his head, causing him to flinch; he clapped his hands over his ears. He could feel himself losing his grip on consciousness the more he focused on Mena's voice.

"Get out. Get out. Get out. Get out!" her piercing screams reverberated around his skull as she pounded at him from within. Gethen let out a low, ferocious growl and mustered up all his strength to maintain his possession. He could outlast her. There was no way she could keep this up. She didn't have the mental strength or fortitude; it was what he loved most about her.

"I'm going to enjoy slicing up your friend," he said through clenched teeth, bracing himself against the internal screams in response. Determined not to lose this opportunity, Gethen pushed himself up off all fours. He swayed on his knees for a moment before he felt steady enough to get to his feet. He had gripped the knife but was surprised to see one of his fingers lift off, then another. He swore under his breath as he used his other hand to close his fingers back around the hilt. Huffing in fury at her insolent show of control. Attempting to stride back into Rosalin's room, he found himself struggling. It felt like he was walking through quicksand with Mena fighting him with each step. Trembling with rage, he turned the knife towards himself and sliced it across his chest. He could hear Mena's screams, only this time they were filled with pain. Taking advantage of her distraction, he lunged towards the room. He was barely a foot in before his knees buckled and he fell to the floor.

"Give it up, Mena! You will not beat me!" He howled silently. Rosalin began to stir as he dragged himself along the carpet with his elbows, determined to fulfil his kill. As he reached the bed, fiery pain caused him to curl up in a ball. It felt like white hot claws were tearing through his brain, causing an agony like nothing he had ever endured. The knife again fell from his hands, and he clawed at his face, breaking through the skin, wanting the pain to end. Inhuman growls erupted from within. Above, he vaguely noted Rosalin's panicked awakening, her screams barely registering as he writhed on the floor. He heard her leap from the bed and run from the room, and he knew he didn't have much time before she alerted the authorities. He raised his head before banging it as hard as he could on the floor, stunning himself, but more importantly, ceasing the clawing. Raising his head again, he brought it down a second time and screamed, "You cannot defeat me!"

As he lost consciousness, he heard Mena's faint whisper, "Yes, I can."

***

Mena opened her eyes, her ears ringing from the subsequent blows. She rolled onto her back and tentatively touched her face, feeling the stickiness of the bleeding scratch marks. Running her hand along the knife wound across her chest she winced, knowing it was a far worse wound. Muffled, high-pitched talking from the living room distracted her she realised Rosalin must be on the phone.

"Rosalin, I'm fine now!" she tried to call out, but her voice was little more than a hoarse whisper. She took her time getting to her feet, surprised at how good she felt. Despite the bleeding, she felt powerful, more in control of herself than she had in a very long time. The grief that had weighed her down for the past year had lifted.

As she stepped out into the living room, Rosalin lowered her phone from her ear.

"Oh my god, Mena. You look terrible!" she exclaimed with a shaky voice, tears welling.

"I'm okay, really. At least I will be."

"I'm sorry, but I've called the authorities. I'm not helping you by standing by and watching you do this to yourself, Mena." Rosalin sobbed.

Mena felt hot tears sting her own eyes as she walked towards her old friend. Rosalin took a step back, her eyes fearful.

"It's okay. It's me. Everything is going to be fine now. You did the right thing; I do need help. I'm so lucky to have a friend like you."

Rosalin gave her a small smile, relieved Mena didn't put up a fight.

Mena wrapped her arm around her friends' shoulders and hugged her tightly, pulling the knife out from behind her back...

Starved

Ace Antonio Hall

The glorious downfall, which started some twenty-four hours after I placed humans at the top of the endangered species list, began with me (or rather her) picking out an ugly fertility statue out of a wastebasket full of weather-beaten umbrellas. My own pathetic umbrella broke from the fierce winds, therefore I rushed into the crisis center with a wet tangled head full of mess and the metal remains of something that looked like a film student's futile execution of a Lovecraftian cosmic entity.

I tossed my useless Cthulhu-like umbrella straight into the wastebasket upon entering the office suite. A chill made me shudder. Someone had thrown away a bone-colored statuette in the trash, and I stared at it for a moment. It intrigued me that it had a scorpion's body with human legs, wings, and a very disturbing lion-like face. I couldn't remember where I'd seen it before, only that the object symbolized protection. Without a second thought, I retrieved it. One person's trash is someone else's treasure and all that mumbo-jumbo.

Ms. Devereux, 32, single, stood at the doorway of her office, crimson coffee mug in pale freckled hand and greeted me. "So nice of you to finally join us, Kathy," she said, calling me by my first name. "May I speak with you a moment?"

Her blue top stretched over a perfect body. Silky black hair framed an oval face that was flawless. She peered at me over the rim of her mug as she took a slow sip, judgmental black eyes and permanently furrowed brows waited impatiently.

"Uh, yeah," I said, looking at my watch. I still had two more minutes before nine. "Sure thing, Ms. Devereux. I just wanted to freshen up first, and then—"

"It'll only take a moment," she said, interrupting, and turned to wobble into her office.

"Oh, um, sure," I said, trading glances with a nosey co-worker, whose eyes darted back to his computer.

I walked into Ms. Devereux's office feeling wet and icky just as she eased down into her soft leather desk chair. She had the kind of office that showed she had expensive tastes. The windows behind her grand mahogany desk went from the floor-to-the-ceiling, there were three soft leather brown couches in a semi-circle in front of his desk. Caravaggio-only prints decorated the walls, and loads of psychology books filled the shelf on one of the side walls.

Opposite that wall held ornate wooden plaques displaying his plethora of master and doctoral degrees she achieved since she graduated high school at an early age of fifteen. One plaque on her wall had a picture of President George W. Bush pinning the purple heart on her father. She boasts incessantly to the office that her family has voted Republican every year since Gerald Ford, except in 1992, when they voted for Independent candidate, Ross Perot. For the first time ever, she said she thought about voting for a

Democrat, for Hilary, only because she said a woman president could shake up a man's world like none other.

It was a rather eccentric place for a crisis management office. Ms. Devereux started typing into her laptop computer. There were pictures of her siblings in glass desk-frames sitting on the well-polished wood. Red, green and yellow lights blinked on her baby Christmas tree by his laptop.

"I heard about your little event yesterday," she finally said.

"Was nothing," I said, grinning. "Just doing my job."

"You weren't on the clock, Kathy."

"I know, but as you say, everything we do represents this agency—on or off the clock—we are the faces of critical response."

"You know, Kathy, I'm so glad you said that."

She stopped typing and sighed. "Did you ask the potential client to put her weapon aside?"

"Yes, but he re—"

"And afterward, did you excuse yourself to call the authorities?"

"I couldn't leave. He may have still been a danger to the people in the department store."

"I realize that you are a Licensed Clinical Professional Counselor, but do you know what you actually are?"

"A person that saves lives?"

"You are nothing more than a 9-1-1 dispatcher, Kathy."

"We allocate more expertise than what an EMD demanded," I said, perhaps louder than I intended.

"I see," she said, pushing back from her desk, and standing. "Well, the fact-of-the-matter is that for the third time this month, somehow, some way, you have found yourself in the middle of a physical altercation. The news stations have zeroed in on that, Kathy, and are now calling you the *911 Vigilante*."

"They're calling me what? A vigilan—"

"And we frankly, can't have that. It looks bad. Makes me look bad, and when I look bad, something has to be—"

It was my turn to interrupt. "So what? You're firing me?"

She bent down and pressed a button on her desk phone. "Security, please send someone up to escort a former employee out of the building."

"Ms. Devereux!"

"I'm sorry, Kathy, but you have forced my hand."

"But—but, I can't lose my job. I need money to plan for my sister's wedding. What am I going to do for income?"

"You should've thought of that before you went out and misrepresented our crisis center."

"I made our center look good. Made us look like we care, you—you self-righteous bitch."

"Get out," she screamed. "Get out of my office now, before I have you arrested for threatening me!"

"What?"

Someone grabbed my shoulders. I shrugged and walked toward Ms. Devereux.

"Why you—"

Loren, the security officer, was in the office with us. He firmly grabbed me. "Kathy! You're making it worse."

He forcibly escorted me out of the office. "Don't worry, Ms. Devereux. I will make sure she leaves without any issue."

"You better get that lunatic out of my presence," Ms. Devereux said.

"Yes, ma'am," Loren said and eased me out of the door.

I went over to my cubicle, face full of tears, and stumbled into my chair. Eyes were poking over the walls of my cubicle from all directions. I flicked off my computer, and after gathering my belongings, left.

The Next Day

It was exactly nine-thirteen that morning when I saw my neighbor threatening to kill someone in the Pathmart Superstore one block down from my rental home in Pasadena.

Mr. Benjamin Behl, fifty-seven, was a tall Vietnam veteran dressed in a white button-up, blue jeans and an apron. He worked in the deli department at Pathmart. I think everyone who bought something from the deli heard about his adventures in Vietnam. When his face wasn't buried in a science journal, practically lived in the gym. He was a highly intellectual, extremely strong man.

When I saw him, I stopped in my tracks, mouth agape. I switched my motorcycle helmet to my right hand and tossed the bag of my sister's baby clothes in a cart filled with items to be shelved.

Hiding in a Kangaroo standard shoulder holster under my jacket was a Ruger LCR revolver. To be honest, Pasadena was a safe place to live. I didn't need to carry my gun, but nevertheless, I never left home without her.

The thing that surprised me the most about the irony of the situation was not that I was about to do my so-called *vigilante* thing again, but the fact that the person Ben was threatening to harm. Of all people, it was Ms. Devereux!

He was in the food section of Pathmart holding her by a choke-hold. They were both sobbing, she more than he, due to the large knife threatening to pierce her small neck.

"Ben," I said, inching closer as I spoke. "You look worried. Would you like to talk about it? Maybe you can let Ms. Devereux go, and we can go somewhere, you and I."

"Let me go, you imbecile," Ms. Devereux said.

Ben's brows furrowed. "Who you calling—"

"Ms. Devereux please," I said, "Just shut up, will you?"

She glared at me as if I were crazy, but remained quiet. Smart lady.

My feet were apart shoulder length, one foot inches behind the other, knees slightly bent. I had to be in a position to respond instantly to a physical threat if needed, except that I carried a motorcycle helmet and had only one free hand.

Sometimes, you have to adapt and react, Ms. Devereux always preached. I stepped forward.

"Stop right there," Ben said.

I did as I was told. "Sure thing."

"How old are you, Kathy?" Ben asked.

I let out a playful gasp. "Now you know you're not supposed—"

"Just answer the question," he snapped.

"I'm thirty," I said, and took a cautious step forward.

Ben took a step back. "You're a lot younger than I thought, wise beyond your years."

"I hear that a lot," I said, glancing around.

"If you're looking for security," Ms. Devereux said, gasping, "Don't. They're busy handling another emergency near the front of the store."

"Listen to me, Kathy," Ben said, "You see me every week and speak to me about your unconventional ideas in science, but truthfully, you don't have the slightest clue about me."

"It's only unconventional conversation because you disagree with epigenetics."

"You new age science thinkers are throwing dogma right out of the window. You have no respect for your elder generations' philosophies."

"What in the hell do you think you're doing, Kathy?" Ms. Devereux asked.

Ben jerked his arm into her neck. "Be quiet!"

She gasped. "This man is about to kill me and your babbling scientific theories?"

I pointed at her. "Shut up, Ms. Devereux."

Ben smiled. It was a tactic Ms. Devereux herself taught me. Calming him, distracting him, was the best way to contain this situation.

"Aw, come on, Ben," I said. "I'm on the same page as you, just more, well, modern. We want the same things for humanity. I want to see a better more resourceful unified world, but you know as well as I do, we're facing the sixth mass extinction."

"Maybe we're being exterminated because someone wants us humans to be extinct. Did you ever think about that? Why do all these infectious diseases keep getting worse and worse? Doesn't anyone think it strange that the FDA claims it's acceptable for us to have acceptable levels of food contamination from sources such as insect fragments, rodent hairs, and insect and rat feces?"

"There's no apocalypse conspiracy brooding here, Ben."

"You know as well as I that fecal matter from vermin bears infectious agents of potentially fatal hantavirus pathogens? It's in our peanut butter, for Chrissakes! No one finds this strange?"

"So what are you saying, Ben?"

"I'm saying that someone or *something* is trying to wipe out the human species, and we're oblivious to their ploy, especially us. Americans are nothing more than zombies, shambling around and moaning about our own meaningless miserable lives, while the real threat to humanity is sleeping right in our own bed."

"What, now we're moving on from terrorists to alien invasions? Return of the Body Snatchers? Come on, Ben, you don't actually believe that?"

"All I know is that you've got to be a mighty naive species, totally narcissistic, to believe that out of all these universes in existence, we—"

"Are the only one," I said, finishing his statement.

"You're antagonizing the client," Ms. Devereux said. "So glad you no longer work for me. You despicable spoiled—"

"Don't," I said, waving my index finger at her.

"You don't know nothing about me, Kathy," Ben said. "Just like this woman doesn't know nothing about me. She comes in here every week, ordering her chicken salad and pickles, always rude to me. Always. Treats me with disrespect. I'm a Vet. Gave my life so she could live free. I don't need her crap in my life! Not when I have to deal with this?"

He held up a crumpled blood-splotched paper in his hands. Dark red liquid seeped from a rip in Ms. Devereux's floral blouse above her left breast. She let out a soft cry of distress. Droplets of crimson trailed behind her on the linoleum floor. A couple of brown trays, overturned bowls, scattered cereal, plastic silverware and spilled milk was on the floor.

"Insurance company says my wife, Delores, had a pre-existing condition and won't cover her," Ben said. "What's one thing have to do with another? Thirty-five years of serving food in this cafeteria to all these demeaning Pasadena snobs to feed my children and put a roof over our heads. Thirty-five years of living check-to-check, refinancing my house three times already and now I'll

202

probably still lose it! You don't understand a damn thing about my life!"

"I'd be angry, too, if that happened to me, Ben," I said, taking a cautious step.

He laughed. "You're young. You ain't got nearly the kind of problems I have."

"Tell me more about them. I can see that you're very angry about them."

"You're trying to appease me, calm me down. Nice try."

"No, Ben, that's not it at all. I just want to hear your side of the story."

The man was so tall he had to hunch over to hold Ms. Devereux.

I gave Ben a sympathetic smile.

Dammit, I should've told the bystanders to clear the area! Too late now. Gotta focus.

I held my hands outward; helmet still in one hand.

Ben took another step back. "You got children, Kathy?"

"No, um, not yet," I said, glancing at the double doors to the west wing of the hospital, the cancer ward.

"Well, I have—had—I had five," he said, blindly moving toward the cash register in the center of the cafeteria. I could tell he was becoming hyperactive by how he kept tightening his grip on the knife, veins throbbing in his hands. I needed to calm him down.

"Tell me more."

He narrowed his eyes. "Eh, okay. Five beautiful children—four girls, one boy," he said, and then pride filled his face. "And seven of the most amazing granddaughters in the world."

His armpits were soaked, perspiration freckled his nose and forehead.

"That's a big family, Ben. You sound like a very caring father, and one who spoils his grandchildren."

He smiled, loosened his grip on Ms. Devereux.

"Get your filthy hands off me," Ms. Devereux said, "I'll see to it that you not only lose this job, but you'll go to jail, and never see your children again."

Ben tightened his grasp on Ms. Devereux. She gasped.

"Shut up, you," he said and slit her below her collar bone.

Ms. Devereux screamed, and blood gushed out of her wound onto the floor.

There were surveillance cameras. Maybe the police were outside, securing the area and escorting people safely out before they went into emergency reaction protocol.

There were a few people hiding down some of the aisles, and about a dozen watching in groups of two's and three's.

"Everyone stay back please," I said.

"Who the hell are you, lady," I heard a man say.

"She's the 9-1-1 Vigilante," a woman said. "Saw her on TV, yesterday."

I shot her a quick glance. "I'm not a vigilante."

"No!" Ms. Devereux said and clawed at Ben's eyes.

Ben may have been old, but his strength proved to be too much for them. He grabbed her hand with the same hand he held the butcher knife and snatched it away from his face. I gasped.

"Don't hurt her, Ben," I said.

He grabbed her by the neck the way an insensitive jerk would hold a pup. Thunder boomed outside and shook the walls of the building.

"Ben, please, no!" I said.

He grimaced and pressed the butcher knife into my former boss's neck. "But Ms. Devereux here, she doesn't care about my Mikey, or anyone else."

"Ben," I said. "Tell me about your children.

"What?" he said, and wiped the sweat from his brow.

"You were telling me about your children. Who's Mikey?"

The lights flickered. The storm was getting worse. I glanced up at the ceiling. When I returned my focus to Ben, he gave me an idiot's smile.

"Mikey's dead," he said. "He wasn't a perfect teenage boy, but are any of them?" His eyes furrowed again. "You—you tell me, was you perfect when you were a teen?"

"No, actually, far from it."

I noticed that Ben started favoring his right knee, his hand reached down to touch it, and he grimaced again. Terrified onlookers continued to gawk; a few people eased up in the bicycle aisle behind me. One of them, a young kid wearing a gray collegiate-style sweatshirt with the words DRUKEN STATE over a football image, was videotaping the incident on his iPhone.

Ben was in a daze, showing that idiot smile again. His hold on Ms. Devereux was still tight.

Say something, I told myself.

"I ran away from home the day after all my scabs healed from having the measles, Ben," I said, "And blamed my parents for conspiring with the martians. For some reason, I thought measles was another name for martians. Go figure. I was eight. So, no, Ben, I wasn't a perfect kid."

"Yeah, well neither was my Mikey. Didn't mean some white cop had to shoot my baby boy in cold blood," Ben said. "Said he was one of them bioterrorists. My son wasn't a terrorist. He was smart, but he wasn't crazy."

I gasped. Not because I was shocked at what happened to his son but because I'd recognized the name. Michael Behl. It was a polarizing case that got just as much exposure on the airwaves as all the cases in India where

205

bioterrorists were using suicidal bombers, except instead of using bombs they were using infectious diseases and spreading the airborne pathogens in public places.

The president came under much fire for banning all flights to and from India. It was a big mess, and Ben's son made it a worldwide discussion on the ethics of profiling the new trend of science thugs. It sounded like some unrealistic conundrum. Science was built for nerds, not thugs. But that was old news now. The news networks have since moved on to Ebola cases and hospital preparedness in America.

"I know it's bad for a parent to have a favorite," Ben said, "But I loved him like crazy—loved that boy like crazy."

"I remember seeing your son on TV, Ben. He definitely didn't deserve that. I'm sorry for your loss."

"You know, Kathy," Ben said. "Mikey was going to go to college—first one in our family—he was so smart at math, could figure stuff out in his head without writing it down, and he and I used to talk about Newtonian physics all the time, but all that is gone. Gone—gone!"

Ben's lips trembled, and tears gushed out. "Took up all of my savings fighting that case in court. Just so the bastard could get off with a measly thirty-day jail sentence. Pushed my wife into having a stroke. And now this?"

He held up the crumpled paper. "A hospital bill for one hundred and seventy thousand dollars! How do they expect me to pay that? I'm just a supermarket deli man."

"Ben, I never told you this, but I work, well used to work, at a place that can help you. We have many resources. It's just down the block."

"Oh, yeah, Kathy? What did you do?"

"I work at a Crisis Unit."

"You did? Well, obviously you don't now. So why even bring it up?"

"They can help you, Ben. Find ways to help you cope. They can help put your life back in your hands, give you choices. I'll even go there with you."

"No, you won't," Ms. Devereux said.

"Ben," a short, stocky man said, emerging from seemingly nowhere. "Let the woman go. You're done here—surely going to get fired. Apply for some government assistance, or the only place you'll be working at is in prison making license plates."

"Government assistance?" Ben said. "And what, Aaron? Raise my four daughters who still live under my roof with all my grandchildren on 450 dollars a week? How am I going to even tackle hospital bills with no more insurance from the job? Do me a favor, Aaron. Go back to cheating on your wife with Bonnie-Sue from jewelry and stay out of this."

Aaron's mouth fell agape. "Ben, you promised not to say anything!"

This guy was agitating Ben. I needed him to go away.

"Ben. Is it okay if I have Aaron write down the number to my job? Aaron, can you get something to write with?"

"Wait," Ben said. His eyes darted back-and-forth sweeping the floor before him as he searched for an answer. "No, Aaron will only call the police."

"Don't you think someone already did that?" Aaron said.

I shook my head. "Maybe not, Ben. Don't listen to him. If someone had called the police, they would have made their presence known already, would've tried to contact you."

Taking another step forward, I said, "Perhaps, because you work here, they are giving you the benefit of the doubt that you are just having a bad day." Again, I took a step.

"No," Ben said. "Stop doing that. Stay where you are!"

He took another step backward. Distracted, Ben slipped from a small pool of Ms. Devereux's blood, stumbling to the floor. Ms. Devereux rolled out of his grasp, got up and ran out of the cafeteria screaming in a foreign language that sounded Mandarin. The onlookers scattered, moving out of her way. Her blood spattered everywhere, on the bicycles, on the baby clothes.

Ben slipped again clumsily, before picking himself up. He ran after her. I swung my arm and slammed my helmet into Ben's weak knee. He cried out in agonizing pain and crashed into a row of bikes. The butcher knife flew out of his hands and went sliding on the floor.

I slipped out my revolver and pointed it at Ben. "Freeze! Don't make me shoot, Ben. Please don't do anything stupid."

I walked over to him, kicked the butcher knife out of reach, behind me. Ben's body was wrangled up in between three bikes. He groaned and awkwardly reached for his knee. Thunder and lightning roared and crackled, and a loud crash like glass shattering came from the front of the store. The few people that were still in the store cried out sounds of fear. Wind thrashed inside of the store. Papers and anything that wasn't tied down started flying all over the store.

A warm buzz tickled my ear, and spine-tingling whispers called out to me.

What's happening?

"Run," I said, to Ben.

He picked himself up and backed up toward a wall of toys and games, eyes trained on my gun. "That buzz ... in my head—"

From above the aisle, a long blue tentacle that was over ten-feet-long with a thickness like an over-sized boa constrictor whipped over and snapped around his neck. Ben

208

gasped and tried to break free, but another tentacle reached over the aisle and wrapped around one of his legs, lifting it.

"Stop," I said. "Stop it!"

The few people who were still in the store scattered. Boxes from the shelves fell to the floor. Screams echoed throughout the different aisles.

Ms. Devereux walked from behind the girl's shoe section. "Time to die," she said, but her lips didn't move.

She spoke to my mind. Telepathically.

Something squawked and garnered my attention. It was Ben. He was still being strangled, but his dark skin had turned purple, and he had fallen to the ground.

"She's a," he said, gasping. "She's a ..."

Ms. Devereux wobbled over to me. She placed her hand on my shoulder and leaned her head forward. I tried to speak, couldn't. My muscles felt tensed, but I was unable to move. Tapping her forehead with mine gently, a long thin tentacle extended from her right ear lobe. I struggled to move. My breathing became labored.

The tentacle pressed against my mouth, and I tightened my lips, clenched my teeth, as the cold, slimy thing pried against my lips. It slipped into my nostril, and I gawked. Another tentacle slipped out of the other ear lobe, quickly, and slipped past my lips. It stretched inside and coursed its way down my throat. It went into my stomach and made me nauseous. I gagged, spittle slobbered down my chin. Everything in me became numb, instantly.

"Nothing is more important than the protection of my family," she said, in my mind.

Ben pointed at me. "It's an ... alien," he said and fell over dead.

Someone in the store screamed.

Were there others like her in the store? Is that why there were no police? Were they all dead?

Ms. Devereux, or whatever she was truly called, shook her head and glanced around. Confusion crossed over her face. While her mind wandered, I felt her psychical grip on me loosening. Pins and needles tingled in my entire body, but the numbness faded.

I followed Ms. Devereux's eyes. No human in our proximity was left alive. They were all sprawled out like dead fish on a beach. A bluish liquid seeped out of the orifices of their bodies and pooled on the floor. One thing Ben got right was that the human's bodies were taken over.

"At first," she said. "I thought I could inhabit this place, but now I see that my kind are truly incompatible for coexistence."

"Why don't you coexist with the demons in hell," I said and fired my gun into her stomach.

"Mother!" a voice said, behind us.

It was a creature that looked much like a human octopus, it had a human head, but its body was clumsy, writhing with tentacles. She bolted toward me, screaming. Long tentacles started extending from her ears. I shot her three times before she got within ten feet of me, shot Ms. Devereux once more in the head, and collapsed to the floor.

I awakened with handcuffs on me, knowing that darkness had consumed me. An army of policemen dragged me away from the store. There were flashes in my eyes, mobs of people cursing me for the cause of the massacre. Many tried to get me to speak, but I never spoke to another human again; not during the trial, during psychiatric examinations, or when anyone visited me in the sanitarium.

Several months later, I sat in my room and glanced out the window at the pretty fall colors, watching the leaves play tag in the wind. My hands rested snug above my large belly. I felt something squirm, and then slap against my tummy, glanced down, and whispered, "Soon."

I turned to see the time from the digital clock on my nightstand, but instead, I stared at the bone-colored statuette I saved from the trash the day I was fired from my job. I'd since learned that it was the statue of Pazuzu, a demon in his own right, but a protector from any entity wishing harm to my baby. I believed it had great power for it seemed to speak to me the moment I gazed upon it. I smiled, pat my stomach again, and spoke to my baby. But it wasn't me that spoke but Ms. Devereux. Somehow, she was in my mind. She spoke to the baby or whatever that was growing inside of me.

"Your mother tried to kill me. But I survived, and so will you. These creatures are nothing more than ghouls, hungry for pestilence. And I, as well as you, my darling, am insatiably starved for human extinction."

A woman came in, the one who treated me as a child. "It's time for your pill," she said, extending her hand to my mouth.

I gave her a struggle just so I could taste her skin when she shoved it in my mouth, and only pretended to swallow it, watching her. Her bleached blonde hair spilled over her shoulders like silk. She wore a white hat, uniform, and even walked in shoes that were as bright as snow. But pure she was not, and soon, when my hands would be free to do as I pleased, I would bite into her flesh to see for myself if she was pure. When she left, I spit the pill out, hungry for death.

When I met Hannah

Shelly Schulz

Marie stood out in the sea of navy and black, wearing a pale yellow dress. Her hair was loose; falling in waves down her back. Nothing like the severe twist she wore it in at the office. She was relaxed, watching the people mill about, and the smile that crossed her face when we made eye contact made my heart skip a beat. She really was beautiful, and I could understand now, why most of the office talked about her in hushed whispers. She was one of the first people to reach out to me when I had transferred to Seattle from the Georgia office. I handed the valet the keys to my car and smoothed my hand down my tie, insuring that it lay flat against my shirt.

"Will!" she called out to me, waving me over. "I'm glad you found it."

"Your directions were solid," I said offering her my arm. I could kick myself with how stupid I sounded. "You weren't waiting out here long?" My gut twisted when her arm slid through mine, feeling the gentle press of her body against me. I turned my attention to the brick warehouse that loomed in front of us. The invitation to the art gallery opening had come a few days after a meeting.

"Not really," she said with another mega-watt smile. "I was just enjoying watching everyone."

We made our way to the line when she tugged on my arm again, leading me past the people to the head of the queue. "We're on the list." Marie said to a man with a clipboard, "Under Jordynn." The man frowned, realizing that Marie had dropped the artist's name, as he scanned the pages on the clipboard, before nodding to a second man who removed the velvet rope.

"Enjoy your evening," He said as we walked through.

People milled around the main floor, the hum of conversation blending together with the quiet strains of a string quartet. Wait staff carried trays of hors d'oeuvres and carefully balanced flutes of champagne. Paintings were displayed on rough easels, softly backlit by standing floor lights. I flagged down one of the servers and handed a frosted glass of champagne to Marie, and took one for myself.

"I'm going to go grab Jordynn and introduce you, and then we can look at everything." Marie rose up on her tiptoes, still nearly a head shorter than I, even in her heels. Her lips brushed my ear as she spoke, her finger smoothing the collar of my shirt. She disappeared into the crowd, and I busied myself people watching.

Seattle was a completely different change of pace from Atlanta. The people were busier; the workload heavier, deadlines approached must faster than the laid back attitude of the deep South. I preferred the weather here; it didn't rain nearly as much as the media wanted you to believe. I liked my coworkers, and my place within Addams, Abrahm, and Bonnom Law Firm. My office overlooked the city; one of the windows framed a view of the Puget Sound.

Most everyone kept their heads down and handled their business, making it easy to avoid the hassle of making small talk with people that I wouldn't associate with outside of the office. Marie was one of the few exceptions to my self-imposed rule.

"Will, I'd love for you to meet Jordynn." Marie had returned to my side, another woman in tow.

"Pleased to meet you," I said offering my hand to the woman. Seeing Marie and Jordynn side by side was a little bit of a shock, the two were polar opposites. Jordynn's bright blue hair was styled into a Mohawk, vividly colorful tattoos adorned pale skin, she wore no makeup but sported a few facial piercings. She towered over Marie, long legs tucked into fishnet stockings and combat boots, and a mini skirt that barely brushed her upper thighs. Her shirt was white, paint splattered and artfully slashed, a neon pink bra peeking out between the fabric tears.

"So you're Will," she said with a shit-eating grin, casting a glance at Marie who blushed. "Welcome to my opening." She released my hand and gestured around us. "If you see anything that you'd like, everything is available for purchase. I'm just glad to see Marie get out of the house."

"Jordynn!" Marie muttered, taking my hand and pulling me away from the artist who was laughing softly. "I'm sorry, I've known her for years, and she thinks she's more of a comedian than an artist."

"She's charming," I squeezed Marie's hand. "Where should we start?"

"Jordynn's art is amazing, and I'm not just saying that because she's my best friend." Marie led me by the hand toward the far end of the room. "Her landscapes are some of my favorites, so we can start there, and then end with the portraits. I think she's got some of her photography as well." We moved through the crowd, ducking between clusters of people.

Along the back wall framed paintings were hung, partitions of white filmy fabric separating them, creating little viewing rooms. Thick oil paint coated large canvases, depicting beautiful scenes. Downtown Seattle, some of the Cascade mountain ranges, another of a sea of people at the local farmer's market, each one as amazing as the next. Love and patience were behind each brushstroke, the colors intentional and deliberate, it was plain to see that Jordynn's love affair with her craft shone through each work.

Photographs were next, unframed, floating against a massive pegboard that took up an entire wall. These were all in black and white, shadows intertwining with light sources, stark images of flowers offset by darkness-illuminated from overhead. Her portraits were cropped at odd angles that only furthered the subject's beauty. There were a few of a man, covered in tattoos, with prosthetic legs, a flag draped over his shoulders. He was nude, looking away from the camera, and I could almost feel the emotions radiating off of him.

"She is amazing," I turned my attention to Marie who was enraptured by the same series. "She must like this man." There were ten pictures of him in total, each different and none where he looked at the camera head on.

"I should hope so," Marie said. "He's her husband." She flagged down a server, switching out our empty champagne flutes for full ones. "Let's move on to the portraits."

The portraits were set up similar to the landscapes, separated by filmy white cloth. Marie had left my side after the first few, called away by a mutual friend, with the promise to return in a few minutes. I wandered from stall to stall, taking in the care and precision that Jordynn used as she painted her subjects. The woman was talented, without a doubt and I had a strong suspicion that I was witnessing something special. I entered another one of the cloth alleys, as I had come to think of them, and paused in front of the portrait.

The subject lounged on a window seat looking out the window, face away from the artist. The golden tones of her hair glowed as if they were spun from the precious metal. Her skin fair, delicate, the brushstrokes gentle enough to convey how smooth it must feel. A book was on her lap, the pages dog-eared, and the hand holding it in place relaxed. Long legs extended out in front of her, one ballerina pink flat hung delicately from an arched foot, the hem of a green skirt kissed perfect knees. The cloth was painted as though it could move at any moment. There was a slight curve in her torso, that accentuated the arch of her breasts under a white blouse, and a silver chain cascaded down her neck before disappearing under the collar of her shirt. My fingers itched to touch the painting, trace along the curve of her pale throat, feel the heat from her skin, the delicate flutter of a pulse under my fingertips. A slight profile was all I could see of her face, high cheekbones, and a full, lush, carnation pink mouth. I breathed her in, my mouth dry, heart caught in my throat, pounding so hard that I knew it was betraying me.

The paint was rough under my fingertips, thick swatches and brushstrokes causing my fingers to rise and fall as I stroked along the painting. I glanced down at the nameplate attached to the painting's frame. It read 'Hannah.'

"Hannah," I murmured, fingers brushing along the woman's cheekbone. "Hannah," I repeated, the name gaining a feel in my mouth, the vowels tripping over my tongue, igniting a fire inside my gut.

"Isn't she beautiful?"

I whirled around, snatching my hand away from the painting, stuffing both hands into my pockets. "It is a lovely painting." Jordynn stood in front of me, arms crossed over her chest. "Is she a friend of yours?"

Jordynn shook her head, "She's straight from my imagination. A little bit from person A, a little bit from person B and a healthy dash of what's in my head."

"How much is it?" I needed to have this painting. I needed to have her in my home. There was something that beckoned me, drew me to her.

"Three hundred," Jordynn said easily, "But you're the infamous Will that Marie goes on and on about, and I like the way you look at the painting. I know you'll take care of it. Two hundred sound good to you?"

"Yes," I reached for my wallet before pausing. "I don't have the cash on me."

Jordynn laughed softly, reaching out to pat my arm. "We'll settle that later. I'll have someone wrap her up; you can take her home tonight."

"Are you sure? I can pay with a card, or go get the cash…"

Jordynn cut me off with a wave of her hand. "You came with Marie. I know you're a decent guy. Pay me tomorrow. I'm all about spreading the joy of art." She winked at me, before turning and disappearing into the crowd.

I turned back to the painting, my heart racing once more. I had found something within this piece that I hadn't realized I had been missing. I drank in every detail, thirsting for just a little something more that I hadn't noticed before. The noise of the people around me faded into nothing, even the quartet was mute as I memorized each swipe of paint on the canvas. A person emerged from behind the display, clad in black, wearing white gloves. He picked up the painting carefully, before starting to head back the way he had come.

"Where are you going with that?" I asked.

"I'm going to wrap it up for you and set it aside until you're ready to go."

"I'm ready to leave, just please wrap it up." I wanted to get home, find a place of honor for Hannah. Minutes ticked on for what seemed like an eternity before the person came back, carrying the bulky package that had been wrapped in brown paper. "Thank you." My valet ticket nearly burned in my hand as I picked my way through the crowd still milling around on the main floor. As I exited the building, two more people entered. I handed the ticket off to the valet and waited for my car to be brought around.

The drive back to my apartment was a simple one, twenty minutes at most, thirty if I missed the lights. It went quickly, the streets nearly abandoned due to the time of night. I swiped my garage key and parked my car. My hands trembled as I withdrew my package from the trunk of the car, closing it securely. Cradling the frame to my chest, I got onto the elevator and took it up to my floor. The paper was a comfort, knowledge that nothing in the trunk could have gotten onto the painting, or marred its perfection.

Once the apartment door was locked behind me, I toed off my shoes and walked back to the bedroom. I set the painting down on the bed and started to peel away the brown craft paper. I tossed it aside, breath catching in my chest when I looked upon Hannah once more. I picked up the frame, holding it to the moonlight that streamed in through one of my windows. The paint seemed to glow, the slightest rise and fall from Hannah's chest. I crossed my bedroom, placing her carefully on the mahogany dresser. She was leaned against the wall, the golden hue of her frame contrasting sharply with the rich, dark tones of the wood she rested on.

I stepped back, sitting on the edge of the bed and just watched her. She looked as though she belonged in my room, in my home, with me. My phone buzzed, and I glanced at it, seeing Marie's number, before putting it aside. I woke up some time later, my bedroom a wash of brilliant sunlight. I sat up, blinking, confused, my face sticking to the comforter a little bit. I got to my feet, sore from passing out half on-half off the bed, still in my suit from the gallery opening, hours before hand. My gaze landed on the painting I purchased, and the muscle soreness melted away.

"Good morning, beautiful," I said out loud. The morning sun made the scene glow, the fevered pitch of illumination matching the blazing sun outside my window. The wood was warm and smooth under my fingertips as I ran a hesitant finger along the bottom of the frame. I would have to keep her in here. She needed to be the last thing I saw before I slept and the first thing I saw when I woke up. She was so calming to me. I glanced at her one last time, before heading toward the kitchen. I had a hammer and nails in the junk drawer, Hannah needed a proper place within our home, and above the dresser would be perfect.

I laid her carefully on the bed so I could move the dresser, and pounded the nail into the wall, taking great care to avoid my fingers. I then moved the dresser back in place, and picked her up, placing her gently where she would stay. The gold of the frame stood out in stark contrast against the flat white paint of the wall, bringing more attention to the beautiful blonde who had stolen my heart. I started when my phone rang, scrambling to pick it up.

After a short conversation with my mother, reassuring her that I was not, in fact, dead in a gutter—and yes I would be meeting her for lunch—I forced myself away from Hannah and grabbed a set of clean clothes before hopping in the shower. I made my way downtown, promising Hannah that I'd be home soon, and found the restaurant my parents had made reservations at.

"How was your date last night?" Asked my mother, the picture perfect image of classic beauty dressed in a pale pink blouse and charcoal gray skirt that fell just beneath her knees. She wore stockings, kitten heels, and pearls at her neck and a massive diamond ring sitting on her left hand. Her hair was in a low knot, swept free of her face.

"It wasn't a date." I corrected her, kissing her on the cheek before taking my seat opposite her. My father sat on my left, dressed in dark tones, suit jacket hanging stiffly on the back of his chair. "I went with a coworker to her friend's gallery opening."

"Sounds like a date." Ruby red lips twisted into a smile as she raised her water glass, took a sip and placed it down. "Tell me about her."

It wasn't a question, nor a request and I knew there was no way to get out of it. "Marie works in accounting; we're on a couple of teams together."

"What's her family like?"

I knew the source of that question. "She's independent and helps her parents out." A glass of water was placed in front of me, and I nodded my thanks to the server. "She's got an apartment in the university district." Money was very much a *thing* for my parents. I fished my phone out of my pocket and pulled up a picture of the two of us from the night before. "This is from the gallery opening."

"She's nice," My mother handed the phone across the table to my father. "Bit of a showy dress though for a gallery opening." She said, "Our meal should be here soon. I took the liberty of ordering for us."

I barely resisted the urge to roll my eyes. My mother, while dressed in a skirt, clearly wore the pants in the relationship. I knew that if I gave her an inch when it came to Marie and our 'not date,' she would run for miles with it. Thankfully, she dropped the subject and started talking about the latest cruise she and my father were taking. Our food came, and that provided a pleasant distraction, and the conversation ceased.

We finished lunch and said our goodbyes. I watched my parents climb into a cab, and I decided to walk. I had a few errands to run. The public market was crowded, but manageable, and I picked up a fresh half of a salmon for dinner as well as handmade pasta. I could make a mean alfredo sauce, and I could grab a loaf of fresh baked bread from the bakery just down the street from my apartment. After the debacle of lunch, I wanted something I could control. The sunlight glinted against a jeweler's display, and I hesitated, the play of the light against the silver captivating me. My feet moved on their own accord, and I reached out, fingers brushing along delicate chains, watching the pendants swing and chime together. The painting flashed into my mind, the silver chain around Hannah's neck, disappearing under the collar of her shirt. I combed through the pendants, trying to figure out which charm was nestled between her breasts. I kept returning to the arrow charm, and I slid the necklace off of the display.

"How much?"

The girl looked up from a dog-eared novel, "Sixty bucks. Its hand cast and I make the chain myself."

I thrust my credit card at her, noting the mobile payment slide on her phone. "I don't need it wrapped up." She gave me back my card, and I put the necklace in my pocket. "Thanks." My heart skipped a beat, feeling the chain slide through my fingers, settling into my pocket, safe and secure. I hurried home, purchases slung into plastic bags, bouncing on my heels as I waited for the elevator. My hands were trembling so it took me a few tries to push the button for my floor. My stomach rolled nervously as the elevator lifted, and sank a little when it came to my floor. Laughter bubbled up when I unlocked the front door, tossing my dinner onto the kitchen counter. I walked back to my bedroom, heartbeat racing, throbbing in my ears.

"Hello beautiful, I missed you." I murmured, gazing upon the image of Hannah. "I saw this and thought of you. I hope you like it." I took the necklace from my pocket, nearly dropping it in my haste. I held it up, letting the arrow spin on the chain, reflecting the midday sun. Carefully, I leaned up and placed it on the upper left corner of the painting. I breathed a sigh of relief when the chain settled against the grooves on the frame. It looked perfect, and I swear she smiled at me. My heart nearly sang, my pulse surging.

She liked it.

I retrieved my laptop from behind the couch after changing out of 'lunch with my parents' appropriate clothing, climbed into bed and pulled up a couple of movies. "I do hope you enjoy the classics," I said getting comfortable. There was no way for her to watch them, not with where she sat, but I knew she could hear them, that way it could provide background noise for her book. I liked that she didn't need to talk too much about things, but we could sit together, and enjoy our own hobbies. The hours stretched by comfortably, as I got lost in the old school glamor of Hollywood, in shades of gray and black, with jumpy cinematography, the words so familiar and warm.

"Are you hungry?" I asked Hannah as I rolled off the bed. My stomach was starting to growl, and dinner would take a little while to prepare. "Let me know if you want a plate, I'm going to go start cooking," I said, and left her to her book.

Cooking was one of the things I excelled at outside of law. For a little while, I had entertained the thought of becoming a chef, but my mother quickly squashed that dream. It didn't take long for my apartment to smell amazing, the heavy cream and cheese from the sauce permeating my senses. I tossed the salmon onto a cedar plank and put it into the oven, the warming wood, and sizzling olive oil creating a symphony of scents. I plated up the pasta and salmon, grabbed a beer from the fridge and hesitated in the doorway of the kitchen. I longed to go back and enjoy dinner with her, but she hadn't shared an opinion on the meal. Instead, I took my place at the table and ate alone.

I did the dishes, the hum of the dishwasher filling the quiet in the apartment. I went back to the bedroom, turning my attention to Hannah. The green of her skirt was one of my favorite shades, a brilliant grass green. I touched it, feeling the waves of the warm, worn cotton under my fingertips, ghosting along the curve of her kneecap. I was being forward, but she didn't reject me.

"I have to work in the morning." I sat on the floor, my back to the bed, legs crossed as I looked up at her. "I'm not looking forward to being gone for so long, but I will tell you all about my day." I smiled as the breeze from the open window moved her hair ever so slightly.

I cleared my throat, watching her, so peaceful and serene. I felt like I could open up to her, share things with her. I talked until I was hoarse, my eyes blurring with the need to sleep. I got up off the floor, limbs protesting the movement. I powered down the laptop, putting it into my briefcase, plugged in my phone and slid into bed burrowing under the blankets.

"Goodnight, sweet Hannah." I reached over and turned off the bedside light, casting the room into darkness.

My alarm brought me crashing back to reality. I woke startled, struggling to catch a breath. She had come to me in my dreams, and we walked the city streets, hand in hand.

Her skin was so warm and pliant against my own, her perfume blending with the grapefruit scent that graced her hair. I rolled over, clutching a pillow to my chest, blinking blearily at the cell phone that continued to bleep pitifully at me. I slapped at it, muttering when it fell silent. I shifted, sitting up, feet hitting the cold wooden floor. I yawned, scratching at my stomach and lifted myself out of bed. I showered, wishing more than anything that it was her hands touching me, rather than my own. The coffee pot came on automatically, and I poured some for myself, tipping more into a second mug. I figured Hannah took hers sweet, and full of creamer. I carried it back to the bedroom, leaving it on the dresser for her, before picking up a quick breakfast and heading out to work.

I had barely settled in and started to go through the papers on my desk when my office door opened and Marie came in. "Do you have a minute?"

"Sure," I said looking up from the document. "Won't you have a seat?"

"I'll stand, thanks," she said, arms crossed lightly over her chest. "Listen, I'm trying to figure out what went wrong Saturday night. I mean I thought you were into the art gallery." She shifted her weight, lower lip worried between her teeth. "You cut out and didn't answer any of my texts. I'm trying to give you the benefit of the doubt, but you can't answer a text—even if you aren't interested?"

"I didn't mean to leave so abruptly, I'm sorry." I turned my attention fully to the woman in front of me. "I was with family yesterday, and when I saw your text it was pretty late, and I didn't want to disturb you." I offered her a small smile, watching some of the tension in her shoulders ease.

"Drinks Friday night then?"

"Name the place, and I'll be there," I said.

"Maloney's on 1st?"

"I'll be there," I said. "I'm looking forward to it."

Work hours blended together in boring moments of black and white. I took pleasure in the time I spent at home, with Hannah. I could tell her anything, and soon I was telling her stories about my childhood, spending summers in various countries, and the school year in boarding academies. How my first word wasn't in English, but rather the Spanish of the nanny my mother had hired to take care of me while she and my father toured the social scene. Guilt swelled in my gut every time I saw Marie. I knew that I would have to explain to Hannah that I was going to get drinks with her, but it meant nothing.

Hannah was the reason why I continued to work in for the aggravating firm.

I had found a dress for her, one that would complement her sun-kissed skin and lithe frame. Her blonde hair would accentuate the lavender perfectly. It was something that was appropriate for meeting my parents without being totally matronly. The box arrived on Friday, and I picked it up from the reception desk of my apartment building. Again, I was giddy, hoping that Hannah would love it. It was a color I hadn't seen her in, and one that I loved so much on women.

"I'm home!" I called out to her, locking the door behind me. "Did you have a nice day?" I loosened my tie as I walked back to the bedroom. She was waiting for me and turned when I entered the room. She had spent the day doing laundry—her hair was up, barefoot, her toenails were painted the same delicate pink as her fingernails. She smiled but didn't say anything to me. It took my breath away every time I saw her. She had grown more comfortable in the house, doing things on her own when I wasn't home.

"I know, and I'm sorry," I said, putting the box on the bed. "I won't be out late, and I'll let her know that I can't

225

see her again. I need to apologize for leaving her so suddenly the night that we met." I opened the box, and pulled the dress from it, holding it up for her to see.

Another beautiful smile crept across her face, her lips curving. I laid it out on the bed for her to get a better look at, while I searched for a change of clothes that would be suitable for drinks with a coworker.

That's all Marie was, a coworker. Hannah was the only woman who captured my heart.

I changed and headed for the door. Hannah had picked up her book, settling down to read. The thought of going out to a busy bar with another woman was almost too much to bear. I wanted to stay here. I retrieved my phone and sent a text to Marie, letting her know that I wouldn't make it. She immediately called, but I declined it, letting the phone take a message. Instead, I sent her a text.

I met someone. I'm sorry to have misled you.

Then I turned my phone off and went back to the bedroom with Hannah. It was a little cruel, but it surely was the correct thing to do. I couldn't mislead Marie, and I couldn't continue to toy with Hannah's affections. I couldn't allow anything to get in the way of our budding relationship. Not anymore.

I called out sick on Monday—the weekend was far too short. I wanted more time with Hannah. We would read aloud to each other, the stories she picked were simply enthralling. I loved the way her mouth formed the words, her voice filling the room expressing character's emotions in a way that simply reading the words on the page couldn't. Tuesday I called out again, blaming my sudden illness on something that I had eaten over the weekend, and I should be recovered in a day or so. I missed court, though I did manage to pass my notes to a colleague who was just as capable as I.

My mother dropped by that Saturday. She drifted into my apartment on a cloud of plumeria perfume and a powder blue dress. She made herself comfortable in the kitchen, making a pot of coffee. "William, I have to say I'm a little concerned."

"Why is that?" The apartment was clean and tidy. Hannah liked to have everything spotless, the scent of lemons permeating the space from a diffuser tucked into the corner.

"The growth on your face." She stroked her own cheeks. "That's not entirely professional."

"I've been working from home." I managed to convince a 'doctor' at a clinic that I was suffering from depression and would benefit from working from home for a few weeks. Just until everything stabilized emotionally.

"How does Marie like it?" She pursed her lips. "I noticed she's keeping her shoes here. Miserable taste in clothing, but at least footwear is acceptable."

I paused, coffee mug halfway to my mouth. I hadn't told my mother about Hannah.

"I'm assuming that the relationship is progressing to your satisfaction," she said, stirring more sugar into her mug.

"Actually, I'm not seeing Marie," I managed to get out. "I met someone named Hannah."

"Hannah," my mother repeated. A flash of anger tore through me at the way she said Hannah's name. I was used to the dismissive tone when it came to other women, but when it came to the one who held my heart?

"Yes," I said, "We met at the art gallery. In a way, Marie introduced us." I licked my lips. "She's beautiful and smart. So graceful and full of light, she's someone that I really love being around."

"What does she do for a living?"

"She's with the Seattle ballet as a dancer," I said. Hannah had been dancing for years, and it was something she loved to do. "She trained at Julliard, and also has a doctorate in classic literature." My mother's expression evened out a bit, and I could tell I had her attention now. "Her parents passed when they were young, and she was raised by her aunt. She's the reason why the place is so lovely." I gestured around my apartment. "She teaches evening classes at a dance studio, so she's here most of the day. I don't know what I'd do without her."

"She's not much of a cook, though," my mother interrupted. "Your refrigerator is full of take-out containers. You've lost weight, Will."

"The summer shows are coming up," I said, needing to defend Hannah. "And I've been caught up in work, so what we haven't been eating the greatest. She's so important to me."

"You met at the gallery?" The mug didn't make a sound when my mom put it on the counter. "Will that was a month ago." Concern clouded her expression. "She's moved in already?"

"When you know, you know, mom." I walked the length of the kitchen, turned and started back. "She's amazing. She dresses beautifully and isn't judgmental about anyone. She volunteers at the homeless shelters on the weekends. The only thing that she does that drives me nuts is she loads the dishwasher wrong, but the way she smiles and laughs about it, makes it seem so stupid."

"William!" A hand gripped my elbow, stilling me. "You're worrying me." She peered at me owlishly. "Are you feeling alright?"

"I'm fine," I said. "I didn't sleep too well last night. Hannah was out late, and I had a hard time falling asleep without her."

"Why don't you go lay down." She hadn't released me. "Rest for a little while, and I'll make some meals for you and your Hannah. I'll stock up the freezer so you don't have to rely on the take-out menus."

I heard movement in the bedroom and knew Hannah had come home while my mom and I were talking. She was so considerate not to interrupt us. It was just one more thing I loved about her. "Hannah's home, would you like to meet her?"

"She's home?" My mother asked as she led me down the hallway to the bedroom. "I didn't hear anyone come in."

"Hannah's really quiet. I know she didn't want to be rude by bursting in and disturbing us." I nodded, following after her. She pushed open the bedroom door and stepped inside.

"William?" My mother turned to me. "There's no one here, darling."

"Don't be so rude, mother." I jerked my arm free and brushed past her. "Hannah, I'm sorry. This is my mother. Please don't hold it against her." Hannah had selected a book and was reading.

"William," my mother said. "Darling, I'm worried about you." She was looking wildly around the room.

"Mother, she's right there!" I pointed at Hannah who had changed back into her green skirt. She was wearing her ballet flats again, and that beautiful white shirt that drove me crazy.

"The painting?" My mother pointed at it. "William, that's a painting."

"That's Hannah!" I yelled back, heat surging through me, my heart pounding. "That's her. I love her. How dare you be so rude to her."

"It's a beautiful painting, but it's not a person."

"Get out!" I roared. "Get out, you despicable woman." I turned to Hannah who continued to read. "I'm so sorry my love. She's just so backward she can't understand our feelings for each other."

"William, please come with me. Let's get you some help."

I whirled on her, staring her down. My mother stood in the doorway, arms crossed over her chest. She wore the most peculiar expression, mouth drawn tight, eyes wide and trembling. "If you can't accept Hannah, then you need to leave."

"I'll let you be for tonight. I'm coming back tomorrow. I need to call Dr. Barringer and see if he as any recommendations for someone who can help you out here."

"I don't need your help. I need you to leave." I snarled at her, feeling my lip curl, spit flying from my mouth. "Don't you ever come back." I lunged at her, incensed by rage, wanting nothing but to inflict the same pain radiating in my chest at her rejection of Hannah, on her. The woman who called herself my mother. She was an imposter. A true mother would support Hannah and me. She would see that we were clearly meant to be. I watched as she turned and ran, her high heels clattering down the hallway, the front door slamming shut.

"I'm sorry my love." I turned to Hannah. "She'll come around, I promise," I said to her. Hannah didn't look up from her book, or give any indication that she heard me. That wasn't like her and only fueled me on. "Are you listening to me? I said I was sorry."

Again, no response from my Hannah.

"Hannah! Pay attention when I speak to you!" My hands curled into fists. I wanted to snatch the infuriating book out of her hands, get her to pay attention to me. I needed to know that she wasn't put off from my mother's remarks. That we were okay, and we could continue to explore our relationship.

"Hannah!"

I lurched forward, stubbing my toe on the dresser, as I reached for the book in her hands. I clawed at it, ripping the pages from her hands. My fingers were coated with white and gray, the emerald green hue of the cover under my fingernails. Still, she said nothing. I reached for her shoulder, but she shied away. Blinded with the emotions surging under my skin, I grabbed at the silver chain around her neck, coming up with nothing. I snatched up the necklace I bought for her, ripping the charm from the chain. "Listen to me!"

Another book was in her hand, and she was smiling as she read.

She smiled as though there was nothing wrong; like she couldn't hear me. Wasn't listening to my pleading, my begging, I would make her listen to me.

I left the room, snatched up one of the knives she had left in the sink—she still hadn't done the dishes. Thundered down the hallway and brandished it at her. "Pay attention!"

Still nothing.

"Damn it, Hannah!" I cried, slashing at the book in her hands. Ripped and tore at it with the blade slicing through the paper as though it was butter. Paper and paint fluttered down onto the dresser, the floor, chips clinging to my hands and shirt. My eyes stung with unshed tears, I never wanted to hurt her like this, but she wouldn't listen. She simply wouldn't listen to me.

I broke down and sobbed, dropping to my knees when the knife embedded in the wall. My hands ached, small cuts on my fingers due to recklessness. I stared up at her in tatters and shreds, my beautiful Hannah who was nothing more than a painting.

Did You See Evelyn Today?

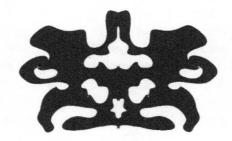

Kelly Matsuura

This story is written in UK English

Amelia came to my room at five o'clock, on the dot, as she always does. It was Tuesday, so she had been at the local op shop all day volunteering.

"Hello, Diane. I brought some more wool for you."

Knitting was a good way for me to pass the time, and Amelia would snag the best of the donated yarn before it went out front for sale. I took the plastic bag she offered and fingered the soft, melon-pink balls inside.

"This four-ply is lovely. Thank you."

"My pleasure." Amelia gave me what I called her 'pageant girl' smile and left the room for a second, returning with the tea tray.

"Earl Grey, or Assam?" she asked, knowing that not once in the two years I'd lived in her house had I drunk Earl Grey. It was a game to her, I supposed, mind tricks to see if she could turn me to her side.

Well, I still had my dignity to fight for.

"Assam, dear." I was only three years older than her, but it was my own little way of taking a stab. I did hold

232

some power after all—I wouldn't be here in her house if I didn't.

"Of course." Amelia poured the tea and handed me the vintage Wedgewood cup.

I recognised it, although I hadn't seen it for a month or more. I held in a sigh, knowing full well what was coming next. Whether I mentioned it was Evelyn's cup or not, Amelia would steer the conversation that way. She was so predictable with her games; it made me cringe with a deep impulse to put my hands around her throat and squeeze tightly before the phrase could escape her dewy mouth.

"Nice," I managed to say quite politely after taking a sip. Amelia did brew a good pot of tea; I gave her that. "Mmm, so did the Benz run okay today? You said it has been stalling sometimes."

"That was Evelyn's tea cup, you know." Amelia cut off my mundane question with her obligatory swing to discussing her sister.

It was enough to drive anyone mad. "I've lived here for two years, Amelia. I know that." I kept my tone even, so I thought, but regardless she huffed at me.

"I was just saying." Amelia looked over the rim of her cup, not at me, but of the paintings on every wall. "That one's my favourite," she told me, nodding to a small landscape that Evelyn had painted in New Zealand.

"You should put it in your room," I suggested. She wouldn't though. As much as she wanted to see Evelyn again, I knew she didn't want to be frightened in her bed or while she was dressing. She liked that Evelyn was lingering in their childhood home, but she wanted her sister contained in this one room so she didn't upset the order of things.

"Oh, Diane. Really." Amelia put her cup down and picked up a ginger biscuit. She raised it with a delicate gesture to her mouth but paused.

"So, did you see Evelyn today?"

"No, Amelia. Not since Sunday." Again, I spoke calmly. It really was exhausting, this never-ending daily routine. Same tea, same questions, same hidden agenda and fake friendship.

But we were stuck together, weren't we? We didn't like each other, but we needed to be here in the house, close to Evelyn. Our lives were deeply entwined, each as crazy as the other. At least Amelia got to go out in the world and have some semblance of a normal life.

"Where does she go, when she's not here?" Amelia asked, topping up her tea with hot water from the pot.

"Well, she likes the ocean. She watches the families on the beach and the fishermen. She has no sense of time like we do," I explained.

Amelia shuddered. "Why the ocean, of all places? You'd think it would remind her too much about...you know."

I didn't like talking about Evelyn's death either, so I merely nodded in agreement. I squeezed my eyes tight to block out the gruesome pictures in my head. Nothing stopped the sudden thumping of my heart in my eardrums, though.

I had found Evelyn that day; her dress torn, cuts all over her skin, bright purple marks around her throat. She'd been dumped there by the rocks where she and I first met, and in her cold hand, she clutched the small, heart-shaped stone I had given her on the day I confessed my love. It was real turquoise, her favourite gemstone. Where was it now? Amelia would know, but I could never bring myself to ask.

It was clear to me who had taken Evelyn's life; only a husband who discovered his wife's true love would hurt her like that and leave her where he knew her lover would be first to search that area.

Roger had paid for his cruel deed, but it didn't really change anything. Evelyn was still dead, and although she returned occasionally to keep me company, we would never have the life together that we had planned.

***

Weeks passed, the routine never changing. Amelia was out most days, volunteering somewhere, golfing or lunching with friends. To the outside world, she must appear to be coping quite well with her sister's death, but her social circle didn't know about *me*.

I had a full-time caretaker to prepare my meals, help me dress and bathe, anything I needed. Gabby was a pleasant enough woman, but I preferred she spend the minimum amount of time possible in my room. She never commented on my living situation, and I was also happy not to discuss it with her. I assumed that Amelia paid her well over what my trust fund covered, thus buying the woman's ignorance.

One Friday, Amelia brought tea at five p.m. and placed a few new books on the shelf for me.

"Margaret from the club recommended this author— Anita Shreve. Looks like the kind of books you read."

"I've heard of her. Thanks."

I never saw much resemblance between Amelia and Evelyn; Amelia was younger by a few years but had the stockier features of the Robinsons' side, whereas Evelyn was thin and graceful like the Cork women.

But as Amelia ran her hand over the back cover of one of the books, she reminded me of Evelyn for a moment. The way she stood, the angle of her head as it tilted to read the blurb.

I looked closely at her hands as well—something about the way Amelia's fingers smoothed the edge of the cover caused me to shiver. Oh, how I missed my darling's warm caress every day.

"Your hands are much like Evelyn's," I told Amelia when she sat down in the other armchair. "I never noticed before."

"Yes, I suppose they are." She held both hands out and examined them front and back. "I wish I had cared better for mine. I always thought she was silly for buying all those expensive creams, but her hands were always so white and smooth. What was that lavender one she always put on?"

"Yardley," I said with a smile. Amelia was right; Eve was fastidious about filing her nails and rubbing ointments into her skin. She didn't like polish, though, she only cared to be healthy and youthful. I used to love watching her apply the cream and gently massage it into each hand. The expression, her intense relaxation when she did it revealed another deeper, layer of beauty to her character. We weren't young when we discovered the kind of love that made us both truly happy, and we never had many opportunities to be together in private. When we did, though, I would sit holding her hands for hours, stroking them as we talked and made plans for the future.

"Diane?" Amelia interrupted my thoughts.

"Sorry?"

"I said, I know I have a tube of that hand cream somewhere. She gave me some for my birthday before she passed, but I couldn't bear to use it then. I'll give it to you."

This was a very generous offer from Amelia. Pilfered books and yarn from the op shop were one thing, but something of Evelyn's was priceless.

"That…that would be lovely, Amelia."

She poured my tea, and I realised too, she hadn't asked what I wanted.

"You didn't ask me…" I started, about to thank her for her kindness. Maybe she was finally ready to change.

236

"Ask you what?" She held out the plate of shortbread rounds. "Oh, about the money?"

"*No.*" I didn't hide my annoyance. The connection I had just felt with the woman for probably the first time, had lasted all of five seconds.

"Do you think she'll ever tell us where it is?" Amelia continued.

Now, this topic wasn't part of her daily chant, but it was on the weekly menu.

"Amelia, she never had it to begin with. Roger made that up."

Roger, Evelyn's murderous husband, had confessed at his trial but had claimed ignorance to his wife's lesbian affair. Instead, he told the court that he was angry at Evelyn for taking sixty thousand dollars that he had hidden in the fuel tank of an old motorbike out in his shed.

"She was running away! She must have…"

"No, she didn't take it! She didn't know he had it," I argued. "I doubt it even existed—he just made it up as a motive because he didn't want to admit his wife loved a woman."

I had gone too far. Amelia tolerated a fair argument about the money from time to time, but I knew better than to mention the unspeakable truth.

Instead of yelling, Amelia stood up straight and erect, so much so, it seemed someone had rammed a broomstick down the back of her skirt. I almost chuckled but bit my tongue.

"Diane. I accept you in my home and share my company with you, but you know very well the rules we are both to live by." All this said most tightly.

"I know you don't want to hear the truth, Amelia, but you ask me every damn day, 'Did you see Evelyn?' 'Did she tell you where the money is?' I can only tell you what I know. Won't you ever just give it up?" I stood too, ignoring the dizziness of rising quickly. "Do you want your sister here because you love her and miss her, or do you just want to get your old wrinkly hands on the *supposed* money!" I had to sit back down, not only was I dizzy, but my heart started jumping erratically. If I didn't calm down, I'd need the oxygen tank, which is probably what Amelia was hoping for.

"I love my sister! The fact that she only appears to you makes me want to throw myself off the cliffs sometimes." She didn't let me respond, just exited the room slamming the door. She struggled to lock it, but it soon clicked into place, and her footsteps moved off down the hall.

I didn't feel sorry for her. She was one of those women who had been born with everything, believed they deserved to be loved by everyone, yet had never truly cared for anyone but themselves.

I took a few breaths to calm myself and slowly sipped the rest of my tea. The pot still had hot water in it, so I dropped my teabag back in the cup and filled it with water.

"God how I wish that damn money was real."

If the money existed and I knew where it was, Amelia would let me go.

***

"The money is real, Di."

I looked up in surprise. Fuming over my fight with Amelia, I hadn't noticed Evelyn appear in the room.

"No, it's not. Roger lied." I felt like I was speaking to Amelia again, but no, my beautiful, untouchable Evelyn was really there in front of me.

"He used to steal motorbikes and strip them for parts or rebuild them," she told me. "That's where he really got the money."

"What? Why didn't you ever tell me that?" I was hit with a mix of emotions, none good.

"I didn't want to worry you. And, we needed the money to run away together. If you knew about it, you would have stopped me taking it."

"I don't believe this." I stood up and paced the room, avoiding her gaze for a moment. She was my Evelyn, but she wasn't. I still saw her, but she didn't react with the emotion or passion of her beliefs that she had when she was alive. "Why have you kept this from me for two years? Two years!"

"Calm down, Dee Dee."

I pointed sharply at the door. "Your *effing* sister has kept me a prisoner here since your funeral…all because she thinks that money is still out there."

Evelyn smiled softly. She drifted over to the door and stopped in front of it.

"This door isn't locked, Di."

I stepped back and sat on my bed. I ran my hand over the blanket covering it, the one I had lovingly knitted the first few months of my imprisonment.

"Why didn't you tell me about Roger's money? That's why he bloody killed you." I don't think I ever swore in front of Evelyn when she was alive. Both she and Amelia didn't stand for cursing.

"I didn't tell you because you needed time. To grieve, and to heal."

"I've been fine for a while now," I insisted. "I'm only a bit loopy sometimes because Amelia keeps me locked in here. How am I supposed to get better when I'm trapped?"

"The door isn't locked, Di. You know that, deep down."

"I need another cup of tea." The water in the pot was cold, but I didn't care. It was something to do while I processed what Evelyn said about the money. "God, I wish

I had some brandy for it." I held my cup to her in salute and tossed it down, imagining there was hot alcohol in it.

"Alcohol is not a solution to anything," Evelyn scolded softly. Roger had been a heavy drinker—I'd forgotten that for a moment.

"Sorry. Look, I know you don't want Amelia to have the money, but if we give it to her, she'll probably let me go. She doesn't want an invalid in her house forever," I reasoned.

"Actually, I want both of you to have the money. I've just been waiting for you to be ready."

I scowled. "Two years? I know you have no sense of time, but you see how she tortures me every day." I guess spirits just see life very, very, differently from their side.

"Really? She tortures you with imported tea, hardcover books, and luxury wool? What's that black shawl you knitted last spring made from? Buffalo yarn?" Evelyn shook her head like a schoolmarm giving a math test. "You know what Roger did to me. *That* was real torture, Di."

"Don't talk about that! You know I can't...." I sucked in too much air and began to cough.

"I apologise. I shouldn't bring that up." She glided across the room to the window and gazed out at the evening sky.

My coughing ceased, and I picked up the conversation. "And don't you take Amelia's side. She's only looking out for herself in this."

Evelyn ignored me and continued staring out the window.

"The sunsets here are so beautiful. Pity you can't see them from this window, though, you'd have to go to the back patio. From there, is the most glorious view of the shoreline. My favourite place in the house."

"Why do you stay in this room then?" I asked. "You always come back here. It's not even your old bedroom, is it?" Amelia told me once that this had been her grandmother's room. After the first time that I saw Evelyn in spirit form here, Amelia and I had decorated the space with all of Evelyn's special things, and I had agreed to sleep here, hoping to see her more and more.

"I come back to this room because you are here. That's the only reason."

"You were in here the first time I saw you…" I began.

"You were in here crying after my service. I revealed myself to comfort you, but you were too broken to understand why I was there."

"I still don't know why you're here!" We had had this argument before, I'm sure of it, but her reasoning always confused me. This time, I tried to really listen. It was the first time she mentioned having taken the money, so that had to be important. "You were in this room, so I moved in here, and then Amelia locked me in so she could find out where the money is."

"No." Again, Evelyn argued back. "Honey, Amelia doesn't believe any of this. She doesn't believe the money is real; she doesn't believe you talk to me. She's just taking care of you because I love you."

"Amelia is a selfish, greedy…"

"The door *isn't* locked, Diane." This was the harshest ghost-Evelyn had ever spoken to me. Her voice deepened and growled.

"Of course it is." I got up from the bed and walked over to try the handle. My hand twisted the old brass knob and the door opened enough for me to see the vase of white roses on the hall table. The delicate scent reached my nostrils and instantly calmed me. My mother had always kept fresh roses in our house growing up; another happy memory I had forgotten in recent times.

"It is open." I turned back to Evelyn, who was smiling at me.

"Yes, it's open."

"I can go get the money, then I can…leave."

"That's right, you can," Evelyn said. "Where will you go?"

"I don't know. I could visit my brother, I guess. He must be worried about me."

"Amelia calls him every week. I'm sure he'd love a visit. He had another daughter a few months ago. Do you remember?"

"I remember." Amelia had brought in some photos of the little girl. Ashley, she was called. I opened the door a little wider. I wanted to check if Amelia was upstairs or not. Gabby's room was on the first floor, so she had no reason to be around until she brought up my dinner at seven-thirty.

"Has Amelia forgotten to lock the door other times?" I asked Evelyn.

"She never locks it. You just feel safer believing that it is."

"Oh." Maybe Evelyn was partly right. I could recall a few times when Amelia hadn't locked the door, but I'd stayed because it was after dark and cold. Better to run away in the summertime when I had the chance. "I should pack some things." I went to my tiny closet to look for a bag.

"No rush," Evelyn said. "We can talk a little more."

"Sure. You need to tell me where the money is anyway. Will I have to travel far to get it? Do I need warmer clothes?"

"It's not far, love. But, there's one problem."

"What?" I turned back from the closet to see what she meant.

"Well, I want you to be free, but I want Amelia to have half the money as well."

"No!" I threw a blouse at her feet. "She's been draining my trust fund for years!"

"Your trust fund and medical pension ran out six months ago, Di." I moved to the door, intending to slam it shut again, but Evelyn flashed in front of me and blocked my way. Well, I wasn't going to attempt putting my hand straight through her.

"Do. Not. Close. That. Door."

"Don't talk like that. Your voice scares me," I told her, sitting back in my armchair and crossing my legs in defiance. "Why did you tell me about the money? Now we're fighting. Again."

"We're not fighting," Evelyn disagreed. "I told you about the money because you're both ready."

"What makes you think that?" Why had she waited so long?

"When Amelia came in before, you talked about me first."

"No, I didn't. She always asks me if I've seen you," I argued.

"I know, but today she didn't. You mentioned me first, you commented on how similar our hands were."

"Oh?" Was that really the first mention of Evelyn?

"She didn't ask you about your tea, either."

"About time she stopped that." But it did make me smile just a little. I had worn her down after all. "I don't see how that warrants thirty thousand dollars, mind you."

"She's earned it for other things. You have both been through so much. I want you to have the money and go live!"

"Where is it?" All this talk of the money, but until I saw it, I couldn't quite believe I was free.

"I'll tell you if you do one small thing for me," Evelyn teased.

"Oh, what would that be?" I couldn't imagine what a spirit would want.

"It's pretty simple. I want you to take the tea tray downstairs to the kitchen, and give it to Amelia. If you actually leave this room and go downstairs, I'll tell you."

**

It sounded like a simple request, one foot in front of the other, right? I took a few quick steps out into the hallway, holding the tea tray tight to stop it rattling.

Passing through the doorway hadn't been so bad, but now that I was facing the daunting staircase, I froze.

"I can't go down with the tray. I'll fall for sure." I looked to Evelyn who was hovering just to my right. I think she was anticipating I would make a run back to the room. I was tempted, yet being out in the hallway and realising I was breathing normal, I pushed myself to keep going.

"You won't fall. Just take your time, and stay near the rail," Evelyn encouraged.

I heard the hallway clock ticking as I took each agonising step down, and I don't know how long it took me to reach the ground floor, but I did.

"Holy Hell." I released the tea tray and it clattered as it hit the surface of the hall table. "Has it really been two years?"

I looked around Evelyn and Amelia's family home with new eyes. Amelia hadn't changed anything as far as I could tell, but perhaps my memory of things had altered while I was trapped in my own world. Everything was slightly wrong; the sofa larger, the green curtains paler in the evening light.

"Gabby?" Amelia's face poked out from the kitchen doorway and she gasped.

"Sorry to startle you," I mumbled. What do you say to someone you have been a complete cow too? The realisation of all that had occurred since I moved in was very slowly coming to the front of my awareness, and it frightened me. Exactly how crazy was I, or had I been?

Amelia straightened her blouse and brushed her fringe behind her ear. "No, it's quite alright. Thank you for returning the tray." She picked it up and lingered, turning her feet as if to leave, then changing her mind.

"Um, Gabby went out for the evening. I've just started preparing our dinner. Would you like to sit in the kitchen while I cook? We could have a glass of wine, perhaps." Amelia captured my eyes, really engaging me, and gave me what I now could understand was a genuine, compassionate smile. Just like Evelyn, there was nothing fake about this charitable woman; I had invented it all. Well, she must have some flaws, but she wasn't a monster who locks women in attic rooms.

"That sounds…" I hesitated only because of my embarrassment at who I was. But, I honestly did want to have a normal meal and conversation. "That sounds lovely. I can set the table."

"Wonderful."

I followed Amelia into the kitchen and while she set about checking the stew and rice boiling on the stove, I found the plates and cutlery and laid two places on the beautiful oak dining table. "Your father made this set, didn't he?" I found it helped clear my mind to reassure myself of little facts I knew about the house, and the two sisters. "Oh, and this burn mark is from the Christmas your cousin Marcus knocked over the candlestick."

Amelia laughed. "Yes, that's true. Did Evelyn tell you that story?" She lifted the wooden spoon to her lips to taste the stew.

"No. I think you did. On Christmas day." I frowned. I remembered her being in my room and telling me family stories, but I don't remember doing anything special for the day. Had Amelia tried to get me down for lunch? Had other people been here, or did she go out to escape me?

"I don't remember well, but that sounds right." She stirred the pot again. "This is red-wine stew. The weather's cool today so I felt like it was time to add it to the monthly menu."

"Thank you, I love beef stew. I always thought Gabby prepared my meals, though. Have you been cooking all this time?" Again, I was embarrassed for being a total mental invalid in her house. How I had done that to both of us, I wasn't ready to admit.

Amelia shook her head, one hand on the counter. "No, not every meal. But a lot of your requests were Evelyn's recipes. It was just something I started doing to be close to her again." She shrugged. Maybe she wasn't crazy like me, but her sister's death was still very painful to her. I should have bonded with her because of it. Instead, I let myself fall on top of her existing responsibilities.

I wanted to say a million apologies, but it was so lovely to just be in the fragrant, inviting kitchen, and to see Amelia as an ally, finally. I hoped she'd understand my further selfishness for the evening. As we ate our meal, I kept expecting her to push for answers and give her her dues, but instead, she simply kept up a lively conversation about the house and her plans to do some renovations the following summer.

"You know, Evelyn always loved this house more than I did, yet she wasn't angry when father left it to me."

"Well, she was already married, and you weren't. She understood the reason. Besides, she loved the holiday apartment in the Blue Mountains. That was hers," I added.

"Yes. It did work out well at the time. I just wish so badly that she had moved back here. If I'd had any idea what her husband was like, I would have insisted."

I remained silent. I could not talk about that man. It was too terrifying.

"More wine?" I asked instead.

Amelia nodded. "Sorry. That's the problem with you and me, the topic of conversation always strays back to Evelyn. Good or bad stories."

I put the wine bottle down and turned to her.

"There's something I need to know."

"Yes?"

"I'm not sure how reliable my memory of this past two years is, but I think you asked me every day if I had seen her. Did you?"

"Yes, I asked." Amelia took a sip and licked her bottom lip. Her eyes showed only curiosity.

"But, do you believe she's there? Or were you humouring me?" Evelyn had told me that Amelia didn't believe me, and I needed to be sure too.

"Well, of course she's there! I don't see her clearly like you do, but I can feel her." Amelia looked over to the large French doors and pointed. "She was over there when I was cooking, but I've lost track now."

"Oh." I was flabbergasted for a moment. Evelyn was real—I hadn't just created her to keep me company in my crazy, closed mind. "She came downstairs with me, but I think she wanted to leave us to talk alone."

"I'm sure you'll see her tomorrow," Amelia said cheerfully. "Now, would you like some coffee cake for dessert? A small slice?"

"Yes, please."

Amelia stood up and took our empty plates. "I'll clean up and put the kettle on. You relax right there."

"Thank you, dinner was lovely. I'd like to start helping around the house again soon. I...I'll try some chores tomorrow while you're out." I didn't know if I could cope, but a burst of gratitude and love for Amelia filled me. I might still be crazy for a good while, but damn it, I would fight to be a real person again. For Evelyn and Amelia too, we were all ready to move on.

***

I spent the night in my usual room but vowed it was the last time. First order of business the following day would be to move back into Evelyn's former bedroom that Amelia had continuously offered to me.

When I opened my eyes to the early dawn I was surprised that it was already morning—I hadn't woken once during the night, and I had not taken my habitual sleeping pill. I had simply forgotten in the strangeness of the evening.

I sat up and stretched, smiling to the three little sparrows perched on the window ledge. I hoped they would continue to visit me when I changed rooms.

"Good morning."

"Evelyn!" For the briefest moment, I saw her as she was alive. Then the sunlight shone through her blue dress, and I had to squint my eyes to see her features clearly. "Thank you, for last night. I don't know why it was so hard for me to face reality, but you believed in me."

"Of course, I always have," Evelyn responded. Her smile was loving, but I missed the depth of passion that used to be mine in her eyes. "You'll both be fine without me. Promise not to be sad anymore and go live your lives. Do all the things we talk about, Dee Dee."

She didn't feel sad and empty about the loss of her life, the way that Amelia and I truly did. I understood, but I had

248

to stop expecting to connect with her emotionally the way I needed to. It just wasn't possible. Instead, now I could see that Amelia and I had our shared pain and memories to hold us together.

"I will, Evie. I promise you. I want you to find peace too. There is something new for you out there, I know it in my heart." I meant it, I didn't know where she would go or what she would become, but I had always believed that good people found their own version of heaven.

She traced my cheek with a hand, the touch so light it felt like only a cool summer wind stirring.

"I loved you," she told me.

"And I loved you." I bit back tears, knowing I would never see her again after this moment.

She leaned forward to kiss my cheek and I closed my eyes to steady myself. To savor her and also to let her go easily. That, I could try to do for her.

I felt her cool kiss, then she whispered softly in my left ear. Before I could say goodbye, she pulled away and when I opened my eyes, I was alone.

***

"I'm so glad the fog has lifted," Amelia said, pouring my coffee. "You know, before, I wasn't in favour of your relationship with my sister, but I did like you. Maybe you think I only took you in out of pity, or duty, but I saw all the good in you. The elements that Evelyn was attracted to."

"I really appreciate that. I honestly didn't expect an easy road with our decision to be together and become a part of each other's families, but most people came around and were kind. You...I understood it was hard for you because you and Evelyn were so close. It must have been hard to see such a big change in her."

Amelia nodded. "I didn't know any women…well, like you two. This town is so isolated to such people and ideas. But, it was also easier to be angry at your relationship instead of being angry at myself for not seeing how Roger was treating her. I would have done anything to protect her if I had known. How could I not have seen it?" A tear fell and traced her jawline before she dabbed at it with a tissue.

"She hid the abuse well." I too, needed to wipe my eyes. It could have all turned out so different if Evelyn had only asked for our help.

"So, did you see Evelyn today? Is she still here?" Amelia asked.

I didn't answer for a second, letting the moment build. Finally, I put my cup down and laced my fingers together on the table in front of me.

"I saw her. She came to say goodbye."

Amelia's expression saddened, I guess wishing she'd had the same chance to talk to Evelyn one last time.

I smiled at her, though, broader and more connected to the world than I had been in years.

"What?" Amelia asked, tilting her head in puzzlement.

"She asked me to tell you that she loved you, and is grateful for everything you've done for me."

"Is that all? Your expression is…curious."

I nodded slowly. "Yes, there's more. She told me where the money is."

Amelia's mouth dropped open, but she quickly snapped it shut.

"Well, then." I lifted my water glass in the air. "Cheers to a fresh start for both of us."

Amelia picked up her own glass and clinked it with mine. "Yes, indeed."

North Side Asylum

Lily Luchesi

From the *Chicago Tribune*:

The following document was found last week from the late Ms. Freya Green's personal effects. Because of the strange, half-written and half-recorded interview and its relation to the circumstances surrounding her passing, we elected to run the entire transcribed piece, unedited, on our website. It has been published in part in print. This is in correlation to her last assignment from us here at the Tribune, *concerning the rumors about the treatment of patients at the North Side Psychiatric Asylum.*

Let it be noted that some of the information is uncorroborated, and therefore cannot be seen as undeniable fact until we can locate her source. More about him after her article. --ED.

***

As I went to meet my informant for this piece, a small prickle of doubt came upon me. After all, there has been a string of murders lately, and the victim selection seems so random that I do fear going out alone at night. Well, tonight, anyway. The victims are always killed on the full moon. Ah, well, I am not being paid to write a piece on that. My piece is a bit more disturbing, featuring the allegations that doctors are torturing patients at a local psych ward. As a former patient at a different hospital in the city, this appalls me, and I want to get to the bottom of this.

These days and in this economy, it is rare that a reporter finds a source willing to give up their information for free, but my source and I have been emailing back and forth for a week, and he is insistent he merely wants to have the doctors punished. That's good enough for me.

The bar is also on the North Side, a small, smoky place not far from the baseball stadium. I find it odd that it's smoky because Chicago outlawed indoor smoking years ago. The lights are low, but it is easy to see. I wondered how I was going to find my informant as I weaved my way through the patrons, looking for a man sitting alone. There were not many and soon I heard my name being called.

I turned to see where the voice was coming from, glad that my last byline had included a photo of me, and spotted a small, stocky man clad in a black leather jacket with custom tan designs at the lapels and shoulders. He was wearing a pair of fitted jeans and the woman in me wanted to see them from the rear. His boots were black leather as well and looked expensive.

He was smiling lightly, holding a glass half-filled with amber liquid in one strong hand. His dark eyes bore into me and through me, as though he knew my every nuance from just a glance. He didn't look very old, maybe forty at the most, and a good-looking forty at that, but he was prematurely bald.

Well, as my mother used to say, stress will make one of two things happen to your hair: it turns gray, or it goes away.

He stood up as I approached and held a hand out to me. I noticed a silver thumb ring and a silver ring on his pinky with an onyx cross.

"I'm James Divina. Thank you for coming to speak to me this evening," he said, his voice pleasantly deep and his grip firm.

"Thank you for *wanting* to speak with me," I replied, sitting down across from him. A waiter approached, and I ordered a glass of red wine. I rarely drank on the job, but when a source wants to meet, it is usually a bar. Maybe they think I'm going to make them the star of the next *Interview with the Vampire* or something. In any case, nursing a glass or two of red wine would make the source feel more comfortable, so that's what I did.

"So, what do you already know about North Side Asylum?" he asked me. I loved it when they got right to the point.

"Know? Absolutely nothing," I replied. "It's all a rumor spread a few months back when that inmate escaped, and after she spilled her guts to a gas station clerk, he killed her, thinking she was going to attack him. He put her body in the backseat of her car. This is why I want facts from you."

"Right...and everyone who ever entered the asylum usually died there," he added.

I stared him in the eyes and said, "Except for you."

"I got lucky," he replied, leaning forward, letting the dim lights reflect in his eyes, turning them into dark, fiery pools.

"You need to understand, Mr. Divina, I cannot simply take your word as fact. Which is why, in my last email to you, I asked that you please bring with you proof that you were a patient there. May I see it?" I asked.

"Of course." He put his glass on the table and proceeded to remove his jacket, revealing a tight black tee over a body that belonged on a romance novel cover. (Well, I am going to have to edit this article before sending it in-- how many glasses of wine have I had?)

He held out his left arm and burned into his skin like a cattle branding was a serial number: JD031373. Below that, also burned in, was: NSPA.

I was speechless, staring at the scar.

"Hot metal rod. Burned it in and immediately cauterized the wound as well," he said as he leaned back in his chair.

"Holy hell," I whispered. "May I take a photo to run with the article?" He nodded, and I took the shot on my smartphone camera, wishing I'd thought to bring a real one with me.

He started to put his coat back on. "So you see, I have permanent proof of my time spent in earth's version of hell."

"I want to let you get on with your story, but my editor likes background. Are you willing to tell me why you were in the asylum?" I asked. "It's okay if you don't want to talk about it. I just had to ask."

"It's fine," he said. "I was just graduating from college when I found out I hadn't made it into law school. It immediately sent me into a downward spiral. Since I was a teenager I've wanted to be a lawyer, and with one little letter, all my dreams went straight down the toilet.

"It started with drinking, progressed to hard drugs, and then when the shame and hopelessness did not abate, I tried to kill myself. My girlfriend found me, called nine-one-one, and called my family. I don't remember any of this, but evidently I was really out of it, kept trying to hurt myself and others. After the hospital detoxed me, they forcibly committed me at North Side." He took a long sip of his drink. "I don't do drugs anymore since coming out, but damn does this feel good while I have to recount what happened to me in that place." He jiggled the ice in the glass. "They use experimental drugs there. They made me hear voices. I think schizophrenia was a side-effect of one of them...or all of them combined did it. I was perfectly normal, albeit depressed and high, before then."

"Did you feel that the forcible committal was necessary for you?" I asked.

His eyes met mine, and he gave me a knowing smile. "Hell no. I was no longer a threat to myself. However, I firmly believed that they got a bonus for every patient they referred to the asylum."

That was what I had been thinking, too. I set my tape recorder on the table (I'm old-fashioned, so sue me) and said, "You don't still hear the voices, do you?"

He threw his head back and laughed, a sound that was simultaneously freaky and sexy. "Funny girl."

I smiled and clicked on the recorder. "Anytime you're ready, Mr. Divina. I won't interrupt, though I may have questions afterward."

He nodded and started to talk.

***

[The following is the unedited transcript of the time James Divina alleges he spent inside the North Side Psychiatric Asylum. Foul language was removed. --ED]

***

My first clear memory is waking up in Resurrection Memorial Hospital, hooked up to IVs and feeling like I'd been hit by a *[bleeping]* truck. I had no recollection of how I'd gotten there, and I had no idea what day it was. I only knew it was Resurrection because their logo was on the IV bag.

The last thing I remembered was shooting up the heroin I'd had in my place, waiting for it to take effect. Nothing happened, and I remember thinking I'd been ripped off. Not being able to get high, my depression returned with renewed force. The self-doubt and hate was immense, and I saw no future or myself. I remember laying on the sofa in my living room, staring at the ceiling fan. You know, I was in one of those older apartments, where there was no air unless you bought your own window unit, and all we had was a fan in there and the bedroom.

I remember removing my belt; I remember getting a chair from the kitchen, and everything after that is lost.

According to my mother—who stopped associating with me after that initial duty visit—my girlfriend had come home the second I lost consciousness from the belt cutting off my airflow. Paramedics revived me, brought me to Resurrection, where they treated the cuts on my throat from the leather, and then detoxed me.

I guess I got violent during the detox, even broke an orderly's nose. I don't remember it. Whatever drugs they'd given me, they were top of the line *[bleep]*. In any case, that on top of the suicide attempt earned me a trip to Resurrection's small mental health center, where I woke up and got the information I just relayed to you, all while being restrained to the hospital bed. A doctor—I can't recall his name: it's been twenty years, remember, and some of the "treatment" I received at the asylum gave me some memory issues—came and examined me.

"You're healing well, Mr. Divina," he told me. "Do you know where you are?"

My mind automatically thought, *in the jungle, baby*, and I had to force myself not to laugh. "Yeah. This is my regular hospital, but I don't know how I got here, or what day it is," I told him. "What happened?"

"Do you remember trying to hang yourself from your living room fan?" he asked me.

I did. "So, it's just been a day, then?"

He shook his head. "It's been a week. Your mother will fill you in on everything, but you have been very volatile since your arrival. We detoxed you, but it was quite the struggle."

"Hence the *[bleeping]* wristbands? No offense, but I prefer black leather," I said, smirking at him.

He gave me that serious stare they must teach at med school. "Do you find what you did funny, Mr. Divina?"

"Suicide? No. Not at all. I don't remember anything else to know if I consider it funny or not," I replied.

He wrote down something on my chart. "You are being moved this evening to the North Side Psychiatric Asylum. It is mandatory that you have a seventy-two-hour hold there, and I am signing the papers for long-term committal until their doctors see fit to release you back into decent society."

I wish I could convey the contempt and disgust in his voice as he said that to me. It was as though he thought I was some subhuman thing that needed to be locked away and examined to see how it ticked, you know?

I was incensed. He was not a psychiatrist to tell me if I needed to be committed. I knew about the mandatory hold, but the committal was out of his hands, and I told him so.

He chuckled mirthlessly. "You are in no position to make those decisions for yourself, Mr. Divina. Your girlfriend would tell you that if she were here."

My girlfriend was Judy Hoover and we had been together since we were sixteen. "My mother said she was the one who found me," I said, my heart sinking. I hadn't thought about who would find me after I did the deed, only that I wanted out of this hopeless life.

"Yes, she did. She saved your life, and you were not very grateful," the doc said.

"I was out of it. I don't remember anything. You can't *[bleeping]* commit me when I have no idea what I did!" I cried.

The doctor did not speak to me again. He left, and my mother came in to tell me how I'd attacked doctors, nurses, and orderlies. No one told me why, and I assumed it was the drugs I'd taken. They hadn't worked because they were contaminated somehow. I tried telling her that, tried telling the police when they came around to interview me. Evidently, I racked up quite a bit of criminal charges while I was "not there." They didn't believe that I remembered none of it and refused to give me the information of precisely what I did when I asked. A judge made the executive decision to continue the committal while I was already in the asylum, saying that what I'd done had obviously been done while I was in what he called a 'disturbed state.' Highly illegal, all of it, but I had no one to argue my side except for a piece of *[bleep]* public defender.

When the night came, and it was time to transfer me to the asylum, my parents said goodbye and I asked repeatedly to see Judy before I left. I wanted to apologize to her for having to find me like that.

I was refused each time I asked, and the orderlies from the asylum laughed as they rolled me, still strapped to the bed, into the ambulance.

"I don't think she'll be coming to see you anytime soon," one said. He had a crooked nose, and I had half a mind to break it again and make it slant to the other direction. Maybe it *was* a good thing I was restrained.

The other said, "Who knows, maybe he *will* see her soon." They both laughed.

It's a twenty-minute drive from Resurrection to the asylum, and in those twenty minutes, I was left alone, strapped to a gurney, staring at a dirty white roof while I could barely hear the two goons cackling in the front. It gave me time to think.

I remembered nothing more from the past few days, but I realized that the guy I had bought the heroin from had not been my usual dealer and that this one had had a crooked nose as well, though he had been a blond, and the man in the ambulance had brown hair.

I shook my head. There was no way it was the same guy. I was just off of some seriously bad *[bleep]*, having tried to kill myself and some hospital staff. My brain wasn't functioning on all four cylinders yet, that was all.

But that *nose*. I'd have a lot of time to think about it in the years that followed. A lot of time to look at it, too.

We arrived at the asylum and I was wheeled into a room with one bed, a small table, and one chair. All nailed to the ground. There were a sink and toilet in the same room, like a fancy jail cell. The window did not open, and the glass was unbreakable, like the high-rise casino windows, from where big losers would like to throw themselves over had the windows been real. The blinds closed with the press of a button, no cords on which I could try to hang myself again.

Crooked-Nose unbuckled my restraints and I sat up, feeling sore and weak from being in the same position for so long. Weren't hospitals supposed to have someone move people, work on their muscles when they were "out of it" or restrained, so that they did not atrophy?

He yanked me from the gurney and to my feet, where my jelly-like legs decided they did not want to support all one hundred and seventy pounds of me and I crumpled to the floor, embarrassed and extremely pissed off.

The two *[bleepers]* laughed at me, and then the other one yanked me back to my feet, shoving me to sit on the thin white cot they called a bed. He tossed a pair of hospital pajamas next to me.

"Get to sleep. You'll begin intake at six in the morning," he said, and then I was alone, locked in a ten by twenty room that needed a severe mopping and a new color scheme. At that moment I knew I had somehow entered hell.

The next morning an alarm blared, apparently to wake up all of the patients. I say patients, but I found out soon that we were really inmates and test subjects, nothing more. I admit freely that, if Crooked-Nose had been the one to open my door, I would have done my very best to make sure he never pushed anyone ever again, but instead a beefy-looking woman came in, reminding me of one of my relatives who ran a farm in Iowa. Close cropped hair, glasses, and a pristine apron over her uniform. I had no idea if she was a nurse, a doctor, or a patient playing around. I did not like the look of her one bit. She reminded me of someone who would assist Dr. Satan in *House of 1000 Corpses*.

"Divina, James?" she barked.

I nodded.

"Get dressed and then follow me," she said, throwing a white shirt and white pants on the bed. I did not care to have her watch me as I changed my clothes (they didn't even give me underwear), but she didn't turn away. The clothes had "property of NSPA" written on them. Like anyone would want to steal those things!

I shuffled along next to her in house shoes as we walked down a long corridor with windowless doors, all of which had numbers on them. I had a million questions, but I figured I'd save them for the doctor since this woman did not seem the talkative type.

Exiting that corridor, she took me into an elevator and we rode two floors up. Judging by the elevator, there were five floors. Three had inmates—excuse me, *patients*—living on them. One was administrative offices, and another was exam rooms and doctor's offices. There was also a basement and sub-basement. We were going to a doctor's office it seemed as we stepped off the elevator.

This floor looked much less intimidating than the one I was currently staying on. At least there was decent lighting and the floors had been cleaned sometime in the last decade. She stopped walking outside a door marked, "Guy Trelawney, MD, Ph.D." On a side note, who the hell is pretentious enough to name their kid Guy?

She entered, grabbing me by the sleeve and tugging me in after her. "Doctor T, Divina is here for his intake."

Inside the room it was awfully hot. I wondered idly if the boiler was overheating or something. The building *is* old enough to still have a boiler room. Dr. Trelawney, another person with whom I would get very well acquainted with over the years, stood up behind his desk.

He was tall but sturdy, with round, *Harry Potter* glasses that magnified his cold gray eyes. He was smiling, but there was nothing nice in that smile. I could easily have pictured ravenous werewolves grinning at their prey like that.

As a lawyer in training (which I had been), you're taught how to read your clients and the opposition. And what I saw in him was pure, unadulterated sadism. He enjoyed seeing the suffering of his patients as they struggled with their own minds. Had I been his attorney, I'd quit. Immediately. I had the urge to run, run far and run fast. It was the same urge I got in middle school when the bigger boys (and they were almost all bigger than me) smiled at me on the soccer field. He had that same sick, sadistic pleasure in his eyes.

"Mr. Divina, please sit down," he said, gesturing to the lounge chair that was across from an armchair. It was different from the usual sofa situation you see depicted in cartoons of shrinks' offices.

I didn't want to sit there, so I went to sit in the armchair when Dr. Trelawney cleared his throat loudly.

"Other chair, Mr. Divina." There was no mistaking that warning in his tone, and I quickly changed seats, feeling odd and uncomfortable in that reclining position those chairs force you into. Both the doctor and the woman watched me as I got settled.

"Look, Doctor, let me be blunt: I have no interest in sitting here and talking about my potty training, okay?" I said. "I was depressed, an addict. I suppose I'm still a drunk, but I can guarantee after that bad heroin I'm never doing drugs again. I was suicidal. I am sure I need some treatment for that, but I don't need to be here beyond the mandatory hold."

Dr. Trelawney chuckled. "I think I'll be the judge of that, hmm, Mr. Divina?" He checked what I assume was my chart. "You exhibited homicidal rages."

"Yeah, from bad drugs that altered my thinking. For all I know, I thought those *[bleepers]* at the hospital were werewolves or vampires. I've never so much as gotten into a scuffle since I was a kid," I said.

"Nevertheless, today is not going to be your sitting here and discussing your youth, Mr. Divina," the doctor said, reaching into a desk drawer. "This is merely basic intake to get you into our system properly."

Then why do I have to sit in this ridiculous thing? I wondered as he rummaged in his desk. My mind was flashing red WARNING signals, but if I tried to run they'd get me and it would just give them another reason to lock me away here.

"Nurse Gemina?" The doctor gestured from the nurse to me.

That was all the communication she needed to walk over from where she had been standing and sidle up next to me. Under normal circumstances, I'd think she was about to check my vitals. However, there were no medical instruments to use: no stethoscope, no tongue depressors, no thermometers, and no blood pressure cuffs. What she did have were more restraints. I immediately jumped up, only to be shoved back down by hands that were much stronger than I would have assumed, even though the woman did look like she could match me in the gym.

She snapped the restraints on both ankles, and I saw that they connected to the underside of the lounge chair I was in. *So that's why he demanded I sit here*, I thought, panicking, as she restrained one of my wrists. My right wrist. I swung out with my left hand, connecting with her jaw. Normally, I would never hit a woman. Usually, though, no woman had ever tied me down without my expressed consent, if you get my meaning.

My life was in danger, and the gender of my oppressor didn't matter to me. I scratched, and I heard her yell. There was blood on two of my fingers. She grabbed my wrist with two meaty hands and twisted. Nothing snapped, but the muscles and tendons that were twisted made me cry out in pain. I knew I had a bad sprain, maybe a torn tendon or two. It stopped my attack on her, though.

When I could see through the gray haze of pain, I saw Trelawney approach with something I did not recognize. It was a long metal rod, with a thin, pointed end. All my hazy mind could think of was one place he might be intending to put it, and it wasn't pleasant. Then I saw in his other hand was a handheld blowtorch. You can buy them for twenty *[bleeping]* dollars on Amazon now, did you know that?

"What the *[bleep]* are you doing to me?" I asked, trying and failing to escape as the nurse twisted my injured wrist and pulled my left arm taut.

"Now now, Mr. Divina," Trelawney said pleasantly, "every patient has to be logged into our system the same way. You don't get preferential treatment."

He lit the torch and put it to the end of the metal rod. It was like a car accident: I didn't want to watch but I couldn't look away as he brought the pointed tip, now glowing red, to my skin and started to carve into my flesh.

At first the pain was so bad, I felt nothing. Have you ever felt pain like that, so deep and intense that at first your mind refuses to recognize what your nerves are sending to it? It hit me as he started to carve in the 'D,' and I screamed bloody murder. It stung, dug, and burned, all without spilling a drop of blood.

I passed out from the intensity of it around the time they were carving the second three in the serial number, and when I awoke it was late evening. There was a tray of cold food on the table in my room, my arm was smarting, and my wrist was taped up in Ace bandages. I looked down at my arm, which had been cauterized and sterilized the moment that bastard touched me, and felt the incessant throb. All I could bring myself to do was curl up in a ball and cry.

I was left alone for two days, except for the orderly who brought me my meals. I checked them over, to be sure there were no pills crushed in there, but if they were, I could not detect them. I thought about not eating, but I needed strength if I was going to break out of the place. When I slept, I dreamed of Judy, but the dreams were distorted, violent. I dreamed I was branding her, and in another, it was she who branded me. Mostly they were of her, bloodied and beaten. The dreams were so real. I could feel and smell the metallic tang of her blood, hear her bones breaking, and feel her nails as she scratched at me, trying to escape. Every time the orderly brought me meals, I asked him to do something to get her to see me, but he never said a single thing to me.

After those two days, along with two painkillers every day, my sprain began to heal. I could move my wrist almost without pain. The serial number on my arm was still tingling as the scar tissue formed, however, and it made sleeping very uncomfortable.

I started to wonder if maybe it wasn't jail. I was not allowed out of my room and only received my meals. If this was a true psych ward, even a twisted one who burned numbers into your flesh, wouldn't I be getting *some* kind of treatment?

On the third day, there was a knock at the door before it opened up and I saw Crooked-Nose standing there, smiling like the devil. His teeth were yellowed and crooked as well, almost like fangs. That was when I knew he had been my dealer. That man had had the same *[bleeped]* up teeth.

Why had he been pretending to be a drug dealer, giving me bad heroin? Or had it not been heroin at all? What the hell had I injected into me?

I stood up slowly as he started to walk towards me. "What the hell are you up to, you sadistic *[bleep]*?" I asked, my nerves trembling. "What did you give me that night?"

He kept smiling; his eyes were blank, like eyes in a portrait. "Recognized me, did ya?"

"What did you give me?" I asked, furious. Whatever it was, it had made me act in such a way that I was locked up in this place.

"Come on, killer. You've got an appointment." He reached for me, and I leaped back, out of his reach.

He came at me again, grabbing my good arm. Despite my sprain being healed, I didn't want to risk hurting it yet again, so I kicked out and knocked his feet out from under him, causing him to fall on his back.

I jumped over him, determined to reach the door and get the hell out of there when I felt a strong grip on my ankle yank me backward. I fell on my face, thankfully not breaking anything, and had the wind knocked out of me. I felt hands on mine, and before I knew it I had been handcuffed, but with the brown leather restraints that seemed to be Psycho Center Chic.

I was bodily hauled to my feet, the bastard nearly dislocating my shoulder.

"You think you can escape?" he hissed in my ear. His breath was rancid. "You'll soon learn otherwise. It always takes a few weeks before you psychos lose your will." He chuckled. "I'm really gonna enjoy breaking your spirit, killer."

He yanked me with him, down the hall and into the elevator again, going up to the doctor's offices. As if there was any actual, real medicine practiced here! I was getting the feeling that we were all locked here, tortured, and God knew what else. There was no help for those who might really be mentally ill, and there was definitely no help for me.

I was taken to a different room this time, a brightly lit one that was too cold, and it looked like a regular doctor's exam room: cot, sink, a cupboard filled with various medical instruments, and a biohazard container.

The only thing in that room that was not in every general practitioner's room was the leather straps attached to the cot, meant to hold patients down who were struggling. My skin broke out in gooseflesh when I saw those and I heard Crooked-Nose chuckle again.

"Scared, killer?"

"Call me that one more time and *you'll* be scared," I said, aware that I was being restrained by a psychopath who could kill me much quicker than I could get to him.

He gave me a long, hard look before the door opened and Trelawney entered with the nurse, Gemina, behind him.

"Thank you, Geoffrey," Trelawney said. "Can you and Nurse Gemina get him strapped in, please? Mr. Divina, how's your wrist?" For all of me, the *[bleeper]* could have been at a garden party!

"Are you kidding me?" I cried. "If I were free right now I'd shove that metal stick right up your skinny little ass!"

He tutted like I was a naughty child. "Ah, Mr. Divina, I see we're going to have to do a lot of work on you." He gestured and Geoffrey and Gemina took my hands, untied them, and lifted me onto the cot. I kicked out, but not even a good one to Gemina's padded stomach had any effect. Before I knew it, I was tied down, unable to move anything but my head. I stared up at the dirty, cracked ceiling and saw a couple of spiders scuttle from one crack to another, trails of web stringing behind them.

I'm high, I thought. *Everything has been nothing but a delusion caused by bad drugs. [Bleep], as soon as I wake up I'm joining the D.A.R.E. program!*

I knew, deep down, that this was no delusion. The straps were cutting into my flesh, my healing arm was itching, and my head was swimming from fear. I thought about dirty scalpels, pliers, rib-cutters, and my stomach did flips.

When I was ten I got lost in the woods. Separated from my parents and older brother, I wandered to try and find my way back to our car. Things were moving between trees, and I heard wolves howling. That was my first experience with true, heart-stopping fear and wolves haunted my nightmares for my whole life. I thought back then that I was terrified, and I now desperately wished to be my ten-year-old self again. Because I now that knew what real fear was, I didn't like it one bit.

"Now, there's no need to be scared, Mr. Divina," Trelawney said. "This won't hurt much. In fact, the only reason we're strapping you down is because we don't know what your reaction afterward might be. Now, hold still. This will only sting a little."

The monster in human skin loomed over me, hands gloved and a long syringe in one of them. Inside was a cloudy liquid. I had no idea what that was, but I knew I didn't want it flowing through my veins!

"You had a very pure form of this drug help you get in here," Trelawney explained. "Too pure to administer more than once. Now, this is diluted with a little Diazepam and Alprazolam."

I tried thinking back to a mock trial we had done in college. Was it legal to mix those two drugs? Was it healthy? I seriously doubted it. I squeezed my eyes shut as the needle pricked my neck, digging deep and injecting its poison into my veins.

That was when the real trouble began, though I did not feel it for some time.

It took me a very long time to feel the effects of the drug they were giving me, and there were chunks of time that I lost, either beaten to unconsciousness or overdosed on many occasions. It's amazing I survived the whole ordeal. I had no idea how many patients were being treated as I was, or if they actually did legitimate psychiatric work here. I assumed they did, because how else were they not shut down yet?

The one thought that stuck with me was that they set me up. Somehow they picked *me* to give that drug to, me to experiment on. And the doctor at Resurrection had been in on it! Who else, I wondered. Who else had set me up, a troubled young man who simply needed help? Why? And how had they decided on me? Who else was wrongfully sent here to be a guinea pig and punching bag?

I was quickly cowed into submission, and within a year I had become a shell of a person, drugged beyond comprehension and as emotionless as a robot. Actually, I think *Star Wars* had robots with more feeling than I allowed myself to have.

If I did not want them to break my spirit, I had to shut down my mind, which was easy to do with whatever they were injecting me.

One day, about two years after I had been admitted, I had an adverse reaction to their newest injection. I believe it was similar to how people act when they're on LSD. I snapped the straps holding me to the table and sent a hard kick right to Gemina's chest, sending her flying backward and into a medical tray. I saw a needle and a scalpel sticking out of her side, blood staining her pure white uniform.

It took three orderlies to get me still, and even when my arms were strapped into a straightjacket, I was still fighting like a wild animal. I had repressed everything so deeply that whatever they'd given me had brought out all my rage.

I was injected with direct Prozac and only then was I able to be transported to a padded cell, where I promptly passed out. When I woke up, I heard the sliding panel (about three inches high and ten inches wide) on the metal door move.

My arms were sore, and I was sure it was not just from the jacket. Lord only knew what I'd strained snapping those restraints. I stood up shakily as I saw Crooked-Nose peering in at me.

"Hello, killer." He had never stopped calling me that, and I was furious each time he did it. It was so mocking, so childish. "All calmed down now?"

My emotions were no longer tamed. If I could have, I'd have run up to the slat in the door and bit his *[bleeping]* crooked nose right off his pockmarked face. "Why do you keep giving me that damned drug?" I cried. "You knew what it did to me the first time!"

He chuckled. "Ah yes. We knew. But do you? Do you know what you did yet?"

I wondered what he was talking about. Yes, of course, I knew. One orderly had an impromptu nose job the first time, and I was pretty sure Nurse Gemina needed stitches this time, and I broke the jaw of another orderly this time.

"You don't, do you?" I heard something rustle and he threw a bunch of papers and eight-by-ten photographs through the slot. "It wasn't the attack on the orderlies that got you in here. You did *this* before you even touched them. Here. Enjoy." I heard his wheezing laughter, and then the panel was shut again.

Curious, I walked over to the papers and knelt before them. Many had landed upside down, and I had no hands to turn them over. That bastard knew it, too. He was probably picturing what I was doing now: using my teeth like a dog to turn them over.

The first one was a photograph, and I wanted to scream, but all that came out was a breathy groan. It seemed all my breath was gone as I stared at Judy Hoover, the love of my life. Or, what was left of her after her soul departed. She'd been beaten to death. One eye was swollen shut like a plum was shoved into her face. The other had been popped, and the goo clung to her cheek, drying and mixing with the blood from a severe head wound. Her lips were swollen, the bottom one tore partway, having been bitten off.

There were a few more photos, showing detailed close-ups of her broken bones, gouges, and bite marks. Whole chunks of her flesh had been torn away by teeth, my teeth, evidently.

The papers were the police report. They claimed that I had attacked her while she sat with me overnight after she'd rescued me. They claimed I had been yelling something about monsters, werewolves. Still with the wolves, ever since I was a kid. I'd destroyed her before anyone could get to me. That was why she never came to see me. She'd never be seeing anyone again.

I had killed her. She saved my life when I tried to end it and then I killed her and I didn't even remember it.

I screamed then, letting out my shame and my grief and my hate in a wordless cry of pain. I cried so hard and long I threw up, and cried some more until I fell into an exhausted, nightmare filled slumber next to a puddle of my own sick.

When I next awoke, I was back in my room. The memories came flooding back to me, the nightmares I'd had about Judy dying were true, and I had been the one to end her life. Granted, I had been out of it, I'd thought she was a [bleeping] werewolf! I knew I watched too many horror movies in my life, and those wolves had always haunted me since childhood.

I didn't cry again. I didn't think I could cry. I didn't want to feel anymore. Now, I wished for the pain and the torture. I wanted the electric shocks, even though they made my hair fall out. Pain was better than this. Anything was better than this. Even insanity.

It was a week later that my soup turned to blood.

Now, when you think of schizophrenia, you think of the homeless people you see on the streets, right? Shouting, having conversations with people only they can hear. Or you think of those people who make tinfoil hats and talk about that ever-present, never seen 'They.' But when it begins, it's not like that at all, as I learned all too well once the new injections started setting in.

For many people, it starts out with either paranoia or voices. For me, it started with visions.

The first instance of it was when my chicken soup was no longer chicken. What I saw in my bowl was viscous blood, with finger bones floating and a bright blue eyeball peeking through the liquid. I shoved the bowl away, frightened, and when it clattered to the floor, I saw it was only chicken soup after all. It had merely been a hallucination.

The next time it happened to me was when I was being strapped to the chair for shock treatment. The tech started to morph, blood dripping from his eyeballs and face turning into something wolfish. I went for his throat, but they stopped me, and my mind cleared once again.

By the time I was seeing giant spiders and moths all over my room and hearing phantom howls outside my window, I realized that I belonged in this place. I was insane, they were making me insane, and this was where I belonged now. The thought was so natural, so normal, that it didn't even make me angry or sad. It just was.

Time unimaginable passed. I can tell you it doesn't feel like twenty years. I try hard to recall it all, and I can't. Probably a side effect of the meds.

Eventually, the visions stopped, and I was relieved. Until the voices started. They were different voices, some I knew and some I didn't. Judy's was frequent, wailing and calling me every name in the book. And I deserved it. Sometimes it was my father, calling me a useless piece of garbage after I didn't get into law school. Once or twice it was my criminal law professor, calling me a disappointment.

However, aside from Judy's voice, and her distorted image in my mind as I killed her, the voice that I heard in my head the most frequently was *mine*. And that scared me.

At first it just called me names, things I already did to myself. Things I already knew. But why? Why was my disembodied voice the one that affected me the most? I thought about telling Trelawney, who was still going strong despite looking like he was pushing seventy. Evil bastards never die young and in pain, do they? In any case, he already knew what was happening to me.

The voice—my voice—explained what I should have realized already.

They picked you because you were a drug addict. That's how they do it. They get their guinea pigs from off the street to test their experimental [bleep] on. You were by far the most responsive, and because of you, Trelawney is about to be a multimillionaire. He'll be rolling in the dough, and you can bet he'll give Crooked-Nose a nice little nest egg for being your torturer all this time. And where will you be? Oh yeah, sitting here, getting electrocuted, and talking to yourself till you die.

"No, I won't!" I cried, looking around for the person who had been talking to me, but obviously there was no one there.

As soon as this drug sells to a manufacturer, they'll get rid of you. They'll take you down to the sub-basement, right below the level where they electrocute you, and they'll shove you kicking and screaming into the incinerator. They'll roast [bleeping] marshmallows over the very flames that consume your living flesh. Or maybe you'll be so crazy by then that you'll crawl on in there yourself, just to escape me and all the other voices in here.

The thought sickened me, and I only escaped the voice—*my* voice—when I slept.

Until I didn't sleep anymore.

I am not sure, but I think they knew I was hearing voices, and they wanted me awake, because the more exhausted I was, the stronger the voice was. That was their biggest mistake, taking their sadism too far. Because the stronger the voice was, the more inclined I was to listen to it, and that other me had some *very* good ideas indeed.

The first idea was to get to know the new night orderly, a young girl with blonde hair. She was badly disfigured, the skin on one side of her face replaced with deep burn scars. I thought she might be a former patient perhaps, but there was no ID branded into her skin. She walked around and treated everyone like dirt, but she seemed to have soft spot for me, always asking me how I was and if I needed anything.

Eventually, I started to joke with her, saying things the voice told me to say.

"How am I? You tell me, *you* don't get electrocuted twice a day, do you?"

"Do I need anything? Yeah, a full head of hair again and a way out of here."

My sarcasm made her like me even more, and sometimes if there was no one around at night she'd stop and talk to me through the panel in my door for ten or so minutes.

It was after these late-night talks that the voice had its best ideas, and it kept trying to convince me to try them out. Eventually, it got me to consider them by one simple fact. *They're gonna kill you either way. How do you wanna go: fighting, or letting them lead you by the [bleeping] hand to your death?*

I wanted to go fighting. Anything to stop the drugs, the torture, and the voice.

The orderly—her name was Jane—came by my door that night as always. She was wearing pancake makeup to cover her disfigurement. She had revealed to me that an ex had tried to burn her face off with boiling water once. Poor baby.

My body was wasted, but when the voice talked to me I felt like I could do anything. Even kill a person with my bare hands, as I already had once before.

Tell her to open the door, the voice said.

"Jane, I'm so sick of only seeing three inches of your face," I said. "Come on, I've been stuck in here for so long only looking at Trelawney and Crooked-Nose. It'd be nice to see someone pleasant for a change."

She giggled. The noise was like nails on a chalkboard. I always hated gigglers. "I can't. What if another orderly sees?"

She's the last one here. You're her last stop before she goes home, the voice said.

"They all left already," I reminded her.

Another giggle. I wanted to strangle her.

"Come on," I persuaded. When I was young I'd had a lot of female interest even when I was with Judy. Even too thin and as bald as Mr. Clean, I knew I still had that charm. "Please?" I smiled at her, and she smiled back, her face turning pink even beneath the makeup.

Sighing, she used her key to unlock the door, the stupid bitch. I was ready, just as the voice told me to be. As soon as the door swung open, I reached out with my bedsheet and smothered Jane's surprised cries until I felt her go limp in my arms.

There's never anyone on these floors at night. Just the guards at the front door, the voice told me. *You know what to do, and if you're quiet, you'll be home free soon.*

I did know what to do. I carried Jane to the elevator and went to the doctor's offices. I used her keys to get into Trelawney's office. Once inside his desk, I found the metal rod, the blowtorch, and a gag. They'd never gagged me. I think they liked it when I screamed and pissed myself at their ministrations.

As I gagged and tied Jane, she began to stir and try to break out of her restraints.

"Sorry, darlin', but those don't come off easy," I said as I heated up the rod. I checked her ID. Her name was Jane Kozlowski, and her birthdate was April second, nineteen-eighty-five. I took the rod to her left arm and began to brand her as I had been branded so long ago. "JK040285" with "NSPA" below it. She tried to scream around the gag, and I wished I could hear her. It would have sounded so sweet!

I unhooked the restraints, retying them so her hands were behind her back. I left the gag in. Down the hall we went, and I found a syringe prefilled with Prozac. Holding Jane's tied hands in one of my hands and the syringe in the other, I made my way back to the elevator and went to the main floor with the administrative offices.

Good! Only one more obstacle to go, the voice cheered.

The elevator dinged when I walked out. The lobby was so nice and clean, to fool the visitors, I supposed. The security guard was half asleep with a porn magazine hidden beneath the desk. The fat of his neck was folded in neat rolls as his head hung to the side. It looked like I might be able to get out of there and not use the Prozac.

Don't risk it. Drug him, the voice said.

So I jammed the needle into his jugular, thankful that was the side his massive head was *not* listing towards. He woke with a cry, but that was silenced as the pure drug made its way into his nervous system.

Jane kept crying through the gag, her tears making tracks in her heavy makeup, revealing the disgusting flesh beneath the veneer.

"Come on, darlin'. You're my *[bleeping]* insurance policy," I said, dragging her out the front doors with me, flashing my middle finger at the security camera as I did so.

I went into her pockets again and found her car keys. A vintage Camaro. How pretentious. Ah well, at least they were fast.

After checking the vivid pink car for anything that could be used as a weapon (a taser and a tire iron were all I found), I shoved her into the backseat and got into the driver's seat. The fresh air, the feeling of a steering wheel in my hands and soft leather beneath my ass was wonderful, the stuff of dreams and memories.

I rolled down my window and turned on the radio. Something loud and angry blasted from the speakers, and I was more than happy to listen to it. It reminded me of the stuff I liked in the eighties, but harder.

As I drove, going into the suburbs right next to the city, the voice spoke up.

The police are onto you for speeding. You lost them for now, but it's time to activate phase two.

I nodded, though there was no one there to see me. I found a Citgo gas station on Lawrence Avenue and pulled in, climbing into the backseat beside Jane.

"You're going to *[bleeping]* listen to me, and if you deviate at all from the script, I will go to your address and your family, even your *[bleeping]* pets, will be cut to pieces. Understand, darlin'?" I said, grabbing Jane by her bleached hair extensions.

I told her what she was going to do and then removed her gag, forcibly kicking her from the backseat. She ran into the gas station, crying. Of course she wouldn't obey me. I didn't need the voice to tell me that. I watched, in mute horror, as the clerk got a gun from behind the counter and shot her three times in the chest. She flew backward into a stand of souvenir hats, blood spraying into the air from her pumping arteries like a water fountain.

Well, that wasn't in the plan, the voice said, amused.

"You told me she'd be safe! That no one else had to die!" I cried to the voice.

[Bleep] happens, the voice said. I could hear a shrug in that statement, and it infuriated me. *Now get the hell out of here, or do you want to go back to the asylum?*

No. No, I did not. And I never will...ever.

***

As James talked, I stared at him in terror. He was not released. He was not innocent. He was an asylum escapee with rampant schizophrenia. None of what he said could be real. It could all be a delusion created by his warped mind.

When he was done talking he looked up at me with those beautiful dark eyes and said, "Now, you're going to go home, write up your article, and send it in. You will not tell anyone where we met. You will not describe me. And in return, I will let you live. Do we have an understanding, darlin'?" He smirked.

My stomach dropped, and I scrambled to get up. He grabbed my hand, and his grip was like iron.

"Do we have a *[bleeping]* understanding?"

"Yes, just please let me go," I whispered, on the verge of tears. And he did. He let me go, so his story could be told. I'm going to edit this article now and go to the police with it in the morning. Maybe they can find him. All I know is I am not leaving my house tonight. I'm lucky to be alive right now.

***

[In correlation to Ms. Green's article. --ED.]

Tribune reporter Freya Green was found dead this morning in her Arlington Heights home, severely beaten and mutilated by an intruder detectives believe is James Divina, a convicted murderer who escaped the North Side Psychiatric Asylum four months ago, after kidnapping an orderly and killing said orderly and a gas station clerk. He left her bloody corpse in her car outside of said Norridge gas station.

The story he gave her is one of his own delusion, and a large reward is being offered by Dr. Trelawney, who has been treating Divina since his admittance to the asylum in nineteen-ninety-six.

Divina is also wanted for four other murders, all committed on the full moon. According to Dr. Trelawney, he seems to have a werewolf obsession since he was lost in the woods as a child. It is unknown if anything he said is true, or simply a schizophrenic delusion.

A note was left on Green's computer, reading, "You asked me if I still heard the voice, and I didn't answer you. Here is my answer, darlin': I don't still hear the voice--I am the voice."

Tortured Minds
A Mills Asylum Story

Gina A. Watson

This story is written in UK English

The hallowed halls of Mills Asylum echoed with the groaning sounds of Ana, a patient, being dragged out of her cell. Each week the doctors pulled her from her cell and used a tactic to change her accusations. For months now, Ana continued to accuse the doctors of unfair treatment, abuse, and torture.

The doctors dragged Ana down the hall towards the bathroom and the wall mirror. As her skin scraped along the cold, tiled floor, they forced her to stand on now shaking legs. Turning her head away from the mirror, she couldn't even bare to look at what they had done to her.

"See, there is nothing wrong with you," the doctor lied.

She finally found the courage to look at the damage. Her reflection, now something she couldn't even recognise stared back at her with red raw eyes. Her face was scratched beyond anything she could imagine, and it had all began to pus. *Why are they showing me this? Are they just gloating? Are they actually proud of the torture they have put me through?* The cracks in her face stung with the tears she had begun to weep. With one jerk from the doctor on her hospital gown, the pain rushed back to her body, the pain they had given her. She knew what was about to happen next, the same thing that happened each time she spoke about the torturous treatment they gave her.

Still dragging her along the cold ground, they turned corner after corner, her knees bumped into walls, but they didn't care. They never cared. She counted each turn they made so she knew exactly which punishment she would be receiving. After counting the fifth corner, she knew what she was about to endure, electric-shock treatment. As the doctor used his key to unlock the large white door, another came and took over her movements. As her body slumped over the doorway, they lifted her and slammed her back down on a hard wooden slab. Quickly undressing her, they threw a bucket of water over her body to reduce the resistance of the skin to the electric current. They strapped her arms and legs to the edges of the table before getting their instruments ready. As Ana turned her head to her left, she watched as the doctors turned on their electric stock machine and attached the prods. Sweat formed on the back of her neck; she knew the prods were the most painful of the electric shock torture.

Once the machine was charged, they didn't even bother placing anything in Ana's mouth to muffle her screams. She found that they enjoy it when the patients scream. She always saw them smile and laugh when torturing her. Both doctors stood on either side of her body; they asked each other where they should start. The one on Ana's right looked down to her ankle and nodded to the other. The doctor placed a prod on each side of Ana's ankle, and the other clicked a button on the machine. As soon as a spark sounded from the prods, Ana's jerked her leg in the restraint and screamed with her mouth closed.

"Ah, you have been a bad patient haven't you? You know screaming with your mouth closed in unhealthy," the doctor to her left said as he kept the prods over her ankles, continuing the piercing pain. "Now now, if you admit that your accusations about this hospital were just a lie, like a good little patient, we will stop this and let you go back to your cell."

Ana couldn't speak. The electric current was traveling all around her body, making it hard to move voluntarily. All she could do was clench her jaw and try to stop from screaming in pain. The doctors weren't happy. They amped up the current and clicked the button again. Pain erupted from her ankle and pulsed harshly through her body, she jerked hard on the table, knocking her back onto the wood. This time she screamed. Her jaw unlocked, and a high pitched scream escaped and echoed through the room. The doctors laughed at her attempts to stop herself. She closed her eyes for a moment and tried to push the pain away, but it was no use.

"Admit it was a lie!" the doctor yelled through gritted teeth. Ana could tell he wanted to beat her to submission, but this was the way they had chosen to punish her with.

She still didn't speak; she couldn't. Ana's body finally stopped resisting and fell limp onto the table. The doctor moved the prod the next time, as he placed the tip of the prod just under her breast, Ana tried to squirm. The doctor looked at his comrade and nodded, having the setting stay on the same second lowest notch. As soon as the current hit her body, Ana began convulsing. The doctor kept the prod on her bruised skin. Ana's restrained body leapt off the table but fell back instantly. Her screams rang out at a constant sound as her throat became dry and raw. As the prod stayed on her skin, the doctor slowly slid it up towards her neck, holding it on her breasts and nipples. Ana's screamed became louder as the electricity shot all around her body. She felt as though she were on fire; her body writhed in pain.

Finally, the current stopped. Ana's body slumped against the slab, and her breathing became shallow. Her body buzzed from the leftover electricity in her limbs.

"Last chance before we move onto the extremely painful area of your body. Admit that your accusations were a lie!" the doctor warned.

Ana tried to move her jaw, but pain stabbed her joints. She wanted out of the room, so she pulled through the pain enough to speak.

"It was a lie. It was all a lie."

"Good. Now, will you behave from now on?" the other doctor asked.

"Yes," it was all Ana could say.

The pain she had been through still pulsed through her body, with each movement it jolted her through her joints and caused her to continue to cry out. The doctors unstrapped her from the table and lifted her onto the floor. The sudden movements of her body made Ana scream again, the pain in each of her joints was worse than the shock treatment.

She blacked out.

***

Waking up back in her cell, Ana felt groggy. Her eyes blurred and her head felt light. Each movement she made caused her head to spin. Ana tried to get off her bed, as soon as she stood, she was walking on shaking legs. When her eyes fell back to her normal vision, she looked around her cell.

The walls, ceiling, and floor were a sterile white, which made it easy to find germs while cleaning. Her bed was pushed into a corner and was made with sheets that were sowed into the bed, making it so people locking in Mills Asylum couldn't hang themselves. In another corner was a dresser filled with clean gowns and medical socks for winter. The cells were searched each morning and night, and if they suspected something of a patient, they will search in the middle of the night too.

Things ran like clockwork around Mills Asylum, and Ana was beginning to understand their system. Each day they picked out the most volatile patients and used the harshest torture techniques to beat them into submission and bring them back to being docile. The other patients suffered other forms of torture, depending on their "illness" that was diagnosed by the doctors at the Asylum. For Ana, they had diagnosed her with Schizophrenia. They began telling her that she was seeing things and hurting herself because of voices in her mind. She didn't believe them; she knew they planted it in her mind and are making her think she has the illness, all so they can torture her for some government experiment on pain and the human body.

Ana heard a few doctors talking once during one of her normal "treatments," they had spoken about results and that the head of the department wanted the results from each patient before moving forward with the second phase. That was when she began her accusations and enduring the more painful torture to try and get the truth.

She looked out of her window at the clock in the yard; it was past 10 am. Someone should have come and got her by now. *Maybe they are leaving me alone today because of the electric treatment last night,* she thought. Ana looked down to her arms, the bruises she had seen the night before were gone. Closing her eyes, she knew she was seeing things; those bruises were there, she could feel them, feel the pain from them. When she opened her eyes again, they were back. Purple patchy bruises all around her arms from where they had been restrained multiple times, other smaller yellow bruises were near the crook of her arm, where the doctors had placed large needles in her veins.

Ana trembled at the memories; she desperately wanted to be rid of Mills Asylum. She was terrified they would successfully break her, snap something in her brain and turn her into the Schizophrenic they had said she was.

The loud sounds of the bolt unlocking on her cell door made Ana jump and sit on her bed like all patients are supposed to do. She dropped her eyes and watched the shoes of the person walk into her room. She recognised the shoes that entered. It was Doctor Harries, the head doctor for the Schizophrenic ward. Usually, he only visited her when something was seriously wrong.

"Miss Jones, how nice to see you this morning," he said pulling a chair behind him and sitting in front of her.

"Yes, nice."

"Not very talkative this morning Miss Jones, what is wrong?"

"Well, when you have large volts of electricity pulsing through your body the night before, you wouldn't be talkative either."

"What on earth are you talking about? Nothing of the sort happened last night."

"Yes, it did! I felt it, I should know."

He sat up in his chair and wrote something on a clipboard his colleague handed him. Ana studied him for a moment before he looked up at her for a moment. He made a groan and continued to write.

"Ana, I think you may have had another Schizophrenic episode yesterday. I heard from your resident doctors that..." he looked down at the clipboard, "you accused them of torture."

"They have been torturing me! Just look at these bruises," Ana held out her arms and legs and made sure he got a good look. "And just look at my face!"

"I hate to tell you Ana, but there is nothing wrong with your limbs or your face. No bruises, no scars or scratches as you so put it in your accusation."

"What are you talking about? There are bruises all over me, purple and yellow ones, all over my body."

"Miss Jones, no there isn't."

Ana snapped. Fury boiled in her veins and she needed to let it out. She grabbed the clipboard from the doctor's hands and threw it out the open door. As soon as she made the move, Doctor Harries stood from his chair and backed away from her, giving Ana the opening to grab the chair. Her hands gripped the dark wood as she lifted the chair above her head and smashed it against the wall.

"We need help in here!" Doctor Harries called into the hallway.

A few seconds later, two nurses came running into the room. One held a large needle; Ana knew what it was, a sedative. Something to calm her down just enough. It's what they always used so they could take her to be punished for becoming hostile. One of the nurses grabbed her arm as Ana struggled against her grip. The second nurse grabbed her other arm, and they restrained her enough so Doctor Harries could administer the sedative.

Ana's body became slow and heavy, her mind turned sluggish, and she slurred her words. She tried to yell at the nurses and doctors. Soon she fell onto the floor, hard. Pain stabbed into the back of her head, she lifted her hand slowly up and felt where she had hit. Blood was slowly pouring onto the floor.

She blacked out.

Stinging pain forced Ana to wake. She tried to move, but she was restrained again. Her eyes burned as she tried to open them. Her vision was blurry, but she could make out some shapes of people in the room with her. She closed her eyes again and wished to be able to see when she opened them again. The blurriness slowly disappeared, and the bright light in the room soon hurt her eyes in a new way.

Once she could see again, she noticed the doctors in the room. Both of them held objects that could easily hurt her. One held a whip that had been changed to make it hurt more; the other held a sharpened prod that could puncture her skin. This was one thing she had never seen before, which caused her to be even more scared. Sweat formed on her neck and hands; her pulse quickened at the sight of the instruments they could use on her. Her breathing became shallow, and nausea swelled in her stomach. On a table beside one of the doctors, was a tray full of syringes, some full, some empty. Ana wondered what they could have planned for her.

"What am I doing here?" Ana asked them. Her eyes flicked from both the doctors about to cause her pain.

"Never mind Miss Jones, we are just going to experiment with your condition to see how it is progressing," Doctor Harries said from behind her.

She turned her head to see the light just illuminate Doctor Harries' face, the shadows under his eyes made him look scary as he stared at her. The sound of something scraping on the metal tray made Ana whip her head back to the doctors in front of her, she watched as they prepared a syringe filled with a green liquid. Ana's eyes went wide at the sight of the large needle. She squirmed in her chair but it was no use, her arms were strapped to the arms of the chair.

The doctor swabbed her arm before inserting the needle into her vein. Ana screamed from the sting; tears pooled in her eyes. They weren't gentle with the needle at all. They moved it around in her vein, causing more and more pain. The pushed the green liquid into Ana's arm, once all the liquid was gone from the syringe, the pulled it out. Blood rose out of the needle hole and dripped down her arm and onto the floor.

"Let the observation begin, turn on the lamps and wait for it to take effect," Doctor Harries ordered his fellow doctors.

"Let what take effect?" Ana slurred, asking the first question that came to her mind.

Her head started feeling light as her vision blurred again. The images of the doctors standing before her changed into shadow men with giant yellow eyes. Ana screamed and tried as hard as she could to get away from the shadow men. They tried to talk to her, but all she could hear was a muffled version of the normal English she was so used to hearing. Ana's pulse quickened. Each time the shadow men came closer to her body, she screamed louder and started to cry.

"Miss Jones, Miss Jones. Can you understand me?" a familiar voice said.

"What have you done to me?"

"Ana, you are having a Schizophrenic attack. You need to calm down so we can help you," the voice said again.

"No, I'm not having an attack! You did this to me! What have you done to me?" Ana screamed out to the voice she could only hear.

She looked around for who was talking to her, but she could only see the shadow men, who were now holding weapons. Her urge to flee came on full force in her mind. She tried to back up in her chair but couldn't move. The shadow men moved closer and began using the weapons.

Ana's leg burned from a whip being lashed onto her bare skin, over and over all in the same spot. She screamed in pain and to be let go. The second shadow man used the sharpened prod on her leg, it dug the point into her, and as soon as it broke into the skin, her screams became worse.

"Miss Jones, we need you to calm down," the familiar voice said.

"How can I calm down? You did this to me! Let me go!"

Another needle dug into Ana's arm, she continued to scream in pain at the feeling. Within moments, her dizziness and blurriness stopped. She closed her eyes for a moment, and when she opened them again, the doctors were back standing before her.

"What did you do to me?" she screamed.

Doctor Harries rounded the chair and stood in front of her. His face was amused, and his eyes were wide. His lips were almost curled into a smile.

"Miss Jones, we didn't do anything to you."

"Yes, you did! That has never happened to me before. You injected that weird green liquid into me and then it happened. What did you do?"

"Men, she isn't going to let up on this, please take her back to her cell," he said to the other doctors.

Ana looked down to her legs, her left one was whipped down to raw skin and was beginning to seep Her left leg was covered in blood. The blood had risen through the puncture wound and was dripping onto the floor. The sight of the fresh blood caused Ana to feel nauseous, her stomach began doing flips and the longer she looked at her, the sicker she felt. As soon as they began to move her from the chair, she doubled over and vomited on the floor and herself.

"Also take her to the showers, make sure she puts on a fresh gown. We don't want her getting sick and dying on us."

Ana growled at Doctor Harries for his comment, and they pulled her off the chair and onto the ground. She knew what was coming next. The doctor grabbed the collar of the gown and began dragging her out of the room. She watched as blood trailed in their path as it dripped from her leg. They either didn't notice or didn't care.

As soon as her skin scraped across the cold, hard tiles, she knew she was in the showers. The doctor turned on the water and pushed Ana under its scalding flow. She cried out as the boiling water flowed across her stinging skin. Tears fell down her cheeks as she rushed to wash the grime and blood off her skin. As soon as the doctor thought she was done, he turned off the water and threw a towel on her. Once she was dry enough, the doctor grabbed her arm and hauled her out of the bathroom while she was still naked. The other patients and doctors in the hall stared at her naked body being dragged towards her cell.

They stopped so the doctor could open the door and shoved Ana inside. She watched as he laughed while closing and locking the door behind him.

Ana was alone; she finally allowed herself to break down. She sat there on her newly cleaned floor and blubbered. Her tears flowed down her cheeks as she pulled her legs up and hugged them. They had finally broken her. They had forced her mind to see things she had never seen before, and that couldn't be explained. Exhaustion pushed on Ana as she lay her naked body on the floor, she pulled her knees up to her chest and cried herself to sleep.

***

She woke the next morning, still naked on the floor and someone pushing something into her back. She turned to find a doctor pushing his foot into her back to wake her up. He grabbed her arms and forced her to stand.

"What do you think you're doing? You were told to put on a new gown."

"I fell asleep; I was exhausted."

"Put on a gown now. I will be writing this in your file, explicitly disobeying doctor's orders, now hurry up and get ready, its visitor's day," the doctor said as he turned and walked out of the room.

Ana staggered over to her dresser, her leg still sore from the puncture wound she incurred the night before. She winced while pulling a fresh gown over her head; luckily it covered the new wounds and bruises on her legs. She hated explaining how she got them to her family. Once dressed, she waited beside her cell door for a nurse to bring her to the visitor room.

The room was filled with long tables with benches that were attached. The tables were filled with families of the many patients of Mills Asylum. All of them didn't know a thing about what happened behind the closed doors of the hospital. Ana spotted the familiar grey hair of her parents sitting at a far table. She tried her best not to stagger as she slowly walked over to her family. Mary and Liam Jones, Ana's loving and supportive parents, waited for her. As much as Ana loved her parents, they were the reason she was stuck in the hell hole that is the hospital. Her parents stood from their seats as Ana approached them.

"Ana, darling, what's wrong?" Mary asked.

"Nothing, Mother, I'm fine."

Ana sat on the opposite side of the table from her parents. They stared at her with concern swelling in her eyes. Her mother looked her up and down and gave a sad smile. Ana reached over the table and grabbed her mother's hands in hers; the warmth calmed her down.

"How has your treatment been darling? Is it helping?" her mother asked.

Before Ana could respond, Doctor Harries walked past their table and overheard the question. He took the chance to sit next to Ana. She flinched at his movement as he sat down beside her. Doctor Harries looked at her with a warning stare; she knew exactly what he meant by it. She isn't supposed to tell her parents about anything that happens in the hospital.

"Mr and Mrs Jones, Ana's treatment here at Mills Asylum is progressing nicely. Currently, we are trying to determine the exact progress of her Schizophrenia and how we will fully be able to treat it in the long-term outlook," he said, lying as much as he could to Ana's parents.

"I'm sorry but, who are you exactly?" Liam Jones asked.

"I am Doctor Fredric Harries; I'm the lead doctor in the psychiatric ward, I specialise in Schizophrenia."

"Doctor Harries, I am curious as to why my daughter was staggering when she walked over to us. She has bruises all over her body. Why has happened to her?" Mrs Jones asked.

"I was curious about that too, we have been monitoring her when she has her Schizophrenic attacks, and she seems to harm herself during those attacks."

Ana whipped her head to the doctor with her mouth gaping wide. She knew he would be lying to her parents, but she didn't know it would be a lie like that one. They are the ones that cause the bruises, and she knew it. He stared back at her with a stern look, mentally telling her not to say anything.

"We have tried to medicate her for her attacks, but nothing seems to be working as of yet. Once we find how bad her Schizophrenia is, we should be able to help her and stop the attacks," he continued.

Once Ana's parents believed everything the doctor was saying, he took his leave but not before giving Ana one last stern look. She nodded to him and said her goodbye and turned back to her parents. Her mother now had tears pooling in her eyes and held her hands over her mouth. Ana desperately wanted to hug her mother, but the hospital rules stated no large contact with the visitors, which meant, only hand holding.

A few hours past and her parents announced their leave. As they stood from the table, Ana stayed seated.

"Goodbye dear, we will come and see you next visitor's day. Hopefully, you will have made more progress," her father said.

Ana nodded and looked back at her mother, she was now quietly sobbing into her hands and couldn't speak. She couldn't sit by and let her mother stand there in despair. She leapt off her bench as fast as she could with her pain and staggered over to her mother. She pulled her into a soft embrace and let her sob on her shoulder.

"Please don't cry mom, everything will be alright."

As soon as the guards noticed the hug, they rushed to Ana's side, surrounding her and her mother. Ana let go of her mother and slowly backed away, knowing what the punishment will be, she didn't care what she had just done. She wanted to be held by her mother again. The nurses pulled her away and restrained her carefully in front of the guests. She mouthed her goodbye to her parents as she was pulled out of the room and back into the hallway of the hospital.

The nurses and doctors looked at her with anger in their eyes. Ana closed her eyes and let them take her away to her punishment. They led her down many hallways and down two flights of stairs. Darkness came quickly down each hallway they passed through, as her eyes adjusted to the light, she realised she had never been in this section of the hospital before.

They dragged her into a dark room and strapped her into a chair. Keeping the room dark, Ana heard all sorts of noises from behind her. With each sound, it caused her to jump and squirm in her restraints. Not being able to see what was about to happen was making Ana's pulse quicken. Two arms from behind her rubbed a cold substance on her own arms, causing her skin to burn. A few seconds later, needles were jabbed into her veins. Ana screamed and cried out with the pinch of the needles in her arms, moments later lights burst on in the room. She watched as a doctor scraped something small across her skin. The path of the object felt as though the skin was being peeled back.

She screamed with the intense feeling along her leg, wondering what was happening. *How is it this painful? All he did was rub something on my skin,* Ana thought as she watched the doctor again. Next, the doctor brandished a small pin. Her pulse quickened at the thought of what the tiny pin could cause in pain. As the doctor pricked the pin into her leg, Ana screamed in agony. The pain was more intense than anything she had ever felt before.

"What is happening to me?" Ana screamed in agony.

"We have injected a rare poison into your veins that makes your body intensify any pain that you feel," the doctor paused for a moment, "This gives us a chance to do the most minimal things to you, and yet it will cause you severe agony."

"Why would you do this?" she asked.

"We are testing this on you. You defied our orders twice in twelve hours; you need to be severely punished, so you learn your lesson."

The doctor said nothing to Ana after that; it was the only explanation she was given before the onslaught of agonizing pain. He continued with the pin pricks around her body, choosing the most painful places to prick. Each of the pin holes only produced tiny amounts of blood, so he was able to go for a larger amount of time without making it obvious she has been injected with the pin.

Ana was now shaking with fear, waiting for the each and every tiny attack that brought her immense pain. Her heart was beating painfully fast in her chest, so fast she felt as though she would have a heart attack if she didn't calm down. Each movement from the doctor caused Ana to flinch, making her wonder where he would touch and inflict pain next. In front of her blurred eyes, Ana noticed the doctor holding something strange. She had never seen anything like it before. It looked like a Flyswatter but the underneath held blunt pins. Ana's breathing became shallow at the sight of the new instrument.

The doctor flicked the weapon onto Ana's leg; instantly the skin underneath felt like it was on fire. Like acid had been poured into the patch of skin. Ana's piercing scream echoed through the entire room, she squirmed vigorously in her chair, trying to get away from the torture of the doctor. The new weapon brought the most painful feeling Ana had ever felt, matched with the poison flowing through her body, she felt as though she was being tortured to death. The skin welted where the new instrument was whipped against her leg. Ana's tears burned her cheek as she sobbed in the chair. With one more whip of the blunted pins onto her other leg, she was gone.

Her sobs became screams, and her tears fell more violently, with the intense pain ringing through her body, Ana blacked out.

***

She woke in the dead of night, her legs felt like jelly and each movement brought more and more pain. The poison was still flowing in her body. Ana was sick of blacking out from the pain, she just wanted it all to stop. She wondered how many other patients had to endure the same suffering as her, how many others had to lie to their families about how they got their wounds and bruises.

Ana curled onto her side and pulled her legs into her chest; she let her fears run free. Her tears burned down her cheeks and she sobbed away her pains. She couldn't take the torture anymore. She couldn't take the constant pressure of doctors telling her she has something that doesn't exist in her mind and being punished for denying its existence. She hated this place, hated everything inside of it, the doctors, the other patients but most of all, she hated her parents for sending her there. Every day there was constant torture, the drugs they forced her to take that did god knows what to her mind and body. She stayed like that until the light shone through her tiny window and as soon as she saw it, she shed her tears again. Ana knew what was going to happen; they were going to take her again.

A few hours later, or so she thought. They unlocked her door to check on her. Ana was still lying there with her knees up against her chest; her tears rolled down her cheeks and wet her gown. As the nurses moved closer to her bed, Ana screamed as she knew what was coming. They were taking her away again. She couldn't take it anymore, so she screamed before it even began. They dragged her down the halls again by the scruff of her gown; they didn't even want to be attacked.

Ana's eyes widened at the sight of the room she was thrust into. There was a large chair in the centre of the room that tilted any way someone wanted; under it was a metal trough with a drain. On a table beside the chair was a multitude of different sized knives. Ana swallowed a lump that had formed in her throat at the fear of what she was about to endure. Her tears were still falling as the nurses strapped her in the chair. The door behind her opened again, and Dr Harries stepped through with a sly grin on his face. He was happy that he was going this to her, he wanted to do it.

"Miss Ana, what a lovely morning this is. How are you feeling today?" He asked as he smirked.

"I was feeling fine until I was strapped into this chair."

"You don't seem fine; your face is red and wet with your tears."

Ana didn't respond. She could think of a few things she would like to say to him but she bit her tongue. Dr Harries shook his head before picking up a needle from the table; he pricked the end into Ana's arm and injected her with something she couldn't see.

"This liquid will paralyse you for an hour or so but you will still be able to feel. We did this to ensure you won't move while we do this."

She struggled in the chair as the drug took effect. She could feel the drug numbing her body to the point where she couldn't move. The nurses dimmed the lights so only the chair was illuminated. The shadows on Dr Harries' face terrified Ana. She watched as he picked up a small surgical knife and slowly dug it into the muscle on her leg. At that moment she realised what the trough underneath her was for. She tried to scream but her face was paralysed too. All she could do was sit there and take the pain. The doctor left the knife in her leg and picked up another one; he did the same to the other leg before slicing small lines down towards her knees. Blood flowed from the gashes and down the sides of her legs. She could hear it dripping into the trough. All over her body the doctor cut small gashes and caused her to flow with blood. Ana was beginning to feel weak; she had already lost so much blood in a small amount of time. She tried to struggle but it was no use. She closed her eyes and tried to take the pain without passing out. Her mind flinched with every incision the doctor caused. Tears flowed from her eyes as she couldn't take the pain.

She counted every small cut that was made on her body. When she reached a number in the twenties, she could feel the drug wearing off. She loosened her jaw and screamed at the intense pain. Dr Harries stopped as he was about to make another incision, he realised that time was up. The sheer joyful emotion that wasn't hidden in his eyes went back to nothingness. Before they released her from the chair, they placed bandages over every cut so she didn't die from blood loss. Ana knew it was only so they could keep torturing her. The nurses in the room moved to stand in the halls while the doctor cleaned up. This was her chance. The doctor unlocked one of her arms to be able to place a bandage around it. As he turned to retrieve another one, Ana quickly snatched a small yet sharp knife off the table and placed it under one of the bandages he had already checked. Once she was patched up, the nurses came back in the room and released the rest of her body. She was still slightly under the effect of the drug that was in her system so she swayed on her feet. They grabbed her and dragged her back to her room.

None of them said a word to her as they shoved her back into her cell and locked her away again. She sat there on her bed and pulled the knife from her bandages. She held it in front of her for a moment and realised what she was about to do. She hated being there, hated being in existence when her life was filled with torture and lies. If she spoke up, she was called sick and a liar and was tortured without remorse. She had no idea why they did what they did in this place but she didn't care anymore. She wanted out and this was the only way. Her parents believed she was sick; they were fed the lies to cover up what was really happening to her. She couldn't take it anymore.

She held the knife above her arm and thought she should at least say her goodbye. She lowered it and cut a small gash where there were no bandages. Ana touched her finger into the seeping blood and wrote on the wall.

You have broken me. Your lies have broken me.
You will pay. Goodbye.

Once her message was done, she gripped the handle of the knife and held it towards her neck. The words she had written were right; they had broken her. Ana pressed the blade to her flesh and pushed as hard as she could, slashing it across her neck. She felt the hard sting as it cut through. In an instant, she found it hard to draw a breath, but she didn't care anymore. They had broken her to the point where she was starting to believe them. Maybe she was crazy. Maybe she needed to end it all.

With the blood pouring down her chest, she grasped the edge of her bed and slowly slumped to the floor. She was running out of blood and oxygen. The pain was nothing more than she has already had to endure countless times. A few moments later, the darkness engulfed her. Even though she was gone from her torture, she wasn't free.

About the Contributors

Jaclyn Osborn – Jaclyn Osborn was born and raised in the state of Arkansas. When she's not writing or plotting the next story, she loves to read and go to Renaissance festivals. The men in her head never leave her alone, but she doesn't want them to. Writing is her passion and she's thankful for each day she's able to live her dream.

All types of genres in the gay literature world interest her, and she hopes to delve into them during her writing career.

Amber Hassler – Amber Hassler is a "Twister of Mystery." Creating a web of twists and turns to make anyone flip the page with enthusiasm, to find out 'Whodunit,' is thrilling for her.

Now living in Sin City she has a little more free time by being a stay-at-home mom of two to follow her passion... writing! She recently had a novella published in *Enchanted: A Paranormal New Adult Novella Collection*, titled "K + L."

When she's not writing, Amber spends her time with her family, reading, or playing a few levels of Super Mario on the Wii U.

Kathy-Lynn Cross – Kathy-Lynn Cross is the author of So Shall I Reap, book one in the Unseen Series. She also has other works in the following anthologies; the first is Twists in Time featuring "Within a Grain of Sand." A novella in the anthology Echoes of Winter, titled "A Spirit's Last Gift" and another in Enchanted: A Paranormal New Adult Novella Collection, called "Tainted Currents."

She has resided in Las Vegas, NV for the past thirty-two years. Forty-five years young, Kathy-Lynn's been married to her Split-Apart for over twenty-one years, with two amazing children. If her fingers aren't creating paranormal chaos, you'll find her baking or reading the next book from her TBR list.

Savannah Rohleder – Savannah Rohleder made her writing debut in the *Lurking in the Shadows* anthology. She's excited to be published once again in this series alongside many talented authors. A lover of stories, art, and logic, Savannah obtained her bachelor's degree in Emerging Media and Communication at University of Texas at Dallas. She in the process of writing her first novel and spends many nights swept away in the worlds of her imagination. She's never without a book and finds herself drawn to many genres of fiction. Currently, she is working as a Web Content Specialist and continues to nurture her love of web development. With so many projects demanding her attention, she feels the need to always be busy and creative.

E.M. Fitch – E.M. Fitch is an author who loves scary stories, chocolate, and tall trees. Her latest novel, *Of the Trees*, is a Young Adult horror/fantasy inspired by haunted cemeteries and the darker musings of W.B. Yeats. She is the author of the Young Adult zombie trilogy: The Break Free Series. She has been published in Pulp Metal Magazine, Under the Bed Magazine, and her short story "Release" was featured in *Lurking in the Shadows*. When not dreaming up new ways to torture characters, she is usually corralling her four children, or thinking of ways to tire them out so she can get an hour of peace at night. She lives in Connecticut, surrounded by chaos, which she manages with her husband, Marc.

Jaidis Shaw – Jaidis Shaw currently resides in South Carolina with her husband and two beautiful daughters (with another baby on the way). With a passion for reading, Jaidis can always be found surrounded by books and dreaming of new stories. She enjoys challenging herself by writing in different genres and currently has several projects in the works.

Jaidis also owns and operates Juniper Grove Book Solutions, voted #1 Best Promotional Firm, Site, or Resource in the 2015 Preditors & Editors Readers' Poll.

One of her main goals in life is to encourage her children to let their imaginations run wild.

M L Sparrow – M L Sparrow is currently the author of four full length novels, a novella and a slew of short stories published in various anthologies. She will write pretty much anything that pops into her head, no matter the genre, and enjoys keeping her readers guessing as to what she will write next, though you can pretty much guarantee that there will be some degree of romance!

As well as writing, she enjoys travelling and has been to some amazing countries, where she never fails to gather inspiration and has an endless supply of ideas for future novels...

Jacqueline E. Smith – Jacqueline Smith is the author of the Cemetery Tours series and the Boy Band series. She attended the University of Texas at Dallas, where she earned her Bachelor's Degree in Art and Performance in 2010. Two years later, she earned her Master's Degree in Humanities. Along with writing and publishing, Jacqueline loves photography, traveling, and nature.

James William Peercy – James William Peercy fell through a portal into the publishing biosphere in 2012. Previously, he had been observing his own worlds and recording them since the age of 10. James continued writing while attaining a degree in Computer Science, getting married, raising dogs, and starting a business. Since all worlds exist simultaneously, he has added two book series, the Cliff Fulton mystery series and the Xun Ove fantasy series.

With a mind constantly moving, he devotes his downtime to writing, enjoying a bit of travel, and adoring his wife. If you like poetry, fantasy, sci-fi, and mystery check out his website.

Liz Butcher – Liz Butcher resides in Brisbane, Australia, with her husband, daughter, and two cats, Pandora and Zeus. While writing is her passion, her numerous interests include psychology, history, astronomy, the paranormal, mythology, reading, art and music – all which help fuel her imagination. She also loves being out in nature, especially amongst the trees or near the water. Liz has published a number of short stories in anthologies and currently has a multitude of projects in the works including her upcoming novel, *Fates Revenge*.

Ace Antonio Hall – Ace Antonio Hall (born July 4th, 1966) is an American urban fantasy and horror writer. He is best known as the creator of Sylva Slasher, a teenage zombie slasher who also raises the dead for police investigations, which includes novels and short story collections. He was born in New York, but grew up in Jacksonville, Florida with his grandmother, Sula G. Wells. He is the youngest son of artist and jazz songwriter, Christopher Hall and RN Alice Hall (Thomas). A former Director of Education for NYC schools and the Sylvan

Learning Center, Hall earned a BFA from Long Island University. While teaching English, he studied to be a certified ACE personal trainer with the Equinox Fitness Club one summer, but never pursued it professionally. Hall currently lives in Los Angeles with his bonsai named Bonnie.

Shelly Schulz – Shelly Schulz has been published in the anthologies *Bitter Blackout*, *Dark Light Four*, *Lurking in the Deep* and *Lurking in the Shadows*. She is an accomplished horror writer crafting stories about things that go bump in the night. When she's not creating hair-raising tales, she leads a Girl Scout troop, nannies, and can be unearthed professing her love for the anti-hero. The brooding skies and dark forests of Shelly's home in the Pacific Northwest supply fertile land for her writing.

Kelly Matsuura – Kelly Matsuura grew up in Victoria, Australia, but always dreamed she would live abroad. She has lived in northern China and Michigan in the US, and over ten years in Nagoya, Japan, where she now lives permanently.

Kelly has published numerous short stories online; in group anthologies; and in several self-published anthologies. Her stories have been published by Visibility Fiction, Crushing Hearts & Black Butterfly Publishing, A Murder of Storytellers, and Ink and Locket Press.

She is also the creator and editor for *The Insignia Series*: a blog and anthology series dedicated to promoting Asian fantasy stories and books.

Lily Luchesi – Lily Luchesi is the author of the bestselling and award-winning Paranormal Detectives Series, published by Vamptasy Publishing, as well as various short stories in the horror, paranormal, and erotica genres.

She's an active and out member of the LGBT+ community, a self-professed nerd, music-lover, and just a little obsessed with vampires. When not writing or reading, she can be found drinking copious amounts of coffee, getting tattooed, going to concerts, or watching too much of the CW.

She was born and raised in Chicago, but now resides in Los Angeles. You can find her on Facebook, Twitter, Instagram, Goodreads, and Pinterest.

Gina A. Watson – Gina A. Watson is an Australian writer who has always loved to tell a story. She started writing her first book in 2012 and has loved writing ever since. Gina studies a Bachelor of Writing and Creative Communication at the University of South Australia in Adelaide. Her favourite genres to write in are: Fantasy, Paranormal, Romance, Young Adult and loves to read in those genres as well. Gina's life now revolves around her boyfriend and family as well as studying, writing and trying to squeeze in time to read.

CPSIA information can be obtained
at www.ICGtesting.com
Printed in the USA
BVHW031837141219
566691BV00001B/224/P